THE CALL TO ADVENTURE

The old man spoke:

"The Keepers grow in strength every day. Their leader, Zaragoza, is close to attaining absolute power. Already their spells bar us from the Keep. Only someone from another world can get inside."

"So that's why we're here," said Jason. "You saved our lives and had us trained to stop the Keepers."

"Only if you agree. You must give your help freely. But decide quickly. There is little time. If they succeed, many will die, including your teachers."

"That doesn't give us much choice," Culter said.

"None at all," Sax agreed. "None at all."

"You guys are nuts," Jason said. "You know that, don't you?"

"Of course," Flos answered.

Bantam Science Fiction and Fantasy
Ask your bookseller for the books you have missed

HEROES OF ZARA KEEP

Guy Gregory

BANTAM BOOKS
TORONTO · NEW YORK · LONDON · SYDNEY

THE HEROES OF ZARA KEEP
A Bantam Book / March 1982

ISBN 0-553-20488-2

Published simultaneously in the United States and Canada

Bantam Books are published by Bantam Books, Inc. Its trademark,
consisting of the words ''Bantam Books'' and the portrayal of a
rooster, is Registered in U.S. Patent and Trademark Office and in
other countries. Marca Registrada. Bantam Books, Inc., 666 Fifth
Avenue, New York, New York 10103.

PRINTED IN THE UNITED STATES OF AMERICA

0 9 8 7 6 5 4 3 2 1

HEROES OF ZARA KEEP

Guy Gregory

PROLOGUE

Deep into the night he sat and pondered, his gnarled hands wrapped like leaves around the silver bowl. Strange objects, gathered from the farthest edges of the world, lay all about, in seeming confusion. A small fire of pine boughs flickered before him, casting shadows around the clearing in the forest.

Though his eyes were old past counting the years, sparks of magic danced in their deep seas of age. His face was gray leather scored with time and his voice cracked as he whispered low chants in an unknown tongue.

For many hours he had sat looking into the bowl he held, but suddenly, as if in response to some unseen signal, he rose to his feet and held the bowl high over his head.

A breeze began to swirl about him, picking up bits of the dark forest, spinning them through the night, but he remained still, as though made of the same wood which formed the trees around him.

Still save for his chanting, hardly audible at first, but growing louder, a sound which seemed to call the gods of darkness.

It had begun.

From far, the wind came rushing through the trees, growing louder and louder, like the pouring in of some powerful wave, crashing closer and closer. It came from all directions, but flowed straight to the old man. It seemed the giant trees would crack and splinter with the noise.

The chanting now was screamed into the wind, with each word torn from him and whipped through the clearing. The tumult grew, as though the wind were angry for being called against its will. The branches of the trees lashed back and forth, cracking and shrieking, and the fire exploded into sparks. Only the coals remained, glowing their hot light into the old man's face, lighting the battle which took place within his eyes.

And, when it seemed the forest and himself were about to be ripped from the ground and hurled into the sky, his chanting stopped.

He lifted his bowl over his head, and, with a final cry that came from deep within his soul, he brought the bowl down with all his strength into what was left of the fire at his feet. Sparks flew and were caught by the wind, to spiral up into the branches, and the ground shook from the force of his blow. The bowl was sunk into the embers, with only the edge above the ashes.

The fire flared and began to lick the bowl. The wind died for an instant; then, as if in answer to his action, there came a rumbling from the sky, and first one, then another, then a third, a fourth, and a fifth bolt of lightning exploded to strike the trees above him. The sound was deafening, but he stood firm. The trees were bathed in flames, yet did not burn. The fire crept through the branches until the clearing was lit with lightning blue. Then the fire touched the branches at the center of the clearing and there was a great roll of thunder, the flames formed a ball and rose overhead into the clouds. The cloud burst above the woods and gushed rain. As the flames were littled into glowing, the old man raised his arms and spoke. The glow wavered, slipped, then fell from the branches, dripping down into the silver bowl sunk in the embers of the fire.

Quickly, the old man thrust his hands into the coals, and, though it seemed to take most of his strength, he ripped the bowl from the ground. His hands were covered with ashes, and black smoke rose from his burning flesh as he stared into the glow.

What he saw took what little strength he had left. He wavered for a moment, then, stiffly, as though all his years had suddenly caught up with him, he slowly set the bowl down on the green moss. He felt around, then picked up four of the strange objects from the ground and held them over the bowl. His hands were shaking, and he nearly dropped the objects as he began his chanting once again.

Then he was through, and he let the objects fall, and slumped down to his knees. His face was now aged beyond time. His eyes were black openings to pain, and they filled with tears. He knew he was too weak to do it all himself. He had not fulfilled his duty, and it might well be too late. The clearing was getting dark.

The old man lifted up his head and spoke aloud. "I must get help." He listened, then spoke again, as though he had heard his first statement answered. "They must come from another world. It is the only hope." Again he listened. "They must be young, for we will have to teach them what they need to know." Silence. "Yes. There is so little time. I will do what I can. I shall get them now."

And the clearing was in total darkness.

I
THE COMING

Culter spun around the corner of the alley, saw that it dead-ended, turned to face them, and everything blew into red and yellow lights.

He groaned as he slumped to the pavement. He knew what would come next. If he had only not been trapped by this damn alley, this closed-in place, this place with no escape.

A boot slammed into the side of his head, and he tried to roll away. Another boot into his ribs, and his arms went numb. He tried to get his knife out, but another kick turned the whole world black. He was unconscious when it stopped.

He woke in pieces, identifying every part of his body by the screaming pain it suffered. His arm was on fire, his side tearing agony, his head pounding with blood. He knew this was the worst he'd ever had. Not just another fight down some dark alley, but the work of guys who wanted him to die. If only there had been a door, or fence, or something. Some little opening that he could use. But it had been closed, and he could hardly breathe now. He made a move to rise.

His mouth filled with warm blood, and his body wouldn't work right. Maybe they were right. Maybe he would die. He turned his head to see out of the alley. His vision was blocked by the figure of a man. Culter tried to smile. Blood ran down his chin. There was no way for him to make a joke while dying.

The man moved closer, some kind of crazy, by the looks

of him: long robe, beard, old face; some nutty wino looking for a buck to get a bottle.

Culter couldn't stop the man. If he wanted to take what money Culter had, he was free to do so. Culter found he really didn't care. He just wanted to lie there in that alley for a while and rest. Forget the getting up. Forget the guys who'd done this. He'd just lie there for a while, and then he'd think about what he should do.

He closed his eyes, and felt the touch of the old man's hand across his forehead. Then water. Cool drops of water. One was running down his cheek, and he reached up to wipe it off. Another fell, and Culter had had just about enough. He sat up.

"Hey," he said. "That's enough of . . ."

He was sitting up. And there was no pain. His arm was whole. His face . . . His side . . . No blood inside his mouth.

"No way," he said, then had a terrifying thought. "I'm dead," he said, not meaning it should be aloud.

"No. You are not dead."

Culter turned toward the voice. The same old man. The wino in the alley. But this was not the alley. This was—and Culter suddenly began to see around him. This was out in the country, trees, and fields, and a dirt road. It was getting dark, but it was clear this was no city. Culter had no inkling where they were.

"If I'm not dead," he said, then quickly smiled. "I'm not disagreeing with you, you understand. I'm just thinking out loud. But if I'm not dead, what am I doing here, and what are you doing here, and where's that damned alley? Where's the whole city, for that matter?"

"Too many questions for too short a time," the old man said.

"Too short a time for what?"

"Answering your questions," the old man said, and Culter laughed.

"OK," he said. "But at least you can tell me where we are."

"That is the one question I couldn't answer even if we had

all night," the old man said. "Which we don't. I must leave to get the others."

"What others? For what?" Culter said.

"But before I go," the old man said as though Culter hadn't spoken, "I give you this," and he tossed something right at Culter.

Culter reached out to catch it, then saw it was an open knife. He couldn't dodge fast enough, but the knife turned in the air and landed, handle first, in his right palm.

"That's pretty cute, old man," he said. "You could have cut four fingers off with that one."

"Not with *that* knife," the old man said. "That is *your* knife, and it will obey only you."

Culter looked down at the knife in his hand. It looked like others he had seen—bone handle, with a blade about six inches long. He liked knives, but this did not seem special.

"What's so good about this . . . ," but the old man was gone.

He hadn't walked away, nor made any sound while leaving. He simply wasn't there.

"Swell," Culter said. "Somehow the old guy gets me out of that alley, brings me all the way out here—wherever here is—and then cuts out. What am I supposed to do now?" and he stood up.

"Come to supper."

Culter felt his heart freeze. A deep voice came from behind him. He gripped his new knife and spun around, keeping low.

"Easy, lad. I mean no harm to you."

A man in leather stood a few yards away, tall, thin, with silver hair and trimmed silver beard.

"I don't have any money," Culter said.

"I don't want your money," the man said.

"I don't even have any credit cards," Culter said.

"I do not want whatever credit cards might be," the man said.

"I don't even have the time of day," Culter said, but knew this man was not an enemy. He began to feel a little foolish, waiting to be attacked.

"I have asked you to come to supper," the man said.

"When you have finished with your games, maybe you'll follow me."

"They aren't games," Culter said. "I've had enough of losing fights for one day."

"Then you should learn how to use that knife of yours," the man said.

"I know how to use it," Culter said.

"Hardly," the man said, and made a move too fast for Culter to react. The knife in his hand was knocked away.

"When you have learned how to do that as second nature, then tell me how you understand the blade," the man said.

Culter turned and looked for his knife. It was five feet behind him, lying in the grass. Beside it was another knife, this one with a black handle. It was the second knife which had disarmed him. Culter had never seen a man throw a knife like that. He shivered.

"And you may return my blade while you are getting yours," the man said.

"Yes, sir," said Culter.

He bent and got his own knife, then picked up the other one. He could feel its perfect balance as he weighed it in his hand.

"My name's Culter," he said, and stepped across and gave the man his knife.

"I am called Bladen. Knifewright of this land. Master of the Bladelore."

"Can you teach me how to throw a knife that well?" Culter said. "Where I come from, tricks like that could come in handy."

"Perhaps it is where you are going that you will need them most," Bladen said. "But we must hurry. My good wife will skin the hide from me if I bring you home too late for supper."

"You sound as though she's expecting me," Culter said.

"Of course," the man said, then turned and started down the road toward a distant cottage.

"I'd hate to drop in unannounced," Culter said, but the man was out of hearing. Culter moved quickly to catch up.

All pain was gone. The evening was clear. The air was good. And Culter was more confused than he had ever been in his whole life.

"Hey! Wait up!" He began to run. "What was all that about needing to know about knives where I'm *going*, not where I'm from?"

But the man strode on, and Culter had to hurry to keep up.

Lyca was now crying. Softly to herself, and gasping in between the sobs. Tears streamed down her face. Her amber eyes were reddened and her platinum hair was streaked with soot. Thin lines of beaded blood crossed her cheeks where she had torn herself through bramble bushes. She knew she couldn't get away. The fire was too big, too wide and high and fast, and it was lashing through the trees toward her.

The fire turned her woods into a place of hell. The small paths of deer and rabbits now led into heat and flames and death. The holes, high up the tree trunks, where the squirrel and chipmunks lived were smoking chimneys of natural crematoria. The gentle streams were boiling brooks of scalding steam. There was nowhere to turn.

She stood now in a clearing where she had been many times, but which, in the light of the burning woods, was now a deathtrap. The wind seemed to come from everywhere and blow the roaring flames across all exits.

Lyca turned slowly, knowing this was where her life would end. Then she saw him. At first no more than a vague shadow in the swirling smoke which filled the clearing, then, as a quick breeze spun past, the smoke thinned and she saw it was a man, an old man, thin and bent, and standing in some kind of robes.

"Where did you come from?" Lyca asked. "Is there a clear way out?"

The old man didn't speak.

"Quick, tell me, please," and Lyca stepped toward him. "If there is a way out, you must tell me where it is. We've got to help each other."

The old man shook his head slowly. The smoke flowed back into the clearing. Lyca coughed and felt her eyes might melt with pain.

"How did you get here?" she said. "Please tell me."

"It would not help you," the man said.

The words were hard to hear. The fire in the tops of the

trees was now a roar of terrible intensity. A giant pine tree fell into the clearing. The flames and sparks burst in the air, and the smoke rolled closer.

"Please," Lyca cried. "You must help!"

Then the sound was over her, and sparks and smoke were all around, and she was falling—into a darkened quiet—a sudden silence, with a silver dripping the only sound. She was lying on her back and felt the drops across her face. She opened one eye, then the other. Above her was the night sky, glowing with the light of stars. The air was clear—no smoke, no forest fire.

Lyca sat up quickly.

She was in an open place, with great boulders all around. There was a breeze, and she realized she was high on a hill. Alone. Then she saw him, the old man, seated a few feet away.

"What happened?" Lyca said. "How did we get away?"

"You shall know all that in time," the old man said.

"Who found us? Who got us out of there?"

"The forces," the old man said.

"You mean like the forest rangers?"

"There is no time," the old man said. "I see that you are all right now, and I have work to do."

Lyca was suddenly aware that she no longer hurt. The scrapes and cuts and bruises were no longer there. Even her throat, which had been raw with acrid smoke, was healed.

The old man stood. "I must go," he said.

"Where are we going?" Lyca said, and stood to follow him.

"You must stay here," the old man said.

Lyca looked around her once again: the hilltop with the boulders; the last light of evening. Nothing more.

"I can't stay here," she said, and felt a cold line of fear crawl up her back. "I'll come with you."

"No," the old man said. "You cannot come where I am going. And you have too much to learn."

"At least tell me where I can find a 'phone," Lyca said. "I've got to tell somebody I'm all right."

The old man looked at her gently.

"Whom must you tell?" he said.

There was no one. It was as though the old man knew that. The distant relatives and friends were not important. Lyca's world had been her woods, and they were gone. She could not phone the tiny friends who'd died there.

"You will find a home here," the old man said, and gestured out across the hilltop.

"I can't live out in the open alone," Lyca said. "I love the woods and nature, but I can't survive alone."

"You will not be alone," the old man said, and he took from his pocket a small object. "I give you this as token." He held out his hand. Without thinking, Lyca reached and took whatever it was—a small carving, white wood—silver-white wood formed as a perfect likeness of a small, silver wolf.

"I don't understand," Lyca said.

The eyes of the carving seemed to burn into hers, as though it were alive.

"Don't be frightened," the old man said. "The wolf is a strong and wise hunter of the hills and forest. It does not fear nor hate a living thing."

Lyca held the small carving in her hand, but was deeply afraid.

"What will I do out here alone?" she said.

"I have told you. You must learn the ways of the forest and the wolves. You will need this knowledge."

"The wolves!" and the fear was turning into terror. "How can I learn from wolves? They will kill me if I am alone."

"They will not kill you," the old man said. "You will see. But I must leave now."

"Wait," Lyca said, but the old man moved away, and then was gone.

"Wait!"

But there was no answer. The breeze began to grow into a wind. The night was deepening. Lyca sat huddled alone up on the hill. Then she heard it, the long note of the calling of a wolf.

"My god!" she said.

Another call, and calls from many places all around the hill.

"They are all around me," Lyca said, and looked for some

place in the rocks to hide. But there was no place among
them for the girl. Lyca clenched her fist in fear and felt the
carving in her hand. She looked at it. The tiny animal now
glowed. Its carved fur was as shiny as fine hair. Its eyes were
yellow.

"Do not fear."

It was the old man's voice, but she could not see him.

"I can't help it," Lyca said, but there was no answer, and
the wolves were all about and coming closer. Lyca sank to
the ground, still holding the carving.

Now she could see the first of the great beasts as it loped
up the hill toward her, a dark gray shadow moving silently,
and a second one behind, and then another. The hilltop was a
silent, moving place.

Lyca sat still. She was beyond terror. The animals came
closer. Lyca looked into twenty pairs of yellow eyes. Suddenly she was washed with calm. The fear was gone, and
slowly she got to her feet. Holding the small carving in her
hand, she took the first step toward the leader of the wolves.

Sax reached down, as best he could, to free his ankle. He
could feel something wrapped tight around his leg, and pain
as though some sharp points were imbedded. His fingers
found what felt like old barbed wire. He couldn't get it loose.
He twisted to the right to see if that would work, but the
points bit deeper in, and the wire was wound tighter; to the
left, but he knew it was too late. He had no more air.

Every instinct screamed for him to fight against the wire.
To pull and tear and rip his flesh. Anything. Or he would
drown.

His head was pounding, the sound of his own blood deafening him, a swelling, bursting feeling in his chest and lungs,
and the pain where more barbs drove into his leg.

A final try at pulling off the wire, but his fingers hardly
worked, and the barbs were deep.

The first swim of the season, out in the lake: a damn fool
thing to do alone, but with the sky clear and the temperature
over eighty, he just could not resist. The water had been cold,
but he had laughed and swum out towards the little island,
slowly, no hurry.

He had seen what looked like something sunken, and had surface-dived to find it. He'd found it. An old dinghy that the winter had destroyed: ice-crushed sides. He had swum around the dinghy, seen what might have been an oar, stood in the muddy bottom for a second while he checked, and had been caught by the wire and the barbs.

At first he didn't worry, and pulled his leg away, which set the barbs as neatly as a fisherman can set a hook.

The water was no more than ten or twelve feet deep. He could see the silver undersurface right above his head. He was five or six feet from the air—five or six feet out of reach. Colors began in his head, and the pounding was intense. He opened his mouth. He had to breathe. Even lake water.

His last look up, and there was a swirl there, as though some giant fish or person had appeared. But it was too late for Sax, and his lungs expanded to inhale the water.

Air. He coughed. And coughed again, and breathed in deeply.

It was air. He opened his eyes. It was quite dark, but then his eyes adjusted. A slice of moon was rising, and gave light enough to see what looked like a great boulder. But Sax knew that it must be a car or truck. There were no boulders anywhere around the lake.

He glanced about. There was no lake.

"You are all right," and Sax spun back toward the boulder and the voice.

He could just make out the figure of a man, not much more than a shadow leaning back against the rock.

"Who are you?" Sax said, then realized it didn't matter. Whoever this man was, he must have been the one who had pulled Sax out.

"It doesn't matter," the man said, and Sax could now see he was old, very old, and with a robe of some sort wrapped around him.

There was no way a man of his age could have pulled the weight of Sax out of the lake and all the way up here, wherever here was.

"Who pulled me out?" Sax said. He felt stupid, but he needed to know what had happened. He should have drowned, and he could feel the wire wrapped around his leg; he reached down to see what damage it had done.

His leg was smooth, without a single wound. No wire, and no blood.

"What's going on?" he said. "Where are we?"

The old man moved, and worked to stand up on his feet. He appeared to be weary and unsteady.

"Take it easy," Sax said, and he too rose. "If you pulled me out, you need a rest."

"I cannot rest," the old man said. "There is still work to do."

Sax moved closer to the man.

"Then let me help," he said. "You—or somebody—saved my life. The least I can do is help you now."

"Not now," the old man said. "Later. Now you must find your teacher and begin to learn."

"Teacher? What teacher? Learn what?"

"What you will need to know," the old man said.

"I've had all the school I need," Sax said, and could picture his great body squeezed in behind another desk for yet another year of schooling, of learning nothing which had any meaning to him now.

"There is still much to learn," the old man said.

"And I can learn it on my own," Sax said.

As he had been learning. After he had graduated, he had begun what he thought of as real education. He had gone into the mountains, built himself a hut, learned the ways of the wilderness, and started teaching himself to climb. He knew he could not stay up where he was. Knew that the mountains were not free as they had been a century ago. Knew that they were all part of some park or wilderness preserve, and, when the rangers found him, he would be thrown out.

But one summer and the winter would be long enough for him to start his training. He was a climber—a rock climber. Not the kind who used the tools and ropes and nuts and all the rest to make new ways up mountains, but the kind of climber who went one-on-one, Sax and the rocks, using only fingers and his toes. His body flat against the cliffs, and the tearing winds and screaming birds—that was what Sax knew his life should be.

"You have learned much," the old man said, "but it is nothing when compared with what you must learn now. You cannot teach yourself." The old man seemed distracted, and looked around himself. "She should be here by now."

"Who should?" Sax said.

"Quadra," the old man said, almost to himself. "I cannot wait. I must leave now. She will come soon."

Sax didn't understand. He was about to say something, then heard a sound, a distant voice, too far away to make out words.

"That is her," the old man said.

Sax turned toward the voice, but could not hear it now. Then he turned back to the old man.

"Who is she?" He saw he was alone.

The moon was higher now, and Sax could see that he was on a hillside. Great boulders lay as though thrown there by gods. The sound of the voice came up towards him once again. He turned. The hillside sloped down into what must have been some kind of quarry, or a natural bowl, but the outlines were too sharp and regular.

The voice came again, and Sax moved down towards it. He had to stop a number of times to listen and to find direction. The way was difficult across the rocks. The boulders here were smaller, but more numerous, and Sax had to work his way with care. He slipped once or twice, then started treating this as though it were a climb.

His massive body gathered itself into a working unit, the muscles flowing easily, the movements slow and sure. He now walked without sound.

"It certainly took you long enough to get here!"

Sax froze. It was as though he'd almost stepped right on the voice. Then he saw its source: three boulders, each six tons or more, piled in a heap, and from the bottom of the pile, an arm, with hand and fingers, sticking out.

The fingers were moving, motioning to Sax to come.

Sax felt sick. What those boulders must have done to whomever lay beneath them was too terrible to picture. The fact that the hand and fingers could still move was something of a miracle, but it would do no more than just prolong the death.

"You going to stand there all night?"

The voice was hardly that of a crushed person, yet it came from underneath the rocks. It was the voice of a woman.

"Give me a hand." The fingers waved and beckoned.

Sax knelt down. It seemed absurd to take the hand, for there was no way he could lift the boulders up to get the rest of her from under.

"Hurry up! It's late, and I missed supper."

Sax reached out slowly, then touched the hand. It was warm and worn, with calluses and scars. It gripped his fingers tightly.

"You ready, boy?"

Sax had no idea what to say.

He tried, "Yes. I guess so."

"Then concentrate," the voice said, and the hand tightened on his own. The hand grew warmer. He wanted to pull his away, but knew that was from fear. If he could help the person underneath the rocks by holding her hand for a few minutes, it would cost him nothing. She could not live too long.

Her hand grew warmer. So did his. He felt a tingling moving up his arm, as though it were falling asleep, yet somehow different. Rather than a growing weakness, it felt like a growing strength.

The sensation continued up his arm and into his shoulder, across his back, down the other arm, down through his legs, even to his feet.

"You ready yet?" the voice from underneath the rocks asked.

Sax was not sure what he should say. Ready for what? But the feeling of great strength was powerful, and he wondered if the voice knew what he felt.

"It's getting late, boy. We haven't got all night, you know."

Then Sax knew what to do.

"I'm ready," he said, and let go of the hand. It fell back to the ground, but Sax no longer cared. He was looking at the boulders which rested on the person with the voice. Six tons. He was insane. He stepped close. The rock had been quarried, and was smooth. He felt along its surface. His fingers found the grooves where star drills had been used. He set himself, and lifted.

The rock moved. Up. Slightly.

"A little more," from underneath.

He moved his feet a little, took a deep breath, and lifted. The rock was up another half a foot. The sound of scrabbling from underneath, then the voice said, "All right, you can put it down now."

The rock began to slip from Sax's fingers. He let go and jumped back quickly, then fell over something behind him and lay on his back, looking straight up at the moon.

"You going to lie there resting all night long?"

He saw the silhouette of a figure above him, a woman. Sax gathered himself to rise, and realized the strength was draining from his body. He was becoming weak. He wasn't sure he even had the energy to stand.

"Come on, boy. Get up."

"Just a second," Sax said. "Let me lie here for a minute."

"Oh, it's all in your mind," the woman said. "You're just as strong as you always were. You're just losing the strength I lent you."

She was right. Sax tested himself and found that he could stand as easily as always. He flexed his arms, and they were fine. It had been the contrast between the strength that he had had for a few moments and the return to normal.

He turned and looked at the rock that he had lifted from the woman. It lay where he had dropped it. He didn't have to try again to know that there was no way he could budge it half an inch. Lifting it had been impossible.

"I don't understand," he said.

"Nor should you," the woman said, and there was almost a touch of gentleness in her voice, as though she, too, were thinking about the rock and what Sax had done.

Sax looked at her. She was of normal height—he guessed at five feet, four—and she stood straight, with her feet planted firmly on the ground. Her arms showed muscles well-developed, yet still with the smoothness of her sex. Sax could not tell how old she was.

"It is time to eat," she said, and started walking.

Sax moved to walk beside her, but found the way through

the rocks and boulders was too narrow, so he settled for staying three steps behind.

"How long were you under that rock?" he said.

The woman's back moved easily ahead of him. Her feet, which he now saw were bare, found stepping places quickly. He realized that she would be a damn good climber.

"A couple of days," the woman said, but didn't turn around.

"How would you have gotten out if I hadn't come?" Sax said.

"I was working on that," the woman said. "But I knew you were coming, so it was easier to wait."

"You knew I was coming?" Sax said in amazement, and realized that he was talking more in one evening than he had talked in a whole year.

"Of course," the woman said. "I'm Quadra."

Which sounded familiar somehow. Then Sax remembered the old man, and he had used the name. His teacher.

"If it was your strength I used to lift that rock, how come you couldn't lift it up yourself?"

The woman stopped, and turned.

"You have much to learn, boy. There are some things you can use yourself, and some things you must give to others. If you are not too stupid, maybe some day you will know which one is which."

Sax said nothing. Quadra turned and began walking once again.

Fifteen minutes later, they came to a house; more of a cottage, made of stone, with a stone roof. The woman felt around her person, then swore softly to herself.

"I must have dropped it."

"What?" Sax said.

"The key, of course."

It was hard to imagine a key for a stone door, but Sax was not about to argue.

"Let me have yours," the woman said, and held out her hand.

Sax had no idea what she was talking about.

"I don't have a key," he said.

"Don't be a fool, boy. Of course you have a key. Fulmin would not let you come here without the key."

"I don't know any Fulmin, and I don't have any key."

"Look in your pocket."

"I just told you. I don't have any key."

"And I just told you, look in your pocket. You have a lot to learn, boy, and the first thing is to do what I tell you."

Sax found himself growing angry. He was not the kind to be told what to do. But he dropped his hand down to his pants and stuck it in his pocket—and felt a rock in there. He pulled it out.

"I told you I didn't have a key. I have only this rock."

Quadra held out her hand. "Let me have it."

"It's not a key."

"You seem to know nothing at all about anything," the woman said with some disgust. "What would you expect a key for a stone door to be, except another stone?" She stepped up to the door and held the rock against it, and it swung open silently.

She handed Sax the rock.

"Don't lose it, boy."

Sax was both embarrassed and angry.

"You mean the way you lost *yours*?" he said.

The woman looked at him. Then smiled. Then laughed. "You are not the weakling I took you for," she said. "There is a little man in you after all."

"And a little woman in you," Sax said. "Even if you do hang around a place like this," and he waved his hand around the quarry.

"Don't go getting any notions about me, boy," the woman said. "I am old enough to be your . . ." but she stopped. "This is no time to talk about this nonsense. Come in," and she turned and stepped into the cottage.

Sax took a quick look back, then followed her. He could see no other choice.

It was broken. Flos had never seen a broken leg, but hers was broken. The pain and the sharp lump right underneath the skin were all she needed. She lay at the foot of a steep hill. Not a cliff, nor a dangerous wall; just a steep hill, on which any kid could run up and down and play all kinds of games. But this was no game. Flos lay on her side and knew that she was in trouble deeper than any she had ever known.

The sun was overhead, and the heat was terrible. There was not a cloud, a tree, a bush, or even a cactus to cast a shadow under which she could crawl: only pebbles and the hard-packed earth. No movement anywhere. Whatever animals might live in this deserted land were well burrowed in until the night and coolness. There was not a sound.

Why had she done it? Why had she packed her things and hitchhiked east? There was no place to go. There was no one she had to see. And she had left her plants with Alice down the hall, and thrown the few things she thought she might need into the backpack, and hitched out of the city, through the suburbs, out into the country.

Out into the desert.

The second day she had gotten the ride that brought her here, a nice kid with an old pickup, and she had gone to sleep and never noticed when he had turned off the main road. When she'd awakened, she'd realized this was dangerous, and asked him if he'd let her out right here. He had argued, but she'd really been afraid, and he'd stopped and told her she should watch herself. Stay on the road and hope like hell somebody came along. He had made a plume of dust driving away, and she had stood there watching it, then looked around.

There was nothing whatsoever anywhere—sandy dirt and small stones, a couple of dead twigs instead of trees, and mountains 'way off in the distance.

The dust from the pickup truck had settled when she'd started walking back. She'd had no idea how far it might be to the main road, and wished that she had asked.

She'd gotten thirsty. The backpack had cut into her shoulders. The sand had gotten in her sandals and ground at her feet. No cars or trucks in sight. Nothing but the sand and stones.

She'd walked for what might have been an hour, then came to a place where she could see a hill. Not much more than a mound of sand a few yards off the road, but it was higher than the road and she might see something from there.

She'd put her backpack down, left the road and climbed the mound, and she'd seen just what she'd seen all morning— endless miles of nothing. She'd felt tears coming, and tried to keep them back.

Damn! Why had she slept! Why had she let that kid bring her out here and . . . And why had she been so stupid as to tell him to let her out? If she had stayed with him, at least she would have been someplace with people. Even if she'd had to fight him off, she would have had a chance to call for help.

But here there was no chance of calling anyone.

She'd turned around to look behind her at the mountains, and her ankle had twisted under her, and she'd fallen down the hill, rolled and bumped and scraped her arms and legs and face, and then hit something buried in the ground and got twisted more and her right leg was under her and all her weight came down and there was a sharp crack and pain flashed through her leg and brain and she passed out . . .

. . . waking to the knowledge that her leg was broken, and that she was alone in the desert sun, unable to move, and that no one knew that she was there. She thought of her backpack on the roadside, then remembered that she'd covered it with sand so no one would see it. The pain returned, and she passed out again.

She woke late in the afternoon. The heat was dry, and sucked the moisture from her body. She had to move. If she lay there, she soon would die. She tried to move. The pain was awful. She tried again, and stretched out her hand toward a rock to pull herself along. She could just reach it. Her fingers closed, and she began to pull. She might make it after all.

She stretched her hand again, and never saw it, the curled and ready rattlesnake up on the hill. Her hand was close, and closer now, and it struck.

She knew what it was and knew there was no point in moving. She lay back and closed her eyes. There was no moisture left for tears.

Cool water fell across her lips. She licked them, then opened her eyes. The thin moon shone down around her. She saw that what had been a plantless desert was now a great field of wheat. Along the edges of the field were tall trees black against the midnight sky, and the sound of a stream somewhere behind her.

A drop of water fell onto her lips. An old man stood above her with a silver bowl.

"You are awake now," he said.

"Yes," Flos said. "Thanks for the water."

"You are welcome," the man said.

Flos sat up. There was no pain in her right leg. She felt it and could feel no lump.

"I don't understand," she said aloud, but to herself.

"I have brought you here to help us," the old man said.

"But my leg was broken," Flos said, and felt again to make sure she was right. "I fell down a hill, and there was no water, and there was a snake, and I just don't understand."

"That is behind you now," the old man said.

"What is in front of me?" Flos said.

The old man smiled in the darkness. "I wish I could tell you that," he said. "But I can tell you that you will be under the care of Physis for awhile."

"I never heard of Physis," Flos said.

A soft laugh came from behind her. "You will," said a voice.

Flos turned and saw a woman standing a few yards away.

"Thank you for coming," the old man said to her.

"It is the least I could do," the woman said.

"Coming for what?" Flos said, surprised at her own boldness.

"For you," the old man said.

"Don't I have anything to say about it?" Flos said.

"I must apologize for that," the old man said. "There was not time to ask you."

Flos remembered clearly where she was before she woke up here.

"No," she said. "I'm the one who should apologize. You saved my life, and I haven't even thanked you."

"You may not want to," the old man said. "Now I must go. I shall leave you this." He stepped close and held something in his hand.

It was a woven circle of something. Flos took it. "It's grass," she said, surprised at such a gift.

"Yes," the old man said. "Soon you will understand."

"Understand what?" Flos said.

"Many things," the woman behind her said, and Flos turned around.

"I am confused," Flos said.

"That will pass," the woman said.

Flos turned back to the old man. He was not there.

"I didn't really thank him for saving my life," Flos said.

"There will be other times," the woman said. "You can thank him then, if you still wish to."

"Where are we?" Flos said.

"I will tell you anything you wish to know," the woman said, "but it is late now, and we have much work to do in the morning."

Flos looked around her. She could see no town or city, nor any place to spend the night.

"Do you live around here?" she asked the woman.

"Not far," the woman said. "You may follow me," and she walked toward the wheat field. Flos moved behind her.

The woman reached the edge of the wheat and held out her hand. The wheat moved softly, as though by a breeze, but Flos felt no wind at all. The wheat seemed to part in front of the woman, and she stepped into the field. It was a path, but when Flos looked back there was no sign of one. The wheat straightened and was one unblemished field.

They had reached what Flos judged to be the middle of the field when the woman stopped and looked toward the sky. Flos saw nothing other than the moon and stars—then something else.

"What is it?" she said, and found that she was whispering.

The woman didn't answer, but continued to look up.

A part of the sky was black, and the blackness was moving. A sound began, the sound of something flapping, great wings or cloth or both, and there was a rush of cold throughout her body.

"What is it?" she said again, and wanted to press close against the other woman as though for protection. She held herself back.

"Zaragoza," the woman said, and the cold grew deeper, as though the very word were evil.

"What is Zaragoza?" Flos said.

"You will be told everything when it is time," the woman said.

Both still looked at the sky. The blackness reached the crescent of the moon, and Flos could just make out its outlines.

"My god!" she said. "It looks just like a dragon! That's impossible."

"Not impossible," the woman said. "Zaragoza rides the dragon every night now." Then, to herself, "There is so little time. So little time."

Flos didn't understand a thing, but knew she shouldn't ask. She would be told that she would learn when she was ready.

The sound of the flapping wings was growing dimmer, and the black form was smaller now.

"He returns home," the woman said.

"Where is 'home'?" Flos asked.

"Zara Keep, of course," the woman said. Then, "We must move on. It is late." She started walking through the wheat again.

They reached the other side of the field, and the woman stopped.

"We are here," she said.

Flos looked around. She could see only trees and bushes growing by a stream. The woman walked toward the largest bush, stopped, held up her hand, and spoke very softly words which Flos could hardly hear; and the bush opened.

Its leaves began to tremble, then the branches parted, and there was an opening wide enough for the woman to walk through. She turned to Flos.

"Welcome to my home," she said, and smiled. "I am afraid it has been a trying night for you. Things should look a little brighter in the morning."

The image of the black dragon flying overhead flashed through Flos's mind. She was not sure that things would look much better in the daylight. The dragon and its rider had been evil beyond anything she could imagine.

"What kind of place is this?" she said.

"It is what you can make it," the woman, Physis, said. "Now come inside, and we shall get some sleep."

Flos looked once more at the black sky, then walked into the bush.

There was a wind, but it blew no comfort to the man up on the steel. Six hundred forty feet straight up, or down from where he sat. One leg curled casually under him, the other dangled down toward the city street. But he was not afraid. He knew this world of iron in the sky, had chosen it instead of all the pain of trying to become a doctor, of trying to get into college, of med school—the pain of standing up and saying, yes, he knew he had a handicap—two of them.

He was an Indian.

But, if that were not enough, there were his hands. One was dead white, the other black; neither the color of human flesh, each like nothing anyone had ever seen.

He had grown up with gloves, and working on high steel meant he could keep them on, the great heavy gloves of the men who worked with girders and cables and torches, gloves which covered his disgrace.

They had told him there were scholarships for Indians available, but he had had enough begging for a lifetime. As a high steel worker, he was taken at face value. If he could do the work, the men accepted him. But, as a boy, he had dreamt of healing people, and giving up that dream had been the hardest thing he ever had to do.

He would come back to the job at night and talk the watchman into going out for coffee, and then come up to the open steel and sit and look out at the city. The wind would often wash the pain away.

But not tonight. Tonight he kept returning to the thought of what he might have been had he not had the blood of a second-class citizen, and the horror of the color of his hands. The new fad of every white proclaiming love for his red brother came too late, and neither white nor Indian could understand his hands.

He held up the right one. White. He held up the left. Black. "Like some crazy clown made up for Halloween," he said.

The wind blew the city's answer up to him, the mocking of the taxis' horns, the indifference of the rest. He got to his feet, feeling no fear of the height. He could walk these steel beams blindfolded without a slip. It really wasn't bad, being a high iron worker. Unless, of course, it was your second choice.

Something moved. Over toward the elevator cage. A shadow, like a man. Jason walked the beam in that direction. Maybe it had been just his imagination.

His feet were sure, but they could not see. And the night was dark, and someone had left a wrench up on the job. Nobody ever did that, but somebody had. His foot hit the wrench, and he knew at once that it was over. All dreams, all fears, all hopes, all pain was finished now.

Jason began the fall, then stopped gently, lying on the ground.

He opened his eyes, saw an old man standing near, and sat up. "What the hell happened?" he said.

"You fell," the old man said.

"I know," Jason said. "But what caught me? How the hell did I get here?"

"I brought you," the old man said.

Jason stood up, and slowly looked around. It was a swamp. Dark trees, and slimy-smelling. "This makes no sense at all," he said. "What happened to the city?"

"You are needed here," the old man said.

"Who needs me? Listen, old man, I want some answers. Last thing I knew I was up on the job, then I tripped on something and fell, and now I'm standing out in this godforsaken place with some old man, and I want some answers."

"There is not time," the old man said, and seemed on the edge of collapse, as though he had been working far beyond his strength and age.

"Make time," Jason said.

The old man looked at him, and seemed to smile.

"I know of no one strong enough to make time," he said. "But it is an interesting idea. I shall study it."

"Don't give me that stuff, old man," and Jason stepped up closer. "Tell me what happened or I'll take you apart."

"You are a violent man, for one who wishes to heal people," the old man said.

Jason froze. "How'd you know that?" he said. "I mean, I haven't told anybody about that. Who *are* you?"

"My name is Fulmin, but that is not important," and he looked into the swamp as though expecting someone.

"How do we get out of here?" Jason said, still concerned by the old man's knowing his deepest dream.

"You don't," the old man said.

"I don't get out of here?" Jason said. "You better think again, old man. There's no way I'm staying in this place."

It was dark. The sunrise should come soon, but the moon had set and the swamp was black. The only light came from a small fire the old man had lit. But now there was another.

"They are coming," the old man said. "And I can go."

"You're not going anyplace without me," Jason said, but stood looking at the other light. It looked like some kind of torch, but didn't bob as it would have if carried by someone. It moved smoothly, coming closer all the time.

"It's on some kind of boat," Jason said, as he saw the weaker reflection from the surface.

There was no answer. The old man was gone. Jason felt a surge of panic. This was no place for him. He might be an Indian, but he was from the city. The only wilderness he'd ever seen was on TV.

The light was closer now, and then it stopped. The sounds of someone moving in a boat came through the trees. Jason crouched down, and felt around for something he might use for his defense. He had no idea what or who might show up, and he didn't want to be unarmed. His hand found a broken root. It seemed tough enough, and he picked it up and held it ready.

He could see figures moving now. Two only. If they didn't see him right away, he might stand a chance. He shifted his weight and tightened his grip on the root. One of the figures spoke to the other. The language was one Jason didn't know. It sounded like something he'd heard in Chinatown, but he could not be sure. The two figures were closer now. Jason would have to time his attack perfectly.

They were on the edge of the clearing and the firelight. Jason jumped at the first figure.

A silent whirl, and Jason felt himself up in the air. Then coming down. Hard. Right on his back. His breath was knocked out of him with a grunt. The figure was bending over him.

"I did not intend that we should meet for the first time this way," said a soft voice, with just a touch of oriental lyric. "On the other hand, perhaps it is best. It clears the air of many doubts and questions."

Jason could breathe more easily now. He decided it was safer on the ground.

"Who are you?" he said.

"I am called Shi," the figure above him said, then motioned to the second person who now stood by the fire. Jason could see it was a woman. "And this is my wife, Inochi." The woman bowed from the waist.

Jason felt himself wanting to return it; lying flat on his back was hardly what he had in mind. "May I get up?" he said.

"Of course," Shi said, and held his hand to help.

Jason was not sure he trusted the man at all, but he took the hand and was about to pull himself to standing when he saw the man was staring at his hand. Jason yanked it away.

Shi looked at him, then said, "I am sorry. I was rude. I was staring at your hand. I see that Fulmin did not need to give you any token. You have brought your own."

"My hands are none of your damned business," Jason said, and pushed himself up and stepped back from the firelight into the shadows.

"I fear I must disagree," Shi said, and Jason now could see that he was tiny. No more than four feet ten, and his wife was even shorter. Yet, despite his size, the man had had no trouble whatsoever throwing Jason.

If he ever needed to learn self-defense, this little man would be the one to come to. But Jason didn't need to learn anything at all, except the way to leave.

"Just tell me how the hell to get out of here and back to the city, and I will split right now," he said.

The little man looked confused.

"I know of no city," he said, "and I am afraid there is no way you can get out of here. Or split anything, although I do not know what it is you wish to split. But this is the Great Swamp, and only those who have lived here for years can travel through it."

"What about that old guy who was here?" Jason said. "Has he lived here for years?"

"No," the man said.

"Well," Jason said, "he's gone, so I can make it, too."

The little man smiled. "I fear you do not understand. Fulmin does not travel as you or I do. He has other means."

"Then get me one," Jason said. "One of those swamp buggies, or whatever you call them."

"I do not call them anything," the man said. "I do not know of what you speak."

"To hell with it then," Jason said. "If you won't tell me how to get out of here, I'll just have to find the way myself."

"You cannot do that," the man said, and his voice was slightly harsh with warning.

"Watch me," Jason said, and started across the clearing toward where the rising sun was making the sky glow. He knew enough to follow the sun. That was the best that he could do.

"No," and Jason turned and saw that it was the woman who had spoken. "You must not go," and she held her hand up to her mouth as though in fear.

"Sorry," Jason said. "I don't have any choice," and he turned and started walking.

The two behind suddenly broke into rapid chatter in their own tongue. Jason had no idea what they were saying, but it really didn't matter. His job was to get home. Wherever that was.

He stepped through the trees which formed the edge of the clearing, then looked out into the swamp. Black water stretched under massive limbs which hung heavy with matted moss. It was not exactly what he'd pick to walk home through.

The man behind him called out something. Jason didn't stop. He might as well get on with it, and he stepped into the muck and slime. His foot went down, then slowed, then held, and he shifted his weight out onto it. And put his other foot out front, and felt his back foot sink. Then his front one.

He tried to back up, but both feet now were stuck deep in the bottom, and he was still sinking. The water rose above his knees, to his hips. He turned his head and called for help, and prayed the two behind him were still there.

The man came first, followed by the woman pulling a long vine down from the trees.

"I decided I would stay," Jason said to the little man, and held his hands out towards him.

The sun rose.

"It is done."

"It has just begun."

"Each one has come. Each one is with the teacher."

"We do not have much time."

"They must have time to learn."

"They must learn quickly."

"It is the only hope."

"Yes," and then the glade was silent.

The old man slowly sank beside the ashes of his fire. Beside him lay the silver lightning bowl, empty now, for it had done its duty. He had collected the five they would need. He had cured them all, and seen that each was with the teacher.

He tried to think what else there was for him to do, but he was tired, and his old head fell forward on his chest, and his breathing deepened, and he slept.

II
THE GOING

The land grew cold, and fear crawled down the cliffs of Zara. The people were infected, and the world was changed. Night visions came and terrified the children. The days were filled with gloom. Things were seen which never were before, and things which had been known were gone.

And every night the dragon flew.

The months passed. Then time seemed to stop. The land and waters and the sky stood still. The storm came.

Not slowly or with warning, but as a deluge hurled upon the ground. Trees bent down and thrashed themselves to splinters. Waves built in every lake and pond, and clawed the shore to sand. Clouds moiled into unnatural darkness in the middle of the day.

The rain lashed and streamed and flooded. The people stayed within their homes and huddled by the fires. But the fires died. The storm went on and on. The wind and rain tore crops up by the roots and scattered them. They drowned the fowl, and sickened sheep, and cows would not give milk. The wet was everywhere and nothing burned.

The people stayed within their homes and knew the cold. The storm went on. Yet, at each midnight, it was still, and the dragon flew. Then the storm returned, and it went on and on.

*   *   *

Thunk!
Thunk!
Thunk!
"Culter."

Culter spun around at hearing his name. There was Bladen, standing in the doorway, wet and looking half-drowned, like everyone these past weeks. He was shaking water from his long cloak.

"Stay your blade, Master Culter. Would you impale your poor mentor on a terrible day like this?" and he smiled his long thin smile.

Culter realized that he was standing with his last throwing knife poised in his hand. He lowered his arm in embarrassment. He had been practicing most of the day. He had set up a wooden target at the end of the long room which they used as a shop, and had been throwing the knives into a circle the size of a man's fist. He had done little else for many days. Since the coal for the forge had become too soaked to burn, there was little work. He and Bladen had polished what there was, then spent two full days coating every blade with grease to keep the rust off.

Each morning he looked at his own—the knife the old man gave him—and each morning it shone just as bright as when he'd seen it first. Apparently even this rain could not dull its lightning edge.

But at last each blade was polished and coated with its grease, and there was little else to do.

"Master Culter," Bladen said, "I have been sent by higher powers to tell you that the evening meal is ready."

Culter laughed. He had grown to like this tall, thin man more than anyone he'd ever known, and to respect him deeply. He watched as Bladen walked to the far end of the room and inspected the three knives embedded in the target. He pulled them out slowly, and came back to where Culter stood.

"Now," he said, "as you know, those higher powers of which I speak," and, without looking, he whipped one of the knives the length of the room into the target, "will not tolerate a moment's lateness," and the second knife flashed through the air, "when it comes to matters of the stomach and her food," and the third knife whispered down toward the target.

There was a crack, and the log that Culter had drawn the target on split in half and fell to the floor.

"However, if you wish to spend the evening killing wooden targets in the shop," and Bladen smiled again, "that is your business, and may the gods have mercy on your soul."

Culter bowed low.

"I hear you, Master, and obey."

"It is just as well," Bladen said. "We are down to the last of the salt pork. After this we eat moldy bread."

It was the first sign Culter had seen of Bladen's being affected by the weather. The man had seemed to have an endless store of good humor, but even that was wearing thin.

"Let me get my jacket," Culter said, and took down a soft deerskin shirt that Bladen's wife had made for him. "Lead on," he said.

But Bladen didn't move, nor did he smile.

"There is one other thing," he said.

Culter stopped. The man was deadly serious.

"I am afraid that it is time," Bladen said, as though Culter should know what he meant. "The teaching has come to its end."

"Are you kidding?" Culter said. "I have so much to learn from you, I could spend five years here and hardly scratch the surface."

"There is no more time," Bladen said. "You will have to work with what you have. What little I have taught you."

"You've taught me a great deal," Culter said.

"For what you need, I may not have taught enough," and Bladen's voice was deeply shaken. "But there is nothing more that I can do."

"I really don't understand what you're talking about," Culter said, but somehow knew he did. He tried to pass it off. "Unless you've had enough of me, I'd like to stay and keep on learning. I think I am of some value around the shop, and I will get better."

"I would have you stay as long as you wish," Bladen said, "were it my choice; but it is not. The time is over."

Culter felt himself suddenly cold. "So what comes next?" he said.

"You must leave tomorrow morning," Bladen said.

"Leave!" Culter said, and glanced toward the door, toward the storm and icy rain which lashed the building. "And go where?"

"I shall give you the directions," Bladen said, "and one other thing," and he walked to the other end of the shop. Culter could see him bend, and heard him open something. There was an old chest down there, which was kept locked. It must be that.

Bladen straightened up, then came slowly back to Culter. In his hand he held a sheath with the beautifully wrought handle of a sword protruding from it. He held it out to Culter. "This is yours," he said.

Culter took the sheath and touched the handle. "It's beautiful," he said.

"I have tried to teach you something of the use of blades," Bladen said. "Use this one well."

Culter started to pull the sword from the sheath, but Bladen grasped his hand and held it tightly.

"Later," he said. "Never draw this blade until you need it."

Culter loosened his belt and slipped the sheath along it.

"But," and Bladen's smile was back, "as I said before, we have been summoned by the highest power in the land, and we are late." He moved quickly to the door and held it for Culter to go through.

The rain washed down and the wind blew, and Culter thought he heard Bladen's voice but wasn't sure. He thought it said, "We shall miss you more than you can know, my son," but the words were torn to nothing by the wind.

Lyca peered out into the rain. It dripped through the forest, and had turned everything to mud. There were no clear scents that she could detect, but the hunting had been good. All burrowing creatures had been driven from their holes, and they cowered under bushes until found.

There was a growl from somewhere in back of her, within

the cave. Not a growl of warning or of fear, but one of knowing everything was wrong. Lyca knew the feeling too, for she had felt it long before the storm began.

It was almost dark outside the cave, even though the difference between night and overcast day was slight during the storm. As the hunting hour neared, the wolves in the damp cave grew restless. They were torn between the drive to hunt, and the desire to stay curled up in the cave until the rain stopped.

Lyca stood. It was the signal for the pack to rise and leave with her. Some of the younger wolves still lay and whimpered. They were wet and cold. Their coats were covered with mud which would not lick off. Their eyes had lost the fire of the pack. They lay shivering in dampness. Even though their bodies were well fed, their very souls were starved.

Lyca felt both pain and anger at the sight. She wanted to go out and do something—stop the storm, bring things back to where they had been when she had come there, the cool nights when she had learned to run, and then to hunt as they did, the days when they had lain about and slept and played, and she had learned the language and their ways.

From an ignorant pup, Lyca had risen rapidly within the pack. She now was second only to the leader, Tor. Whatever skills she lacked were replaced with intelligence.

And the power of the token she still held, the small carving of the white wolf, now strung around her neck with rawhide lacing.

She looked out into the rain again, hoping against hope that Tor would come. He had gone, with two others, almost a week before, to find how things were in another place, across the fields to the great plain where the storm might not be raging.

But he was not there, and Lyca knew that he would not return. She would be the leader.

As though this were what she was born for. It had become too hard to think back to where she had been before the forest fire, before the old man summoned her, before the pack. Her life was here now. It held a sense of purpose and completeness she had never known.

She felt herself a wolf, and she was happy.

Until the storm. Then there was no happiness, only wind and rain and evil, an all-pervading sense of evil, heightened every night by the dragon's flight.

The first time they had seen it had been while they were still strong and powerful. They had moved up to Howling Hill, and, despite the rain, circled and called their calls into the storm. Suddenly it stopped, and they heard the sound of flapping. All had looked up, and seen the thing.

The younger pups had panicked and run down the hill. Lyca and Tor and the older wolves had stood their ground. Tor indicated he did not know what it was, but was prepared to fight till death if it attacked.

Lyca stood in amazement when she saw it closely, like something from a book illustration, with great wings and snake's head jutting forth, and heavy legs and talons curled for flying, and a long tail whipping as some kind of rudder in the air.

Possibly, something was riding it. She could not tell, but there was a black cape flowing from its back, then it was gone.

The storm returned, and the pack crept to its cave. Nothing was passed between them about what they had seen, but the sense of evil was so strong they could still feel it. The evil lasted through the days and days of storm. It was still there, although Lyca had learned to deal with it as she did the damp. She no longer thought about it, but continued with her duties as though nothing had gone wrong.

But it was just a trick of mind, for she well knew that things were terrible. Yet, as leader of the pack now, she could not let the others know she felt that way.

Lyca looked once again at the pack lying in the cave. Their eyes were pleading now for her to tell them they could stay and not go out to hunt.

Lyca could make them go. With snarls and snaps, and even kicks, she could get the pack to move. But she felt their fear and cold and she knew pity. She made the sign that they could stay. The pack moved closer to each other for whatever warmth was there. The cave grew silent.

Lyca was restless. Something was in the air. Something which came to her almost as clear as calling. She did not understand. Her hand reached to the small carving which hung on her neck. The wooden wolf was warm, not the warm of being next to her, but something of its own.

She lifted the thong from around her neck, and looked closely at the thing. The tiny yellow eyes were glowing. The fur was silver white. The carving was alive.

It spoke to her. Not words, but in the way of wolves. The silent knowledge passed between two animals. The important messages made no sound. It was thus that the small living wolf was speaking, and Lyca understood.

She turned to the pack, indicated she would hunt, herself, and turned and left the cave. The night was wet and cold and muddy, but Lyca didn't care. She began to run, the long, loping stride of a wolf at hunt, flowing through the night.

The quarry was almost a lake. The deep holes were flooded, and they could only work the walls. Sax would have liked to spend the time inside the cottage, but Quadra took them out each day to cut and haul as though it were not raining.

The only sign she gave of noticing the storm at all was in her humor. It got worse.

They saw no one, except for the monthly trip into the village for supplies. On the way back home each time, Quadra would mumble to herself about how all the villagers just threw away their time in endless blabber. Better to save their breath for good and honest work.

Sax had learned to keep his mouth shut during these short journeys, and most of the rest of the time, for Quadra was as reticent as he was.

The two worked well together, saying nothing. The only times they spoke were when they had to, and it was these occasions Sax learned to use for questions. Quadra had a tendency to assume he knew it all, and that led Sax to making many errors.

"Not there, you idiot!"

"Not that way, fool!"

"When will you *ever* learn!"

"You're hopeless, boy!"

Sax had learned that the words were harsher than the meaning. Quadra was not cruel; quite otherwise. She would lay her hand on a great rock and let her face show what she felt, a kind of tenderness, as though the cold hard stone were warm and living.

"They are part of the way of everything," she said when Sax had mentioned it. "They are not like us, but they are part of the whole pattern, and we should understand that, boy."

Then she was silent for three days, as though to make up for the length of that speech.

"The bones," she'd said another time, when they were hauling the massive cubes of rock towards the loading place.

"What bones?" Sax asked.

"Rocks are bones. Nature's bones."

"But they're not connected," Sax had said.

"Neither is your spine, boy."

"But my spine is held together by other things."

"So are rocks," and that was all she'd said.

They had come one morning to the loading place and it was empty.

"What happened?" Sax had said. "There were a hundred tons of rocks here yesterday."

"They came last night," Quadra answered.

"Who came?" Sax said.

"The builders," Quadra said.

"But I heard nothing," Sax said.

"They make no noise."

"They move a hundred tons of rock without a sound?" Sax said.

"You said it yourself, boy. You heard nothing."

"What are the rocks used for?" Sax said.

"The castles," Quadra said.

"What castles?" Sax said.

"The castles they are building," Quadra said.

"Where?" Sax said.

"Wherever there are castles being built," Quadra said.

"I don't understand," Sax said.

"Maybe someday you will," Quadra said. "Right now it's

not your business. Your business is to learn, not stand here chattering."

Twice more the rocks were taken in the night; then the storm came. Quadra and Sax continued moving the quarried cubes of rock up to the loading place, but no one came to take them. It was as though the sense of evil blocked their passage.

Sax had always been big and strong, but working with the rocks had made him a giant. His arms were knots of strength, his back tremendous. His legs were powerful, his stomach muscles ridged like a living washboard.

"It's your brains I worry about," Quadra said. "You haven't any."

"I haven't been dumb enough to get caught under three boulders by myself," Sax said.

Quadra glanced at him, then mumbled something about not respecting age, and went on with her cooking.

The night was colder than the rest. The days and days of rain had saturated everything, and the stone cottage hardly held the fire's warmth.

"Will it ever stop?" Sax asked.

"Everything stops sometime," Quadra said, and that was all.

The dinner was good, with mushrooms the size of dinner plates, broiled dark and juicy.

"Rain's good for something," Quadra said, sitting down to eat.

"Has it ever rained like this before?" Sax said.

"Probably," Quadra said. "Before I was born."

"I didn't think there *was* a time that long ago," Sax said, and grinned.

"Mind your tongue, boy!"

"I'm not a boy," Sax said. "I'm a man."

Quadra looked up quickly, and stared at him as though testing the thought.

"Not yet," she said; but gently, "nearly, but not quite."

"I will be a hundred before you stop calling me 'boy'," Sax said.

"When you are a hundred, I will be long gone," Quadra said.

"You'll live forever," Sax said, feeling a sudden sadness at her words.

"I have already," Quadra said. "Now eat your dinner."

They ate in silence, Sax filling his large plate four times.

"I suppose we'll work the west wall tomorrow," he said, as he pushed his stool back from the table.

"I shall work the west wall, yes," Quadra said, and stood and cleared the table.

"What's that mean?" Sax said.

Quadra went to the sink and rinsed the dishes in the pan. "Just what I said. Can't you hear now?"

"I heard you say that *you* will work the west wall. What about me?"

"You will be gone." Quadra's voice was low.

"Gone? Gone where?"

"To the gathering, you idiot. Don't you know anything!" She did not turn around to face him.

"What gathering? What are you saying?"

"The gathering. It is the time. Now you must go."

"You don't make sense, old woman."

"I make sense, boy. It is you who do not understand."

"Tell me." Sax found himself cold with apprehension.

"You must go to do what you were brought here for," Quadra said. "It is time now."

"What am I supposed to do?" Sax said.

"You will know," Quadra said. "But you may not know enough to do it."

"I'm not that stupid."

"I did not mean that you were stupid. I only meant that there has not been time to teach you everything you need to know."

Sax had never heard her use that tone. Their jokes and insults had come easily, and let them cover up what they had grown to feel. Now Quadra was letting down the walls, and Sax sat quiet.

Quadra turned around and leaned against the sink. "Give me your key," she said softly.

Sax reached in his pocket and brought out the stone that the old man had put there months before. He rose and brought it over to where Quadra stood. She took the stone and held it in both hands. Then closed her eyes and bowed her head and there was silence.

Sax didn't move.

There was a growing sense of power in the room, as though the stones from which the cottage had been built were giving forth their strength. Quadra stood still, but sweat began to form and stain her face. The candles on the table dimmed. The room was almost dark.

The candles flared, and the cottage shook, and Quadra gasped, then held the stone out in her open hands. "It is all I can do," she whispered. "That, and what I've taught you."

Sax took the stone. It was ice cold, despite Quadra's sweating hands.

"You can borrow my strength once a day," Quadra said. "Through that key," and she nodded towards the stone. "But only once a day, and you will need to rest right after using it. Do you understand that?"

Sax looked at the stone in his hand.

"Is there something special I must do?" he said.

"Just hold that key and see me in your mind," Quadra said. "I will hear you, and I will lend you all the strength I can. But it may not be enough. Distance will weaken it. Certain magic may make it fail. I cannot say that it will always help you."

Sax put the stone into his pocket.

"Thank you," he said.

Quadra seemed to shake herself out of some dream, then looked at Sax with the old fire in her eyes.

"Why are you standing there, boy? Why are you not ready for the trip!"

"What trip?"

"The trip you must take this very night. Get your things. I shall prepare something for the journey. I hope you have sense enough to eat without being told."

Sax smiled. Things now were almost normal.

"If it is edible," he said. "Of course, your cooking . . ."

"Out! Go get your things!"

Sax left to put his few things in a knapsack. He returned a

few minutes later, took the package Quadra held out, and put it in the sack.

"Where am I to go?" he said.

"Go to the village first, then west from there."

"To where?"

"To the gathering, you idiot. I told you that already."

"Meaning that *you* don't know where it is, old woman."

"I have no need to know," Quadra said, and Sax was certain there was moisture in her eyes. "Now get out of here so I can get some sleep."

"You never sleep," Sax said. "You just stand in the corner with your old broomstick, woman."

Despite herself, Quadra smiled, then quickly wiped one work-worn hand across her eyes, and said, "Now get! Out!"

Sax went to the door and opened it. The rain washed down. The wind threw it full into the room.

"And close that door, you miserable . . ."

Sax was outside. The door was closed behind him. The rain flowed across his face, and blended with the tears. He turned and left the quarry.

Despite her chubby little body, Flos ran well. Not the long strides of a fine athlete, nor the effortlessness of the lean, but she ran without sound and, even though she bobbed a bit, she covered ground.

She had learned such running from Physis. She'd learned other things, but sometimes she was depressed at her own ignorance. Just when she thought that she was making progress, Physis would show her something new or ask a question which revealed the magnitude of what she had to learn. It was inconceivable that the learning period was over.

"I have just begun," Flos said when Physis told her.

"But there is no end," Physis said. "You could go on learning through five lifetimes and still not know it all."

"But I would like to spend this one with you," Flos said, then was embarrassed by the show of emotion. Flos preferred to show her love for plants, rather than people.

"I would have you as apprentice, if I could," Physis said. "But the word has come, and it is time for you to go."

"I do not understand this gathering," Flos said.

"It is Fulmin's doing," Physis said, "and, if Fulmin says that it is time, then it is time. Fulmin is the wisest of all the magicians."

Flos sensed something deeper in Physis's tone. "Fulmin seems to mean a lot to you," she said.

Physis looked at her quickly, then smiled and turned away. "He does. And did, but that was long ago." Her voice told clearly that the subject was now closed.

"How will I find the place?" Flos had asked, "and who will gather there?"

"You will know it when you reach it," Physis said. "As for the others, they will be the ones who came with you that night."

"No one came with me," Flos said, "except the old man—I mean, except for Fulmin."

"There were four others," Physis said. "You did not see them, but Fulmin brought them here."

"Why?" Flos asked.

"He will explain," Physis said.

"I wish I had learned more and faster," Flos had said.

"It was the best that we could do," said Physis, and they had worked at packing Flos's things.

The rain made everything sticky and wet, and the satchel Flos would carry felt heavy.

"With your appetite, you soon will lighten it," Physis said, and laughed.

"I guess I never will be thin," Flos said, and patted her fat tummy.

"There are plenty of thin people in the world," Physis said. "A little more of you won't hurt at all."

But it had been almost impossible to leave when it came time, and both had cried and hugged each other tightly.

"Give my love to Fulmin," Physis said.

"I will," Flos said, and wiped her eyes and started walking.

"You will never make it at that speed," Physis called.

"Then I will come back here," Flos said.

"When it is finished," Physis said. "If you do not fulfill the task, there won't be any here to come to. Please hurry."

Flos took one last look at the great bush in which they had lived all those months, then turned and took a deep breath, and began to run.

At first the rain was hardly noticed in the swamp. The dripping trees and growing mold were normal. The storm was like the thrashing of the water when an alligator caught its prey. The wind was like the beating of the egrets' wings.

But then the changes came. Small hummocks disappeared, and larger islands started shrinking. The stairs leading from the house walked down into deep water, rather than to land.

They might have to move if this kept up. This house was hardly built for such a storm. But, together, Shi and Jason kept the roof from leaking, and Inochi wove new mats to brace the walls. Yet their work seemed pointless as the rain continued.

One night Jason dreamt of walking in the sun. Warm and dry, he began to run. But couldn't. Something suddenly was on his chest and holding him. He woke, staring into two round green eyes less than a foot away.

A swamp cat. Bigger than most dogs, and feared above all animals which roamed the swamp; teeth that could tear a deer in half, and claws six inches long, it was sitting on his chest.

Jason lay motionless, working out his moves. If he could get his right hand free, he might hit something vital on the cat; but the odds were excellent that he'd die trying.

The cat sat on his chest and looked at him. It never blinked.

Then it moved. Without a sound, it leaped off sideways to the floor, and in one bound up to the windowsill, where it sat and looked at Jason.

The cat was dark gray, with one white and one black paw on its forefeet. Its eyes were phosphorescent green.

"You must be some kind of joke," Jason said, almost a whisper. "You come in here with those two paws and find the one man in the world to match them."

The great cat sat and looked at Jason.

"And if I move, you'll tear me into pieces," Jason said. But somehow he felt that wasn't true, felt that, if he moved, the cat would still sit there—would not attack. He didn't want to test his feeling. He wanted to lie there until the cat had gone.

There was a small sound at the doorway to his bedroom, and the door pulled back and Shi stood just outside. The cat's hair rose and its lips pulled back to show its dagger teeth. But it didn't move.

"Did he hurt you?" Shi asked, not taking his eyes from the cat.

"No," Jason said. "He woke me up, then went over to the window. Now he just sits there."

"I have not taught you much about the swamp cats," Shi said, keeping his voice calm and soft. "That is because they never come near humans. This one may have been driven here by the rising waters."

"What will he do?" Jason said.

"I do not know," Shi said. "Maybe nothing. Or maybe he will kill."

The cat screamed.

There was no other way to think of it. Jason felt ice inside his stomach at the sound. He had heard the noise from distances since coming to the swamp, but never close up. Even Shi moved back.

The cat screamed again.

"It speaks to you." The soft voice of Inochi, standing now behind her husband, looking at the cat.

"What does it say?" Jason asked, knowing Inochi could communicate with animals as no other person he had ever known.

"I do not know," Inochi said. "Maybe *you* do."

"I don't have your powers," Jason said, but somehow felt she might be right. As he had sensed the cat would not attack him, he now sensed that he could understand.

It came to him in a wave, and he said, "No!"

The cat looked at him.

"I won't go," Jason said.

The cat looked at him.

Jason knew that he was shivering. The message was clear, but he could not imagine following this swamp cat out into the storm.

"I am afraid you must," Shi said. "If you can understand his cry, then he has been sent for you. I fear that you must go."

"Where?"

"The cat will lead you," Shi said.

"I'm supposed to go out there with a killer cat to show me the way?"

"You are not helpless," Shi said. "You have learned well, these months with us. There is much more to learn, but you can defend yourself."

"You have some of the powers I have taught you," Inochi said. "You take some of each of us with you."

Jason felt he was being tested, as though he must follow the cat to prove he was a man. The cat was looking at him.

"I shall fix you food," Inochi said, and went away.

"I shall pack your things," Shi said, and he, too, left.

"It's just you and me, fella," Jason said. The cat growled, low. "How about 'girl'? It's just you and me, girl." The cat sat there and looked at him, then lowered her ears slightly.

"Well," Jason said, "it's a start," and swung his legs out of the bed.

The cat watched him. He stood up. The cat didn't move. He put on his damp clothes. The cat waited.

Shi came back and handed him a pack. "There is both food and clothing there," he said.

"Thank you," Jason said. "I shall be back soon."

Inochi stood behind her husband. "We will be here," she said.

They stepped back from the doorway.

The cat jumped down and padded silently across the room toward them, then through the bedroom door and across the floor until it reached the main room of the house.

Jason followed, opened the front door, and watched the cat bound down the steps into the boat moored at the bottom. It sat in the back.

"May I take the boat?" Jason said.

"Of course," Shi said. "I had it waiting."

"Then I guess I'm off," Jason said, and looked at his two friends. "I owe you a lot."

"It will only be worth something if it can bring you back," Inochi said, and stood on tiptoes to kiss him on the cheek.

Shi bowed deeply from the waist, but said nothing. Jason felt his throat constrict, and he bowed too, then lifted his pack and walked quickly down the steps. The cat sat watching.

III
THE GATHERING

Lyca stood on top of Howling Hill. There was no moon, for the rain still fell. The wind blew her hair back, streaming in the darkness. She waited, but she did not know what for. Was it some premonition that Tor was coming back? The message from the tiny carving of the wolf had been to run. Run to Howling Hill. Run, then wait.

The storm grew worse, as it did each night at midnight, and Lyca knew the rest. The sudden calm. Then the flying. She heard its wings. Coming for the hilltop.

She moved beside a boulder to be hidden by its bulk. The moon shone through the ripped clouds, and she could now see the thing with its great wings flapping in the cold night air, and the streaming cloak from on its back.

Lyca was sure that she could see a figure, but then the beast was overhead and all she could see was the black body and the wings. It seemed to hover, then circle slowly over Howling Hill. As though looking for something. Her.

She did not move. It circled once again, and the stink of the thing settled down around her, and she could hardly breathe. Then it gave a cry, and rose into the upper air, and it was gone.

Lyca did not move until the storm returned, with winds of force to tear her from the hilltop, and rains which were as though made out of ice. Lyca was almost beaten to the ground, but she stood and held her face up to the storm, and

the tiny wolf against her chest grew warm, and she knew
what to do.

She turned, and then began to run, slowly at first, not
much faster than a walk, picking her way down the hill and
through the rocks and boulders. Then, as the land began to
flatten, she increased her speed to a trot, which shifted into a
long, liquid stride that she could hold forever.

Her platinum hair streamed out behind, and she felt the
wind as good instead of evil. She had learned well the ways
of wolves, and recognized each smell and cry she heard about
her. She did not stop to hunt or eat, despite the ease with
which she could have caught her prey. She kept on running.
The land turned into woods, then into forest. The path she
followed narrowed, then it disappeared, but she kept on as
though she'd run this way a thousand times, and was not
tired.

She reached a stream too wide with flooding waters for her
to leap. She would have to find another way across. The
sudden stopping broke her concentration. For the first time
since she started, she wondered where she was. She looked
around, but it was dark within the forest and she could see
nothing that she recognized at all.

But the urge to go on didn't cease. The warm figure of the
tiny wolf still touched her chest and sent its message. She
started up the stream, but found no crossing. Then she turned
and followed it the other way. There was no path. Brambles
grew across her way, and she tore through them, heedless of
the scratches. Rotten logs gave under her weight when she
stepped on them, and she fell a dozen times as she searched
on.

Then she found a path, a deer path, and she could run
again. She smiled, and almost laughed aloud, and started, but
got no more than a few feet before the trap was sprung. A
great, heavy, metal thing leaped from the sodden leaves
which hid it, and closed about her ankle. Pain surged through
her leg, then through her body. It was agony before she fell
into a pit of fire and of blackness. She lay on the ground
unconscious, and the rain washed her blood into the earth,
and the wind blew her platinum hair into the mud, and the
forest stood again in darkness.

*   *   *

While Lyca had stood waiting in the cave before climbing Howling Hill, Sax had been making his way out of the quarry, to the path which led down to the village. While she had waited for the dragon's flight, he had walked silently between the darkened houses, and out the other side and on towards Zaratown. He had never been there, but knew that it lay west of the village, and he assumed that whatever gathering there was would be held in the largest town around.

The storm resumed after its midnight pause, and Sax pulled the collar of his jacket tight, but never slowed his pace. He walked with certainty, as though seeing in the dark. He wasn't sure how he did it, but the ability had grown as he had worked with Quadra and the rocks. It was as though he somehow knew the ground on which he stepped just as he did it, as though the path spoke to his feet and told them where to go.

The landscape, had he been able to pierce the darkness, was less rocky now. Farmers' fields, with stone walls lining them, ran beside the road. The path had widened and become almost a highway, albeit dirt, and not asphalt.

Sax thought back to what he'd known before that day he almost killed himself by swimming, and felt that it might be some other life, as though it meant nothing when compared with working in the quarry and learning from old Quadra every day. He smiled to himself, then felt a twinge of sharp regret at leaving, but there had been nothing he could do. She had virtually thrown him out. But he'd be back when this fool gathering was done.

It was not yet daybreak when he got to Zaratown. The dark houses huddled close, as though in fear. No light shone. No movement—not even a dog to bark and warn them of his coming. He stopped outside the town gate. He was right. There were no dogs barking at all, yet there was no way a stranger could come close to any town without the dogs telling all the world about it. But Zaratown was silent.

"Something stinks," he said aloud, but quietly. The silence seemed to agree. "If there's a gathering in there, it will have to start without me," Sax said, and began circling the town. He reached the other side without seeing any sign of life at all.

"Now what?" he said.

Keep going.

It was as though Quadra were standing there. As though her voice were real, instead of in his head. He almost jumped. The words came back, and he knew he must go on, that Zaratown was not the place. The gathering still lay before him.

He set out again, keeping west, until he reached the river, which was raging from the waters of the storm, spreading everywhere, its whirling, surging, foaming water making white flashes in the night.

Sax stopped. Icy sweat began to form across his forehead. His hands began to clench against his side. His breath came faster. He was afraid.

"No," he said. Then, louder, "No!"

There was no answer.

"NO!"

Images of underneath the water, reaching for the wire twisted deep into his leg, knowing he was trapped and couldn't reach the surface—he was drowning as he stood along the bank.

"NO!" and he shook himself, and wiped his face and breathed as deeply as he could. Slowly his hands calmed down, and the sky began to lighten with the dawn. Sax rubbed his face, looked around and found a rock, sat on it, and ate a sandwich from his pack. It helped.

He stood again and faced the water, then started looking for a bridge.

He found it upstream. It did not stretch from dry land to dry land now. The river flooded over both its banks, and the bridge was isolated, like an island, arching up from flooded land to flooded land.

Sax would have to wade across to reach it. He didn't know how deep the water was. He moved back from the river to a tree, where he was able to tear off a six-foot branch. He stripped the twigs and leaves and tested it for walking. It would work. Then he began to cross.

The water was not very deep around his ankles. If it kept up like this, he was all right. The bridge would carry him across the really deep parts, and he seemed to be able to manage wading without fear.

The water deepened. The sweat broke out again. He probed ahead of him and kept on walking, now only fifty feet from where the bridge began.

His stick dipped in a hole that he couldn't see beneath the surface of the water. He stopped and probed, and worked his way around. The current now was stronger, the water to his knees. He was amazed at the power of the water, at the pulling on his legs and feet, at the feeling of walking against some awful force.

His muscles strained. He moved through the flood. If he slipped now, he would be washed downriver. In that current, there was no way to get out.

Five feet more. Probing with the stick. Forcing one foot forward, then the other. His stick hit the first boards of the bridge.

He was standing on it now. He breathed deeply and crossed the river.

He had to wade through flooding on the other side, but the water was more shallow on this side, and he was not in danger.

He was on what would have been dry land if the storm had not soaked everything through days ago. Sax threw himself down and lay in the dampness, panting, trying to deal with his new fear. As a big man, Sax wasn't used to fear. As a rock climber, he had made himself do things that washed out the last trace of cowardice. Before his getting trapped by wire under water, he had never been afraid of water at all.

But that was over. He knew that he would have to deal with terror beyond his control. Deep water was now his nemesis, rivers his nightmares. It was a part of him now. He lifted his great fist and beat the ground.

He lay there for some moments, then, in a voice purposely like Quadra's, he said aloud, "Get up! Now get up, boy." It got him to his feet and walking, but it didn't calm his anger at himself, at this weakness which he couldn't fight. He moved into the forest.

"If I'm supposed to go west, then, damn it, I'll go west," he said, and walked in a straight line, through underbrush and nettles, thorns and whips, smashing his way through thickets, knocking down old and rotted trees. He kicked at logs and strode through the shower of bark and twigs he made, and tore up bushes by their roots.

Sax was his own storm, and he was mad. He wrenched a small tree out of the ground and hurled it at another. Blind fury drove him now. His stride grew longer, and the sound of his pounding feet was loud. A giant was loose in the forest, and the animals fled in fear, deer down their path to safety, leaping over Lyca on the ground, and Sax was right behind, almost stepping on the girl. He stopped, and all his anger drained away as he looked down at the wounded form caught in the trap.

He knelt beside her and looked at the wound. The trap had smashed her ankle into splinters. The flesh was torn, as though by teeth.

He inspected the trap. It was crude, but horribly effective, and Sax could see it was the type that could not be opened without closing it all the way, which meant cutting off the foot of what was in it.

The girl moaned, but did not wake.

He had to act. The anger he had felt at his own fear began collecting once again inside him, but this time it was focused on the trap, on this thing of iron and of teeth which had destroyed this girl.

He stood and took his jacket off, then squatted down and took the jaws between his hands. There was hardly room between them for his massive fingers, but he worked them in until he had a grip.

Yet he did not pull, not at once. Instead he closed his eyes and brought his thoughts together, let the blood flow into muscles he would need, felt them swell and signal they were ready. He took a long deep breath, tightened his fingers, and began to pull. .

The trap held firm. Muscles built power. The trap whined and shook. Great ridges ran across his back, and sweat poured down his face. The trap gave a little.

Teeth grinding tight and fingers bleeding from the rusty iron, with one terrible surge he tore the trap in half, then fell back and lay there trying to get air. The girl moaned again, and brought Sax back beside her.

Her leg was bleeding from the wound, but not too badly. The splintered bones were visible, and Sax was almost sick. He had to get her to a doctor, but he didn't know which way to go. He tore his shirt into long strips, then looked around for something straight and hard. Three sticks he used to make the splint, and bound it tight.

He picked her up and held her. "I'll find somebody," he said, and looked both ways along the path. There was no sign which told which way to go.

He started west.

The cat sat in the boat's bow looking straight ahead, as Jason poled smoothly through the swamp. He knew this part as well as any place he'd ever been. Shi had taught him every tree and hummock. The storm had drowned much of the normal landscape, but Shi had taught him how to read the signs now under water.

An alligator drifted by, only its eyes above the surface. The swamp cat didn't blink, just stared ahead. Jason kept poling. He had difficulty believing the cat could actually guide him by her gestures, but he had no other map, and certainly no knowledge of their destination.

Yet Inochi hadn't seemed surprised that the great cat came and summoned him. There had not been time to think or talk about it, but Jason felt that somehow she had known.

"I wish *I* did," he said, and the cat turned its head and looked at him. "I wish I knew just where the hell we're going," Jason said. "It's not my idea of fun to come out here and ride around this swamp just because some nutty cat jumps on my bed."

The cat turned back to facing front, and didn't answer him.

"Swell," Jason said. "You're going to be just wonderful to travel with."

The cat's tail flicked, as though to tell him tend to business and quit the chatter.

Jason estimated they had been out two hours when the cat suddenly stiffened, looked back at Jason, then crouched to spring. The boat passed underneath a low-hanging branch, and the cat was gone. A blur of gray, and it was through the branches overhead, and almost running, even though high in the air.

"Hey," Jason yelled. "If you expect me to keep up with you, you'll have to slow it down a lot."

The cat stopped. Jason poled the boat in the direction that the cat had taken, and, on the other side of a small island, found the shore. It was the edge of the swamp, something Jason had not seen since coming here.

He brought the boat to a firm place, climbed out, and looked around. The swamp blended into a deep forest here. The only difference between the two was lack of water and the type of trees, but the green filtered light and the dripping leaves and the underbrush were similar.

The cat growled, and Jason looked above him. The cat was standing on a branch some twenty feet away.

"You think I'm going to climb up there and follow you, you're crazy," Jason said, then had a sudden flash of working on high iron; a sudden sickness, as though he were dizzy, as though he were standing on a girder and then falling. He looked down at the ground to make the image go away.

"What was that all about?" he said to himself.

The cat growled again.

"OK. OK," Jason said. "You go, and I'll do the best I can down here. We've come this far together, let's keep going."

The cat moved forward, and Jason started a slow jog.

The trees overhead grew thinner, and the cat dropped down and led the way along the path. Jason said nothing, needing all his breath to maintain running.

He was breathing too hard to hear it, but the cat stopped dead up ahead, ears up, tail lashing, hindquarters lowered for the spring. Jason stopped, tried to catch his breath, then heard the noise. Somebody swearing—crashing through the forest, swearing.

Jason moved up beside the cat, and put his hand on its tense back before he realized what he was doing, but the cat seemed to accept the touch, and there was a slight relaxing of her stance.

The sound came closer, obscuring bushes up ahead were

pushed apart, and there came a giant. Not quite a giant, a large young man with something in his arms, and he saw them and stopped.

"That your cat?" the young man said.

"Sort of," Jason said.

The cat growled.

"Then get it out of my way," the young man said. "I'm coming through there."

"I don't think I'd do that, if I were you," Jason said. "I don't really control this thing." He patted the cat's back.

"Then I'll have to kill it," the man said.

"Hey, wait a second," Jason said. "What did she ever do to you?"

"I haven't got time to argue. This girl is hurt." He looked down at what he was holding in his arms.

Jason suddenly realized what the limp bundle was.

"Where are you taking her?" he said.

"To a doctor. I don't know where one is, but she's got to have a doctor."

"What's wrong with her?" and then he saw the makeshift splint and torn-shirt bandage. The strips of cloth were bloody, and the foot hung limp. "Maybe I can help," he said.

"Are you a doctor?"

"No," Jason said. "But there aren't any doctors I know of for miles around. I know a little healing."

The young man stepped forward. The cat tensed and sprang.

"NO!" Jason yelled, and knew it was too late. But the cat had heard, and somehow twisted in mid-air and missed its target its landed some way past the young man and the girl. Jason could feel sweat spring out and run down his back.

"I thought you said you couldn't control that thing," the young man said, obviously shaken by the cat's attack.

"I didn't think I could," Jason said. "I'm not sure I can," as he saw the cat crouched down again and waiting.

The young man looked around him.

"Where shall we put her?" he said.

They were in a clearing. Tall trees stood all around, and made almost a perfect circle. There was a bed of moss not far away.

"There," Jason said, then looked quickly at the swamp

cat. The young man moved, but the cat held its ground. The young man lowered the girl onto the moss. The cat still sat.

"I guess it's OK," Jason said.

"It is now," the young man said, and turned to face the animal. "If it even begins to *think* about a fight, I'll break its neck."

The two stood facing each other—the cat and the giant—and neither blinked. Jason turned toward the girl. He loosened the strips of cloth and took them off. The sight of the wound was sickening.

"What did this?" he said.

"A trap. I got her out, but I can't fix her leg."

Jason studied the ankle. He closed his eyes and tried to think of all that Inochi had taught him, all the cuts and scratches she had healed, all the swamp animals that came to her for help, and how she did it. He had never even seen a wound as bad as this.

"One other thing," the young man said without taking his eyes off the cat. "If you hurt that girl in any way, I'll kill you. Is that clear?"

Jason didn't answer.

It was time for going deep within himself. Time to search through every bit of knowledge, every word Inochi said. Time to draw on every talent he could muster.

"You hear me?" the young man said.

The wound was too much. It was beyond what Jason felt he could handle on his own. He sat back, and was about to tell the man to go to hell, go find a doctor by himself and leave Jason alone.

The girl moaned, then screamed. It was almost the sound a wolf would make while hurt and dying.

The cat snarled at the sound, but didn't move. Jason looked at the girl on the moss. Her cry had driven deep inside him. He leaned forward and touched her with his hand, his black left hand, gently, down her leg and over the torn ankle. The girl moaned softly and tried to pull away.

"Easy, little one," Jason whispered. "Easy," just as though she were a wounded pet. "Lie still."

The girl lay still.

He let his hand stay on the burning flesh, and closed his

eyes and concentrated all his strength and knowledge in his hand, the black hand which he had learned could heal.

But how much?

The wound was fire. He focused everything into the sense of healing, everything he was and could be. His very soul poured to his hand. His hand began to ache. It was her pain, passing to him, and it was working.

His hand throbbed, then the pain intensified. He wanted to yank his hand away and free himself from all this pain, but didn't. He clenched his teeth, and concentrated with everything he had. The pain burned in him like lava, yet he still held firm. Sweat was pouring down his face, and every muscle in his body screamed.

His fingers felt the bones and flesh coming together. His body shook as the pain reached his brain. The swamp cat whined, and dropped flat on the ground, but Jason didn't see or hear. All he knew was agony, writhing through his body and his mind. He could not go on, but he could not go back.

A final surge of blinding white flashed through him, and a wolf howled somewhere in the woods. Jason had no more to give. He was empty now. He fell back from the girl into soft blackness, which wrapped his tortured body tight in quiet and in peace.

Culter stumbled through the rain and mumbled to himself, talking about how he'd gotten here. Minding his own business being beaten to a pulp, and then some crazy wino comes and brings him out to here. Still no explanation for where "here" was. Even Bladen hadn't really made it clear. He had talked of Zara, and Zaratown, but those names meant nothing.

"That in New Jersey?" Culter asked, and Bladen hadn't answered.

Culter knew there was more meaning here for him than in the world he'd known. It was not the fact that he had learned about the blades—every kind of fighting edge from tiny knives to swords made for both hands—and how to make and use them. There was more, more even than Bladen and his wife; there was something about the land that Culter liked.

"Except this storm!" he said, looked up into the gray rain, pulled his soaking collar tighter, and walked on.

Something about the simplicity of living in another time, a time when each man had to know how to maintain his life. Not simply fight, as Culter had, with those who thought of other humans as just prey, but where each man had to know the source of food, and how to build his shelter, and how to live with others, not just spectate all the time.

Maybe it wasn't simpler, maybe it was more complex, but maybe it meant more than drinking beer and watching television.

"It means walking in this stupid rain, not knowing where you're going!" Culter shouted at the trees, which dripped their endless drops down in his face and made him splutter.

Culter was lost. He had been lost for some time now, but had delayed admitting it till now. He had followed Bladen's instructions to go north along the river. But the river was so swollen and spread out that, in working his way around its waters, Culter had been thrown far off the path. He had tried to maintain some kind of parallel with the river, but had even given that up now. It must be getting close to noon.

"Lunch time," Culter said, and looked for some place not too wet to sit and eat whatever Bladen's wife had made. It was salt pork, sliced thin and placed between two slices of dark bread.

"That's a sandwich," Culter said, when he had taught her how to make them. "How could you live without knowing what sandwiches are?"

"How could you live without knowing how to use a sabre?" Bladen had countered, and his wife had never said a word.

In fact, she never spoke at all. At first Culter thought that she was angry. Permanently angry. Bladen always said that she demanded this or that, or she would skin them both alive or have their heads. It was almost a week after coming there before Culter realized that Bladen's wife was mute. It was another week before he found she was a gentle woman, who worshiped her husband. It was another week before Culter began to feel her love for him, and he could not believe it.

One month had passed before Culter knew that he was home, the only home he'd ever had, with the only parents he would ever know.

"And they send me out in a storm like this to wander all

alone in some dark woods,'' he said aloud. ''How could they be so cruel,'' and he took another bite of sandwich.

The wind picked up, and Culter hurried to finish his eating. He heard a crack high up above him and looked up. A branch had broken, and was banging its way down.

Culter jumped up and back and saw the branch fall like a javelin right through a hornets' nest and straight down to the ground.

''Move!'' Culter shouted to himself, and started running, then realized that he'd forgotten his knapsack. He ducked back and saw it lying by the hornets' nest. The sound and the curling fog of hornets told him everything he had to know.

''No way!'' he said, and turned and started running. Not fast enough. There was a sudden buzz, then pain burned on his neck. Another. Another.

''Where's that damn river when I need it?'' Culter yelled, and upped his speed.

He saw what might be a stream ahead, and ran toward it. Over the bank and down into a pile of soaking leaves. There was no stream, only a ditch which would hardly help him now.

He scrambled in the leaves, trying to get some traction to start running once again. He kept slipping and sliding down.

Somebody laughed.

Culter spun and saw a figure standing a few feet away and laughing.

''Hey,'' he said, and found he had no breath. ''I . . . hey . . . hey, listen . . . listen, you got . . . you got to get out of here,'' and he found his footing and turned again to run.

''Why?''

A girl's voice. Whoever that was underneath that cloak was a girl, and Culter felt protective.

Until another buzz hit him right on the forehead.

''Damn!'' he yelled. ''Run! It's the damn hornets!'' and he ran.

No sound behind him. He stopped and turned around. It was worth a sting or two to see if the girl was still all right.

The girl was hard to see. She seemed to have lowered the hood of her cloak, but somehow she'd covered herself with smoke. Culter had heard that beekeepers used smoke to quiet bees. Maybe that was what she'd done, although it made no sense to him at all. There was no sign of any fire, or of any other source of smoke around.

Then he saw it wasn't smoke. It was the hornets. Culter felt sick. The girl's face and head were covered with the insects. He started toward her, not sure what he could do, but knowing she would die if stung that many times.

"You'd better stop there." It was the girl's voice from inside the swarming hornets.

"What can I do? How can I get them off you?" Culter said.

The girl laughed.

She must be crazy with fear or pain, Culter thought, and took another step toward her.

"Don't," the girl said. "I can handle them as far as *I*'m concerned, but I'm not sure I can keep them from stinging you."

Culter stopped. He wasn't sure he understood, but the girl's voice had the tone of one who knew what she was saying, as though she were in complete control.

He waited. The hornets flowed over the girl's face and head and shoulders, and Culter could hear her low voice talking. He could not hear the words, and somehow knew he wouldn't understand them if he could.

The hornets stopped, then lifted in a single mass away from the girl's face. A swirling mist of hornets circled once, then once again, then, with a final humming roar, they rose and flew away.

Only the dripping of the rain sounded now around him. Culter found that he'd been holding his breath, and he exhaled in a long sigh.

"You OK?" he said.

"Of course," the girl said.

"I mean, they didn't sting you," Culter said.

"Why should they? I did nothing to harm them."

"Neither did I, but they didn't give me any chance to explain that in detail," Culter said. "In fact, we never discussed the thing at all. I just ran like hell, and they came tearing after. And," and he touched his neck, "some of them won."

"They stung you?" the girl said, and sounded worried.

"Only a few," Culter said.

"It can be dangerous. These are not regular hornets, you know."

"No," Culter said. "I didn't know. How do you tell a regular hornet from any other kind?" His head was aching now and he rubbed his neck again.

"Come," the girl said. "There are ressel plants back there," and she nodded off behind her.

Culter followed. His head was aching more, and he seemed to have something in his eyes, like water that would not come out. It made it hard to see clearly.

"Here," the girl said, and knelt down. She picked a single stem of a deep purple plant, then stood and came to Culter. "You don't look too hot," she said. "Sit down."

"Before I fall down," Culter said, and smiled, but he found a stump and sat down on it.

"Now this won't hurt," the girl said.

"You sound like a dentist," Culter said.

The girl hesitated.

"How do you know about dentists?" she said, then, "No. Don't talk. Wait till this ressel has a chance to work," and Culter could feel her fingers on his neck, then on his forehead. The pain lessened, the ache began to leave, and he could see again.

"Hey," he said. "You were right. It didn't hurt," and he rubbed his neck and could feel no swelling, "and my headache's gone, and now *I* sound like some commercial."

"How do you know about commercials?" the girl said.

"Anybody who's ever watched TV knows . . ." and Culter stopped.

"See!" the girl said. "You're just as surprised as I am."

"You must be from home," Culter said, and stared at the girl.

"The West Coast," the girl said.

"How'd you get here?" Culter said.

"I was out in the desert," the girl said, then laughed. "I'll tell you sometime when we have three or four hours. But how'd *you* get here?"

"Walked," Culter said, then laughed at her confusion.

"That's how I got *here*," and he stamped his foot down on the ground, "today. How I got to this country or this world or this time, that's easy. Some punks stomped the life out of me, and some old geezer found me there and, for kicks or something, thought it would be fun to see if I could turn into Sir Lancelot, or maybe Roland. On the other hand, it might be Ali Baba and that bunch he hung around with. The old guy didn't say."

The girl was looking at him.

"Where are you going now?" she said.

"That's a little hard to say," Culter said. "I am going north, up the river, then I am turning west when I get to the ruined mill. Of course, the ruined mill may have washed away, and the river seems to be turning into a lake, and I have no idea which way is north or west or up or down. Other than that, I know exactly where I'm going."

"To the gathering," the girl said.

Culter looked more closely at this girl. He saw a pudgy, freckled, round-faced girl about his own age, wrapped in a great cloak, but with bare feet. Her pink toes peeped out from layered dirt.

"You're not wearing shoes," Culter said.

"I can't run in shoes," the girl said. "But you didn't answer me. I said you're going to the gathering."

"That doesn't sound like a question to me," Culter said.

"I guess it isn't," the girl said. "But you must be one of the other four."

"What other four?" Culter said. "And how come you know more about me than I do?"

"My name's Flos," the girl said, and held out her hand.

Culter shrugged, then shook it. "You don't answer my questions any better than I answer yours," he said. "I'm Culter."

"We'd better get going," Flos said. "I have a feeling we may be late already."

"Just where are we going?" Culter said.

"To the gathering, of course," Flos said, and started off.

"Hey, wait a second," Culter said, and he got up and joined her. "You know where this gathering of yours is?"

"No," Flos said. "But it should be easy to find."

"Yeah," Culter said. "You just go north along the river till you get to this old mill, see," but the girl had started off again, and he moved quickly to keep up.

The cat was standing over him when Jason woke, but, as soon as she saw movement, she padded across the clearing and sat down.

"You may not think that cat is yours," a voice said, "but *it* does. It's been standing guard over you since you passed out."

Jason sat up. The giant—the young man was sitting some ten feet away, and smiling.

"How's the girl?" Jason said, looking around.

"I'm OK," and a tall, platinum-haired figure stepped from the trees. "Now," she said, and limped slightly as she crossed the clearing.

"It still hurts," Jason said.

"Only a little."

"I don't know how you did that," the young man said. "It was some kind of miracle."

"No," Jason said, then looked down at his black hand. "As an old woman told me once, it's just knowing how things work and being part of them."

"And having a black hand like yours," the young man said.

Jason felt the flame of anger flash through him, but he held it back. "Let me see that ankle," he said to the girl instead.

She came to him, and he touched her leg and could feel the aching. He didn't think he had the strength to take it from her.

"It should go away in a few days," he said, and then noticed her feet. They were more calloused than any human feet Jason had ever seen. They were more like the pads of a great dog. Or wolf.

He looked up at her.

"You can feel the pain in my leg?" the girl said.

"Yes," Jason said.

"And you could feel what it was like after the trap?"

"Yes," Jason said.

The girl's eyes shone, then clouded with tears. "There's no way I can thank you for what you've done," she said.

"Forget it," Jason said, and then stood up. The crying embarrassed him. "I've got to go."

"Where?" the young man said.

"You wouldn't believe me if I told you," Jason said.

"Maybe we can all go together," the young man said, and rose.

"Not where I'm going," Jason said.

"Where's that?"

"Following the cat," Jason said, and looked at the animal. "OK, girl. Let's get moving." The swamp cat just sat there and looked at him. "Let's move it out," Jason said. "Haul tail. Be on our way." The cat just sat there. Jason didn't know what he should do.

The young man laughed. "Well," he said, "if your cat won't move, maybe you'd like to come with me. I'm looking for a gathering."

"What kind of gathering?" Jason said.

"I don't know," the young man said.

"Where is it?" Jason said.

"I don't know," the young man said.

Jason looked at him. He looked at Jason. Both started laughing and couldn't stop. They fell forward and held each other up, but the laughter made them weak, and they fell down onto the moss.

The girl stood looking down at them and frowning.

Jason looked up. "Well," he said, "what are *you* here for? Looking for a McDonald's?" and he started laughing harder.

But the others didn't.

Jason stopped. "What's the matter with you two?" he said.

"You just said 'McDonald's'," the young man said. "Where'd you hear that name?"

"Hear that name? You crazy?" Jason said. "I had a Big Mac the night I fell . . ." and then he understood.

"You're from home!" the girl said.

"My name's Jason."

"Mine's Sax."

"I'm Lyca."

They chattered about where and when and how, and then their voices died and they were looking at each other.

"Now what?" Sax said.

"I think I know what your gathering is," Jason said.

"Yes," said Lyca. "The gathering is us."

"Where are we supposed to gather?" Sax said.

Jason glanced over at the swamp cat. She was stretched out and seemed asleep.

"If that's any indication," he said, "the answer is, right here."

"So we're the gathering, and the gathering is here," Sax said. "But that doesn't answer my first question. Now what?"

None of them could answer.

A cold wind blew through the clearing.

"Well," Jason said, and stood, "at least we could have ourselves a little fire to stay warm," and he started picking up small sticks and branches.

"Right," Sax said, and did the same, and soon there was a good pile.

"Of course," Sax said, "it's soaking wet. There's no way for it to burn."

"Watch," Jason said, and went to the trees around the clearing, and checked them out. Finally he found one that he liked, an old dead hulk which was about to topple.

He pulled at it. It didn't budge.

"Hey," Sax said. "Let me do that," and he came to the old tree, took a look, then wrapped his arms around it, strained, and ripped it from the ground. "Where you want it?" he grunted, still holding the tree.

"Over by the others," Jason said, and Sax waddled, with the massive trunk held in his arms, to where the other wood lay. He dropped the trunk and stepped back, breathing deeply.

Jason just shook his head in amazement at the strength of the young giant, then stepped forward, squatted down, and started digging.

He first tore off some bark, then the wet pulp underneath it.

"Anybody got a knife?" he said.

A whisper, then a thunk, and the handle of a knife was sticking from the tree trunk, not two inches from his hand.

Jason didn't move.

He heard the scream of the swamp cat from behind him, then a sort of growl, and then he turned and faced whoever was attacking.

At the edge of the clearing stood a young guy reaching for the handle of his sword, next to him, a small round girl, and bounding at them the swamp cat. She leaped, then fell short, tangled in long whips of bramble bushes. Jason had not noticed them before.

He caught a movement in the corner of his eye, and saw Lyca slide along the edge of the clearing, toward the two strangers. She moved as smoothly as an animal out hunting.

Sax was standing now, and had picked up the largest branch from off the pile. His arm pulled back to launch it as a deadly missile.

But everything was wrong.

Jason was certain of it.

"No!" he shouted, and stood up and reached to stay Sax's arm. "NO!" louder now, so Lyca would hear too. "They are all right! They are all right!"

Too late.

Lyca leaped at the small girl, and Sax threw his heavy branch.

Lyca never made it. Tendrils of the same brambles which had snared the cat now lashed out from the tangle and caught her leg. She tripped and sprawled, and instantly was covered by the brambles.

But the branch Sax threw went straight and caught the young guy in the head, and he dropped to the ground before he could draw his sword.

"No!" Jason said, but Sax seemed not to hear, as though the sight of Lyca lying on the ground was just too much. He picked up another branch to throw.

Jason moved swiftly and in silence around to face Sax, and he shouted up, "No! Don't do it." But the giant's eyes were glazed with anger, and his arm went back, and he poised to hurl the branch right at the girl.

Jason struck. His white right hand shot out and flicked against the temple. Sax looked down at him, then slowly sank down to his knees, then fell, face forward, on the ground.

Jason spun around. Only the small girl was left standing. She looked frightened, but with a set to her mouth which indicated she would fight. Whatever the odds, she would not quit.

"You are one of us?" Jason said, half question, half in answer.

"I was told to come," the girl said.

"So were we all," Jason said.

"You are from home?" the girl said.

"If you mean McDonald's, yes, we are from home. All of us."

There was a sudden scream, and the swamp cat gave a final struggle in the brambles.

"Him, too?" the girl said.

"It's a 'her'," Jason said, then felt foolish. "But that's not the point. We have to get them out of there. I don't see how both of them fell in the same bramble bush at the same time."

"They didn't fall," the girl said, but said no more.

"I'll wake this guy up," Jason said, and nodded at Sax. "But see if you can get the girl loose first. I think seeing her like that was what made him so mad."

The small girl folded both her arms, closed her eyes, and stood there.

"Did you hear me?" Jason said. "I said . . ."

"I heard you," the girl said. "Now just shut up and let me do it."

Jason shut up.

For the bramble bush had started to untangle. One by one, the long barbed stems unwrapped themselves and seemed to draw within, as though the bush had grown out suddenly, and now was shrinking back to its real size.

Lyca was the first one freed. She sat and rubbed the places where the thorns had cut.

"You OK?" the small girl said.

Lyca looked up. "How come I didn't see that bramble bush?" she said.

"It saw you," the small girl said. "I'm Flos."

The bush kept retreating till the cat was able to jump out. She looked both surprised and embarrassed at her failure to rip the enemies to pieces. She came to Jason, and stood silently. He scratched her neck.

"It's OK, girl. You did your best. They weren't enemies, it turned out." He bent and touched Sax with his left hand, closed his eyes, concentrated for an instant, then withdrew his hand.

Sax opened one eye. "You hit me," he said.

"You almost messed up the whole gathering," Jason said.

"They were hurting Lyca," Sax said.

"No," Jason said. "See for yourself. She's fine."

Sax looked across the clearing. Lyca and Flos were bending over the still form of the other guy. They were both talking quickly about what to do and who they were and where they came from.

Sax shrugged. "You win," he said, and rubbed his head and slowly stood. "But how'd you know they weren't enemies? When that guy threw that knife, I figured we had had it."

"I don't know," Jason said. "I honestly don't know, but I knew they were our friends. That's all I can tell you."

"I'm sorry I conked the other guy," Sax said, and they both went to where he lay.

Jason checked his head, said he was only knocked out, brought him to, and they sat and watched him sit up slowly.

"Who won?" he said.

"You did," Jason said.

"I was pretty sure I had," Culter said, rubbing the lump on his head. "Somehow I always win whenever someone knocks me out. It's a trick."

"How come you tried to kill me?" Jason said.

"Huh?" Culter said.

"How come you tried to kill me with that knife of yours? You just walked in here and tried to stick a knife in me."

"No way!" Culter said. "I wasn't trying to kill you."

"It looked that way to me, too," Sax said.

Lyca nodded.

Culter shook his head as though to clear the final cobwebs, then stood up.

"If I had wanted to kill you," and he walked over to the log that Jason had been working on, pulled out his knife, and turned toward them, "if I had wanted to kill you, I could have done a better job than that," and his arm moved like a whip and his knife whispered, and buried itself handle deep right between Jason's feet.

Jason didn't move. "I get your point," he said.

"No," Culter said. "You *didn't* get my point, *that's* the point."

Jason laughed. "How come you threw the thing in the first place?" he said.

"You asked for a knife," Culter said.

"You always throw one when somebody asks?" Jason said.

"Where I've been the last few months you do," Culter said. "It's faster."

"I can see that," Jason said.

Culter came back, picked up his knife, and introduced himself, as did the others.

Jason went back, dug in the log and brought out just enough dry pulp to start the fire. Soon the other branches dried sufficiently to burn.

It was getting dark. The five sat in a circle, although Lyca kept farther from the fire than the rest.

"Well," Culter said finally, "it seems this is the gathering, and we are gathered. Now what?"

"Zara Keep."

From the edge of the clearing by the tallest tree, the voice of the old man.

"It is now time for Zara Keep."

The flames hissed low, and the air was dark, and the wind was very cold.

IV
THE TASK

"There are five Keeps," the old man started, having taken the seat beside the fire he was offered. Jason had tossed on an extra branch, and the light grew brighter. "Zara is the central one."

"I have heard all this," Culter said. "Bladen has told me."

"I have not heard any of it," Lyca said, but did not explain that wolves did not know history. They communicate through a sense of things, and Lyca had picked up that danger lay east of the Howling Hill in some great building, but there were no details possible without a spoken language.

"I shall tell it from the start, so that you shall know everything you need to."

"How will we *need* to know any of this stuff at all?" Culter said.

"I shall explain in time," the old man said.

"Let him tell it," Sax said.

"Listen," Culter said. "Every time this old wino . . . pardon me . . . this old gentleman, every time this old guy shows up, my whole world changes. This is the first time I have had a chance to get my two cents in first."

"He saved your life, didn't he?" Flos said softly.

Culter spun and looked at her.

"How'd you know that? I didn't tell you anything."

"You didn't have to," Flos said. "I think it was the same with all of us."

"Well," Sax said, "*somebody* got me out, and this man was there when I woke up. I guess he did it."

"I was in a forest fire," Lyca said.

"I broke my ankle," Flos said, "and was bitten by a snake."

Jason said nothing, but the terrible sensation of the falling came back cold deep in his stomach.

They all were silent, each thinking of his or her own way here.

"I shall go on," the old man said. "As some of you know, my name is Fulmin. I am the Watcher Of The Keeps. I report to the Council."

"What is this Council?" Culter asked.

"The wisest people in the land," Fulmin said. "I can tell you no more."

"Go on about the Keeps," Flos said.

Fulmin began again. "I shall tell it from the start. In a time before time, when all things were one with one another, when the plants and earth and beasts and men could talk and understand and were at peace, in this distant time, this land began, and was so for generations. Centuries. Millennia. For eons. And it was good. It would have remained so had not the Masters come."

Fulmin's voice had dropped almost below their hearing. He had difficulty going on, then shook his head, straightened his back, and looked deep into the fire.

"What masters?" Flos said gently.

"The Masters," Fulmin repeated. "Beings from another place and time and understanding. Beings who cared little for our world."

"Why did they come then?"

"We believe that they were driven out of where they came from, but we don't know for sure. They came with great powers, and they ruled this land. There were five of them, and each one built a Keep to live in. Zara is the central one of these. The other four are Sulg, Quum, Wolt, and Vect. Each is located at the four points of the wind."

"They must have brought all kinds of soldiers with them," Flos said.

"They brought only themselves," Fulmin said. "Themselves and magic."

"They controlled everything with magic?"

"No. Only the basic elements. The rest was done by servants. They used some of our people to build the Keeps, to maintain them, and to wait on the Masters."

"So," Sax said, "this place is ruled by the Masters."

"No," Fulmin said. "They ruled a thousand years, then disappeared."

"Disappeared?" Flos said.

"One morning they were gone. All five of them. We do not know why or where, just that they're gone."

"So you are free again," Flos said.

"And careless," Fulmin said. "We rushed into returning to the ways of old. We danced and sang and laughed and never thought that things were not the same, that there were some of us who had been changed. By being servants, and the sons of servants, and their sons. These people didn't want the ways of ancient times. They wanted to be Masters."

"But they were just people like yourselves," Flos said.

"With two differences. They wanted power, and they had the books."

"What books?"

"The Masters' books. When the Masters left, they took nothing. They left their clothes, their furniture, their weapons, and their books, and their books are most important of them all."

"What's in those books?" Flos said.

"Their magic," Fulmin said, and the fire glowed across his old lined face. "All the power they had wielded was written in those books for anyone who wanted it."

"So the servants now control the land," Sax said.

"Not yet," Fulmin said.

"But you said that anyone who read the books would have the magic of the Masters."

"But they must first *read* the books, and no one can do that," Fulmin said.

"The books are written in some other language?" Flos said.

"Yes," Fulmin said. "We cannot read them."

"Then there's nothing to worry about," Culter said, and broke a stick and threw the halves into the fire.

"Unfortunately," Fulmin said, "that isn't true. There is the Crystal. They have learned how to use it."

"What's the Crystal?" Culter said.

"A stone, about the size of a large egg. It is said to look like nothing special. But it has one great power that we know of. It allows anyone who holds it to understand the language of the Masters."

"You say these servants . . . what do you call them?"

"The Keepers," Fulmin said.

"You say these Keepers know how to use the Crystal," Culter said. "Then how come they haven't taken over everything?"

"You must understand magic," Fulmin said. "They have begun to use the stone to translate the books of the Masters' magic, but it takes time and terrible effort to use the spells. It is so with any magic. Knowing what to do and being able to do it are often two different things."

"How do you know they have the Crystal and have started using it?" Jason said.

"The first clue," Fulmin said, "was when we couldn't enter any of the Keeps. When the people brought supplies up to the gates, they were turned away. This, in itself, would have meant little, but one of the farmer boys slipped off and tried to climb the walls. He said he wanted to see what they had inside. Instead, the instant he touched one of the stones at the base of the wall, he was thrown ten yards back on the ground, and almost broke his neck. Since then, of course, we have sent scouts to check the story thoroughly. It is quite true. There is no way any of our people can get in the Keeps."

"You say 'our people'," Jason said. "Does that mean other people might get through?"

"The Council thinks so," Fulmin said. "They believe that the spell being used works only for our people. Someone from another world might get inside."

It was clear to everyone at the same instant.

"Us," Culter and Flos said in unison.

"Swell!" said Jason.

Sax and Lyca held their peace.

"Yes," Fulmin said.

Everyone was silent.

Fulmin went on. "There are other signs that they have magic power. They destroyed the roads up to the Keeps, which indicates that they do not need anything we have for their survival. Then this storm, of course."

"They made this rain?" Flos said.

"Yes, but they do not control the lightning yet."

"Can anyone control lightning?" Flos asked.

"Sometimes. If the need is great enough, and the cause good, there are those who are allowed to use a small part of its power."

"And you're one of them," Flos said.

"Perhaps."

"How close are the Keepers to controlling everything? To taking over the whole land?" Flos asked.

"They gain in strength each day. Their leader is Zaragoza, of the central Keep. He seems closer to attaining absolute power than any of the others. He has not done it yet, but it will not be long."

"He is the one who flies each night," Flos said.

"Yes."

"And that is his dragon."

"Yes. We have no dragons here at all, which Zaragoza knows. He also knows that we can fight any force natural to this land, but are helpless against forces from another."

"But we don't have dragons in our world, either," Culter said.

"Once upon a time," Fulmin said and let the words hang.

Culter wiped his forehead of a thin film of sweat. He wasn't sure what all this meant, but it would be a biggie.

"Zaragoza is bringing in forces from other worlds, and, when he has enough, he will be in control. He will be another Master, right?" Flos said.

"But with a difference," Fulmin said. "The Masters did

not rule with malice. We were not harmed. Zaragoza and the others want to make us into slaves. There is no crueler master than a former servant.''

''How long before they have the force necessary to control you?'' Jason asked.

'We do not know for certain, but the signs say soon. We are mobilizing all the people for the final fight, but there is little chance that they can win. Zaragoza and the others will bring in an evil greater than whatever strength we have. There is little hope.''

''We are part of it,'' Jason said. ''That's why we're here.''

''Yes,'' Fulmin said.

''You saved our lives, had us trained, and now you want to use us.''

''I could not bring you to this world if I had to interrupt your lives,'' Fulmin said.

''You mean we're dead,'' Sax said.

''I mean that you would not be alive were you back where you came from,'' Fulmin said. ''Jason is right. I placed each one of you with a teacher who could take the skills you had and make them greater. We wish we had more time for you to learn much more.''

''What about the using us part?'' Jason said.

''Only if you each agree,'' Fulmin said. ''We will not fight tyranny with tyranny. You will not be forced to do this thing for us. I have brought you together to *ask* your help, not to make you give it.''

''What will happen to Inochi and Shi if we don't?'' Jason said.

Fulmin looked at him.

''Those who have helped the Council will be singled out for special punishment after the Keepers win the war,'' he said.

''They will die,'' Jason said.

''Yes,'' Fulmin said. ''They will die. Quickly, if they are lucky.''

''And Physis?'' Flos said.

''She, too,'' Fulmin said. ''All the mentors.''

There was silence in the clearing.

Then Jason said, "If someone gets the Crystal away from them, then they may not be able to bring other forces in. Is that right?"

"So far as we know," Fulmin said, "they have already begun the process. There are strange beings now in Zaratown. We think they are experimental. They are not warriors of any kind. But soon they will find how to bring in warriors, and the war will then begin."

"Then there is not much time," Culter said.

"Very little," Fulmin said.

"And," Sax said, "if we steal the Crystal, then they can't read the books."

"That is correct," Fulmin said.

"But suppose they've written down the formulas?" Sax said. "What then?"

"It can't be done," Fulmin said. "Magic can only be recorded once. It can't be copied. That is why copies never work."

"If you have some magic, how come you can't do this?" Culter said.

"The little magic I possess is purely natural," Fulmin said. "I can travel on the wind. I can heal by using lightning in a potion. I can move through time for certain things, as I did when getting you. But these cannot be used against evil. They are of no use in getting the Crystal from the Keep."

They had let the fire die, and it glowed orange. The rain had slowed, and now it stopped completely. The moon came out and they looked up at the clear sky . . . and saw the black silhouette against it flying. The sound of the wings came closer, and the smell of evil was around, and Zaragoza rode his dragon through the night.

"He doesn't give us much choice," Culter said, almost to himself.

"None at all," Sax said. "None at all."

"You guys are nuts," Jason said. "You know that, don't you."

"Of course," Flos said.

"And you?" said Lyca, looking with her yellow eyes reflecting the dull fire.

Jason rubbed his chin, then held out his two hands, the left one black, the right one white, and saw the hopelessness of home, and the kiss of Inochi when he had left the swamp, and he looked across the clearing at the cat.

He cleared his throat. "I guess it's worth fighting for," he said.

They slept. Fulmin stood throughout the night, and held his cloak up high. The rain never reached the ground within the clearing.

They woke when it got light, shared what little food they had, and then began their planning. Each was anxious to know what they should do, but none of them had any good suggestions.

"We just don't have enough to go on yet," said Jason.

"Is there a map of the Keep?" Culter asked.

"I do not have one," Fulmin said. "I have never been there. I have heard various descriptions, but I fear the Keep is much too big for you to profit from what I could tell you, except that it is rumored that the Crystal is kept at the highest point of all. I assume that means the room up in the central tower."

"How do we get to the room in the central tower?" Jason said.

"That you must find for yourselves," Fulmin said.

"How do we get to the Keep in the first place?" Sax said.

"There are two routes," Fulmin said. "North through the mountains, then double back along the river to the Keep. It is a ten-day journey, at the very least."

"There may not be ten days, from what you've said," Jason said in a low voice. He was thinking of Inochi back in the swamp, preparing a hot breakfast.

"That is true," Fulmin said. "There is another route, but it is both dangerous and possibly impassible."

"Tell us that route," Sax said.

"From here, go east until you reach the river. Then follow it north, upstream, through the gorge, until you reach the cliffs. There was once a path which ran up the cliffside until it reached the tunnel. But it may have been destroyed, and it is said the tunnels have been blocked by boulders."

"I think we should go that way," Sax said. "How long would that one take?"

"Two days at most," Fulmin said.

Sax looked around the group.

"Do we all agree we take the cliff route?" he said.

Jason had a sudden sense of falling, and he put both hands out on the ground.

"Yes," Culter said.

Then Flos and Lyca.

"And you?" Sax said to Jason.

The sick feeling wouldn't go away, but he had another picture of Inochi's face, and Jason nodded.

"Well," Sax said, and stood up, "that's settled. At least we know which way we're going."

The knowledge put new life in them. They gathered all their things and took an inventory. Four knapsacks, some hardtack and biscuits, half of a salt pork sandwich, six dried figs, and tinderboxes. A sword, a knife, a stone, a carving of a wolf, and a small bit of grass.

"It isn't much," Sax said.

"It may be just enough," Fulmin said. "It's the best that we could do."

"At least we can make a few things by ourselves," Sax said, and walked into the forest, where he could be heard tearing down a small tree.

"He doesn't waste much time," Culter said. "I'll give him credit for that."

Sax returned, dragging the tree behind him. "Can I borrow your knife?" he said to Culter. "I want to trim these branches off and use this for a staff."

"Maybe I could trim them with my sword," Culter said, and reached for it.

"NO!" Fulmin said. "You were instructed not to draw that sword unless you needed it."

"I need it now," Culter said, his hand on the handle.

"Not for this," Fulmin said. "That sword is only to be used when your very life is threatened."

Culter looked down at the sword in its sheath as though he weren't sure he wanted it beside him. Then he shrugged, and said, "Let me do that," and took his knife and started stripping the limbs of the small tree Sax was holding.

"We could use a rope," Sax said, "if we're to do some climbing."

Flos stood up. "Somebody help me get some vines," she said, and Jason rose and followed her into the forest.

"I'll get some meat," Lyca said, and moved off silently into the trees.

The staff was finished, and Jason and Flos were back with yards of vines, but there was no sign of Lyca yet.

"How do we tie these things?" Jason said, holding one end of a vine and scowling.

"Give me the ends," Flos said, and crossed her legs and sank down to the ground. "Just keep the vines untangled, and feed them in to me." She held out her hands for the first vines.

Jason gave her three ends. Flos laid them in her palm, closed her fist lightly, and pulled the loose end through. The vines were braided.

"How did you do that?" Jason asked.

"It's hard to explain," Flos said, "and we're in a hurry. Just keep the vines coming, and I'll make the rope."

So Jason fed the vines to her, and, as they passed through her closed fist, they twisted in some way, and came out braided.

Sax took the braided end, stretched it between his hands, then braced himself and tried to break it. It held. Sax smiled. "That's what I call a rope," he said.

Flos sat there with her legs crossed, smiling, pulling the vines into more rope.

"If Lyca brings in meat," Culter said, "we'd better build this fire up," and he searched around for dry wood which would burn well.

The rope was finished, and Culter cut it in half; one half went to Sax, and the other one to Jason.

Lyca returned. She was carrying four rabbits in her hand. "This should be enough for now," she said, and dropped them by the fire. She was panting, and seemed tired from her hunt.

"I'll fix them," Culter said, and took his knife to start the cleaning. He picked up the first rabbit and examined it. Its neck was broken, and there were teethmarks deep under the fur, as though some dog had caught the rabbit and shaken it to death.

His first thought was that Lyca found it, an old kill of some wild dogs or wolves, but the rabbit's body was still warm. There was no explanation.

Culter looked at Lyca. Her yellow eyes looked back at him as though asking him for silence. He shivered, then shook himself and returned to the task of cleaning the rabbit.

Sax made a small spit to cook them on. The group waited.

"There is one final thing," Fulmin said. "I will send the swamp cat with you to the cliffs. I cannot ask her to go up with you. That will be her choice, but I can have her guide you as far as the cliffs themselves."

At the smell of the cooking game, the great cat had come closer, and now it sat by Jason. He reached out and stroked its neck. "Does she have a name?" he asked Fulmin.

"She may," Fulmin said. "But I do not know it. It is said that all swamp cats have names, but they reveal them rarely."

Jason looked down at the cat. She sat there watching the small carcasses turn slowly.

"She's more interested in that food than telling you her name," Culter said. "Of course, I'm not sure how big cats go about telling people anything, even their names."

"There are ways," Lyca said, then looked as though she wished she hadn't spoken.

"There's no hurry," Jason said.

"The meat's done," Culter said. "Let's cut it up and let's get going."

The meat was cut in strips and packed into the knapsacks, and they all stood and looked at the old man.

"Why can't you come with us?" Flos said. "At least partway?"

"The Keepers seem to have a way of knowing where I am," the old man said. "It is better if you leave me now. I am always safe so long as I am in the clearing. So are you, but once out in the forest, they can find me easily."

"You don't think they will know we're coming."

"I hope they won't."

"So do we," Jason said. "Let's go." He turned and walked into the woods, the swamp cat two bounds ahead.

The others checked their things, then followed single file. The old man stood alone beside the fire in the clearing. His eyes were filled with hope and tears.

V
THE KEEP

The only sounds within the forest were the sounds they made—the cracking of a stick stepped on, the swishing of the bushes pushed aside. Occasionally someone slipped and said something, but otherwise they didn't talk.

They followed the cat. She wound her way along game paths, crossed streams which now were swollen into little rivers, climbed muddy banks, and led under trees weighed down with water so their branches almost touched the ground. It was a soggy journey, and they were in a foul mood when they came out of the forest to the river.

The cat stopped. She seemed to have lost her bearings, as though the flooding had destroyed her path.

They stood by what now looked like a lake, if it had not had such a current swirling down.

"Do we have to cross that thing?" Sax asked.

"I don't think so," Culter said. "The directions were to turn and head north from here. On the other hand, if I were you, I wouldn't trust my memory. The last time I tried to follow anyone's directions I got so lost I found you guys, and now look at me."

Sax never took his eyes off of the river.

"Let's eat," someone said, and there was general agreement.

"No point in a fire," Culter said. "It's raining too hard."

"Just someplace dry to sit," Flos said.

But there was no dry place in sight, so they chose the next

best thing, a fallen tree which served as something of a bench high off the ground.

"It'll keep your fanny out of the river at least," Culter said.

They sat along the trunk and took out pieces of the rabbits Lyca had killed. The meat was cold, but good, and they were hungry.

"Save some for later," Flos said. "I have a feeling there won't be much game where we are going."

"I will get some more this afternoon," Lyca said, and ripped off a piece of meat and swallowed it.

"Don't you ever bother chewing it?" Flos said.

Lyca looked surprised for just a second, then she blushed, and mumbled something about being very hungry. But Culter noticed that she ate more slowly after that, and chewed her meat with care.

They finished, repacked their knapsacks, checked their gear, and started up the river bank. There was no need for Jason to go first, for the flood had hidden all the landmarks, and the swamp cat was lost here. Anyone could lead the party now. Flos started first.

She was in front later in the afternoon when she disappeared around a bend, then came back screaming—running, slipping, looking back, and screaming.

Culter was some yards behind her, and held out his arms to catch her as she ran. She ran into them, and he held her tightly.

"Easy," he said. "Easy does it." His voice was soothing, but he freed one hand and reached down and drew his knife. "Easy," he repeated, looking over Flos's shoulder for whatever had scared her.

The others had caught up, but Flos was not articulate. She held tight to Culter and sobbed into his chest.

"What's wrong?" Sax asked.

"Don't know," said Culter. "She just came back screaming. I can't get her calmed down enough to talk."

"Let's take a look," Sax said, and started forward.

Flos sobbed deeply, then tried to take a breath, sobbed again, then spoke. "The snakes!" she said. "It was the snakes!" She started crying once again.

"Whoa," Culter said. "Hold it, girl. Calm down. What snakes? How big? How many?"

"Lots of them," Sax said, coming up behind him. "There must be a thousand or so there. They seem to have come down to get away from the water, and they're trapped between the river and two streams. I can see why she was frightened."

"I thought you were our nature child," Culter said gently. "How come the snakes got to you?"

Flos looked ashamed. Tears streaked her face, and her eyes were red, and her nose was running. She wiped it on her sleeve.

"It was the way . . . ," she started. "It was what happened in the desert. When I was in the desert and I broke my ankle and the rattlesnake . . ." Culter could feel her shaking up against him.

"It's OK," he said. "It's OK now. No snakes are going to get you."

"We've got a problem," Sax said. "I don't see any way around."

"Back through the woods," Culter said.

"No good," Sax said. "The streams coming out of the forest are so deep and strong that there's no way to cross them except where they spread out by the river. Every foothold there is covered with a dozen snakes. We could walk miles back up into those woods before we found a place where we could cross."

The group was silent.

"Anybody got a bright idea?" Culter said.

"It seems we have a two-part question," Jason said. "The first part is the getting past the snakes. The second part is doing it so this girl doesn't know it's happening."

"What kind of snakes are they?" Lyca said.

"I don't know much about snakes, but these are big and mean looking. There are moccasins in there, if I remember my Boy Scout book properly."

"There is one slight possibility," Sax said. "It's got a lot of holes in it, but, if we could get a rope up high enough, we might swing across."

"Tarzan," Culter said.

"Without the sound effects," Sax said.

"What's the point in swinging on a vine if you don't give the yell?" Culter said, and tried to sound like Johnny Weissmuller.

"You better stick to knives," Jason said.

"Or whistling," Sax said.

"Nobody appreciates real talent," Culter said. "But you said this was only a possibility. What's so hard about swinging on a rope?"

"Getting the rope up there to swing on," Sax said.

"Let's take a look," Culter said, and they all worked their way around the bend, and stopped and stared.

They were standing on a low bank of a stream which poured out of the forest. It was so swift that it had obviously worn itself deep into its bed, and was well beyond wading across. Most of the rocks which might have been used as stepping stones were under water. The few exposed were writhing with a dozen snakes. On the other side of the stream was a small island. Its surface seemed to shift and slide all by itself. Then they saw that it was not the land that moved. It was the tangled mass of snakes which lay across it. Beyond the island was another branch of the foaming stream, and, beyond that, the far bank, looking to be some ten or fifteen feet high.

"I figure it's about seventy-five feet across the whole thing," Sax said. "Give or take a yard or two."

Sax had been right about not going back into the forest. The rush of water from the stream indicated that it probably went some distance before becoming shallow enough to cross. The thought of more snakes crawling down its banks toward the river was not pleasant.

"If we can cross here," Sax said, "we're OK. If we have to find another way, there's no telling when we'll get there."

"You said we could swing across," Culter said.

"Yeah," Sax said. "I said we could, if we can get a rope up there," and he pointed up to a long branch of a tall tree which jutted out above the island.

"That must be fifty feet up," Culter said.

"It has to be, to give us enough rope to swing across," Sax said.

"There's one other thing," Jason said. "To swing across, we have to be up in the air, ourselves."

"Right," Sax said. "Look behind you." He pointed to another tree, with a thick branch about twenty feet above the ground behind them. "I have it figured," Sax said. "If we stand on that branch, we will have enough swing to get across to that other bank."

"And how do we get the rope back?" Culter said.

"We'll tie another rope to it, and someone here will keep hold of it and pull it back each time."

"Have we got enough rope?" Lyca said.

"I think so," Sax said. "What we haven't got is a way to get it up around that limb."

"Throw it," Culter said.

"You can try," Sax said, "but fifty feet's not easy, and there are small branches in the way. I don't think it can be done."

"If someone could climb up there . . ." Flos said.

"There's no way across from this tree to the big one," Sax said. "There must be a ten foot jump, and I'm not about to try that fifty feet up."

The group stood looking at the problem.

"How about the cat?" Jason said.

"She could get there," Sax said, "but how can we tell her what to do? She may like you, but I doubt that she could understand complicated directions like these would have to be."

Jason called the cat to him, squatted down, and told her what they needed. The cat rubbed up against Jason's leg, but showed no comprehension.

"Even if she went up there," Sax said, "how could she tie the rope around the branch?"

Jason spoke to the cat again. Again the rubbing, this time with a whine, but the cat did not understand a word. "Well," Jason said, and stood up slowly, "I guess you're right. Maybe someday she and I will communicate, but this one's way beyond what we can do right now."

They stood looking at the trees and branches. They did not want to look down at the snakes.

"Come!"

The voice was Lyca's, and they turned and looked at her. She was speaking to the cat. The cat stood still, her tail waving back and forth behind her. Her eyes were locked with Lyca's.

"Come!" Lyca repeated, and the cat's tail now lashed. She sank down on her belly and began to growl.

"Come!" Lyca said again, and the cat began to crawl toward her.

"Hey," Jason yelled, but Culter reached out and touched his arm.

"Leave her alone," he said. "She knows what she is doing."

Lyca now turned and walked back the way that they had come. She disappeared around the bend. The cat crawled after her, and she too was gone.

"What the hell was that?" Jason said, and almost started after them.

"She knows what she is doing," Culter said.

"How the hell do *you* know?" Jason said, angry at his sense of helplessness.

"I don't know," Culter said. "But I'm sure I'm right. At least give her a couple of minutes to see what she can do."

"Let's get the rope out, just in case she does succeed," Sax said, and he opened up his knapsack and pulled out a length of rope made from the vines. "You've got the rest," he said to Jason.

Jason got his out. By the time he finished, Lyca was back, followed by the swamp cat.

"She understands what she must do," Lyca said.

Jason went to the cat, but she showed no sign of any harm. She rubbed against his leg, and almost purred. "How'd you talk to it?" he said to Lyca.

But Lyca looked away and didn't answer.

"Let's see if she is right," Sax said, and went to the cat. He held one end of the twisted rope out to the animal. "Here you go," he said.

The strong teeth gripped the rope tightly, and the cat walked slowly to the nearby tree, then sprang straight up, caught the branch above her, and was in and climbing faster than they could believe. She reached the place where she

must jump, and with no effort whatsoever cleared the gap and
was in the tall tree where the branch they needed was. She
crept out along the branch to right above the island, still with
the rope tight in her teeth, then stopped.

"She doesn't know what to do next," Lyca said. "I could
not tell her."

"Can you tell her to put the rope down on the branch?"

It was Flos. Obviously shaken by the snakes, beads of
perspiration lined her forehead, and her cheeks were white.
She was making a great effort not to panic, but she knew she
couldn't stay here very long.

"If the cat puts down the rope, it will fall," Sax said.

"Give me the other end," Flos said, and Sax handed it
across to her. "Now tell the cat to let go."

No one moved, but each turned and looked at Lyca.

She was upset, but there was no choice, and she looked up
at the cat and made a sound. Not words, nor anything they'd
ever heard, but the cat tensed, then opened its great mouth.

The rope dropped across the branch, but didn't fall. Instead,
its end became alive and whipped around the branch, then
intertwined with itself, and was a knot.

"I think that will hold," Flos said, and pulled hard on the
rope. It held. Then Sax tried it, and it proved strong enough
for him. He tied the second rope to the end of the first, so he
could retrieve it.

"I guess that's it," he said. "Now, who's the first one
over?"

Suddenly the snakes seemed closer to them all, and bigger,
and the island more alive. They would have to swing down
close to it to make it far enough across to reach the other
bank.

They looked at each other.

"Ah, *nuts*!" Culter said. "I'll try it." He turned and
started climbing to the big branch overhead. The others
followed.

"It should work," Sax said. "We're high enough to get
the right arc, and . . ."

"Shut up!" Culter said. "Either it makes it or it doesn't.
We might as well find out," and he gripped the rope tightly
in his hand and pushed hard off the branch.

It was almost slow motion, Culter hanging from the rope as it swung down toward the living island, right toward the snakes.

"Lift your legs!" Sax shouted, but it wasn't necessary.

Culter had pulled both legs up as far as possible, and was almost lying flat out in the air. He reached the island, and cleared the snakes by just about a foot.

"Go!" Sax shouted, as Culter on the rope swung up and toward the farther bank.

Then he was up and over, and standing on high ground. He turned and waved, then pounded on his chest and gave a Tarzan yell. The rest broke into laughter.

Culter let go of the rope, and Sax pulled on the one attached to its end, which brought it back for the next swinger.

Lyca went next, and Sax showed her where to hold the rope a little higher up than Culter had. She cleared the snakes with three feet to spare, and Culter caught her on the other side.

"Who's next?" Sax said.

They looked at Flos. She was almost shaking with fear.

"Look up," Jason said. "Don't look down until you get to the other side."

Flos said nothing, but took hold of the rope, and they could see that she was both terrified and determined.

"Ready?" Sax said. "I'll give you a push."

Flos took a deep breath, closed her eyes tight, then nodded. Sax pushed, and they watched Flos swing down toward the island, over it, and up to the other side.

"Open your eyes!" Sax shouted.

Flos almost missed. She kept holding the rope as it swung up over the bank, then stopped and started down again. Culter caught her just in time. He had to pry her hands free of the rope.

Sax pulled it back, and Jason took it and made the swing across.

Then Sax.

He swung up over the edge of the bank, let go, and stood there laughing.

"Well," he said. "We . . ." The bank on which he stood

gave way. He started sliding backwards, down toward the rushing waters of the stream.

He threw himself forward and grabbed a tuft of grass. His fingers dug into the ground, but still he slid. His nails made deep grooves in the dirt as he slid backwards.

Jason was the first to move. He jumped and did a dive along the ground. He caught Sax's wrist. Sax stopped sliding.

Jason pulled. Sax was too heavy, but the others were there now, and their combined strength brought him back to firmer ground, where he lay panting.

"Listen," Jason said, trying to get his own breath, "if you're going to do much of that, man, you've got to lose weight."

They laughed, then lay awhile and rested.

Finally Flos stood. "We've got to go," she said, and the others realized that she was still frightened of the snakes back on the island. They were wasting time, too.

They stood across the river from Zaratown. Sax pointed out the bridge that he had crossed two days before, but only the very top of it showed now. Beyond was the town itself, and it was not empty.

Figures moved in and out of the town gate, and soon someone was pointing at the group. Others came running out, and there was quite a mob.

"Let's go," Culter said. "I'm not crazy about being the center of that much attention."

The group continued on along the riverbank. But now the figures from the town were gathering across from them, and it was obvious that there was great excitement.

"It's too far to see them clearly," Flos said, "but there's something strange about them."

"They aren't human," Lyca said.

"How can you tell?" Culter asked.

"I can see them," Lyca said, then was quiet.

They continued on. The riverbank was getting higher, and the distance across was less, as they reached a place where the water rushed through a narrow canyon.

The figures across the river were now closer, running and stopping and pointing at them all the while.

"Fulmin said the Keepers brought them here," Jason said. "He said that they weren't warriors."

"Assuming these are the same things, and not a new batch," Sax said, "and assuming that the old man was right. I have no idea what *he* means by a warrior. These look as though they'd love to get to us."

Sax was right. The figures on the other side were now close enough for them to see them hold their fists up high and shake them, then stamp their feet and jump up and down. In their hands they held what looked like swords.

"If we get to a bridge up ahead," Culter said, "we're in big trouble."

"They don't have hands," Flos said, and the group stopped and looked across the roaring river.

They were just close enough to see them now. See that, what they had thought was a hand was something else, like a large sucker on a growing limb. But it still held a sword.

"I can't see their faces," Culter said. "They've got them hidden in those cloaks they're wearing."

"I think it's just as well," Jason said.

Culter shivered. "Let's keep moving," he said.

They went as quickly as they could, and reached a place where the river widened.

The things across the river stopped when they saw there was no way they could cross. They lowered their hoods and screamed.

"I guess those are their faces," Jason said, but looked sick.

"Where did they come from?" Flos said with a frightened voice.

"I don't know," Culter said, "but I'm not going to ask them."

"I wonder if the rest of the Keepers' people look like that," Sax said.

They all were silent. The thought of coming face to face with horrors like the ones across the river was too much. It was one thing to try to steal some kind of crystal from a keep, and even have to fight some soldiers, but having to deal with pure evil in whatever form it came was more than any of them bargained for.

The things across the river kept on screaming, and the sound was terrible.

"Let's get out of here," Culter said, and they walked on.

The rain continued all the afternoon, and it matched their mood. Culter found himself walking beside Lyca. They were a little behind the others in the group.

"You didn't say anything about those things across the river," Culter said. "You just said that they weren't human, and that was all. Frankly, I'll admit they scared the hell out of me."

Lyca didn't answer.

"I mean," Culter went on, "I'm not really sure that I could fight those monsters if I had to."

"You would," Lyca said.

"How do you know?" Culter said.

"Because," Lyca said, "we will all do what we have to."

"Speak for yourself, John," Culter said. "I'd rather *run* most of the time."

Lyca looked at him, her eyes yellow in the dull light of the coming evening. "You underestimate yourself," she said. "You may be more than you know."

"And I may be less," Culter said, but something in her tone made him wonder.

"I'm sorry," Lyca said, and shook her head as though to clear it. "I guess I haven't been much good as company. I'm not used to being around people."

"What about your teacher?" Culter said.

Lyca looked at him, then seemed to relax just a bit. "I didn't have a human teacher, as you did," she said.

"What kind of teacher was he?" Culter said, thinking of the creatures they'd just seen. For an instant, he wasn't sure which side the girl was on.

"The wolves," Lyca said. "I lived with the wolves."

Culter had a sudden memory of the warm rabbit with the teethmarks on its neck. "That's why you hunt so well," he said, keeping away from anything more dangerous. Such as *how* she hunted.

"Yes," Lyca said. "It is easy for me now."

"If you lived with wolves," Culter said, "how come you're coming with us now? I mean, I think most of us agreed to get this Crystal because, if we don't, the people we have lived with will be killed. At least, that was my major reason. But no one will kill your wolves if the Keepers win.''

Lyca was silent for a moment, then said quietly, ''I have learned that it is best to be with others. To work together, live together, love together,'' and she stopped, then went on, ''and fight and die together, if necessary. Although I lived with the wolves, I am still a human, and part of this group, even though we just met yesterday. If the pack . . . I mean, the group is going, then I go too.''

They walked on in silence, which Lyca finally broke with a soft voice so low that Culter almost missed it. ''And I have been alone too long,'' she said, then said no more.

The noise of the river was increasing. They came around a bend and saw why. The valley narrowed into a gorge, and the water boiled through it like a maddened force.

''I guess we keep going,'' Sax said, as they gathered around to plan the next move. ''Fulmin said the Keep's up there,'' and he pointed toward the gorge.

The going was more difficult, and finally almost impossible. In normal times, there might have been some kind of bank beside the river which they could have walked on, but, in this flood, there was no land at all, only giant boulders, with the water lashing up the sides and tearing at their footing.

If any of them slipped, they would be gone, caught in a pull that no strength could combat. Each was well aware of what that meant.

''Rope together.'' Sax shouted to be heard above the tumult of the water.

They tied off, leaving about fifteen feet of rope between them. It didn't overcome the difficulties of moving among the boulders, but it cut down the risk.

Now we can only break our legs or heads, Culter thought, as he jumped across onto another boulder.

They reached a wider part which still had something of a shore beside it. Actually, it was three gigantic boulders side by side, which made almost a tabletop to stand on.

''It's getting too dark to see our way,'' Sax shouted to the others.

"Then let's stay here," Culter shouted back.

The others nodded, and Culter was aware how tired everybody was. No one had complained, but their faces were drawn tight, and their mouths were set, and their eyes dark under their brows.

They looked about to see where they could huddle for the night, and found a windfall, a dead tree wedged between the boulders; apparently washed down the river by the flood, but hurled up here where it had had a chance to dry.

How can it dry in all this rain? Jason thought, then looked up.

He could not see the sky. There was an overhang above them a hundred feet or more. It stuck out just enough to keep the rain from falling.

"This will be OK," he shouted to Culter. "Except for conversation," and he grinned.

They got a fire going with the tinderbox in Sax's pack, and took out the food they had and heated it. Lyca had been able to catch another rabbit in the afternoon, and this was roasted on a spit and eaten quickly.

"I hope there's food where we're going," Culter shouted in Sax's ear.

Sax leaned close to him and shouted back, "I hope we're still alive to eat it."

"Wonderful thought," Culter said to himself. To Sax he shouted, "Yeah. I hope so, too."

The noise prevented any further talking, but none of them had the strength or inclination to sit around and chat. Within minutes after eating, they were all asleep.

They had left no guard.

Sax realized this the instant he woke up, but it was too late. The rain had stopped, the moon was out and bright, and the dragon was directly overhead. Or so it seemed, for, when Sax looked up, he saw only the overhanging rock above, which might mean that the dragon and its master had not seen the group down on the boulders.

"What is . . ." Culter started, waking from his sleep.

"Shhh," Sax hissed, "the dragon."

Culter looked up and saw what Sax had seen. They were protected by the rock.

The sense of evil lessened, then was gone.

"It went down the river," Culter said.

"Which means," Sax said, "that it will be back later."

"We may not be so lucky that time," Culter said.

"Get everybody up," Sax said. "We have to hide." He rose and started looking for a place.

The best that they could come up with was to rope together once again and lower themselves down behind the boulders. This left them hanging right above the rushing current of the river, but, if they didn't move, they could not be seen.

They were not too soon. The shadow of the beast came up the side wall of the gorge, and it would keep on going if it didn't see them. But it slowed, then started in a circle.

How did the Keeper know that they were here? If he could find them when they were hidden this well, there was no chance whatsoever they could ever get the Crystal from the Keep.

Then there was a cry. Not from the sky, but from the surface of the boulders.

The swamp cat stood in the middle looking up. They had not hidden her. And, apparently, it was the cat that slowed the dragon and its master.

It circled. They could not see it, but the shadow hovered on the wall, then fell as the dragon dove. A wave of stinking wind passed over all of them, and there was an awful scream from the rock. Then it was gone, and all they heard was the river underneath them surging past.

They waited a few minutes to be sure that it was gone, then climbed back to the boulders' top.

Jason was first over the edge, and first to the cat's side.

"How is she?" Culter said, coming up behind.

Jason didn't answer, but his left hand was searching the cat's body carefully.

They stood around until Jason sighed and sat back. "I can't find anything," he said.

But the cat lay on the boulder as though dead. Only the slightest lifting of her chest showed that she lived somewhere inside.

"May I look?" Flos said.

"Yes," Jason said, and moved aside.

Flos knelt and laid her hand gently on the cat's head. She closed her eyes and didn't move. Then opened them. "It's a spell," she said. "I don't know what kind or what to do about it, but I can feel the magic in her mind."

The cat lay still. The rain began again. There was nothing they could do. They stood, but then they left, one by one, to find their sleeping places. All but Jason, who sat beside the cat and laid his hand upon her neck, and didn't move.

Sax was the last to leave. "You better get some sleep," he said. "It may be rough tomorrow."

Jason didn't answer. Sax shrugged, then went and curled up on the rock. Jason let his hand send him every tiny sign of life within the cat. He could sense every beat her heart made. He could feel the blood pump weakly through her veins. He learned her whole life process, but could not find the key to break the spell.

It was cold, and the wind blew the rain to where he sat, but Jason never moved. The night grew darker, and he could not see a thing, but his hand held still in case there was some sign, some little thing which would give him a clue what he might do. But it never came.

As the deepest dark before the morning sealed him into its blackness, Jason knew that it was hopeless. The cat would die. There was no way to get her out of there for help. If she stayed, she would die of starvation. Even if Jason left the group to be with her, he could not feed her. She was too large, and there was no food anywhere around.

When the others woke, he would have to leave with them, and the cat would die. Jason's eyes began to burn and tears flowed down his cheeks, and he bent his head and laid it on the cat's soft fur, and said, "Come on, baby. Come on. Don't die," and his tears ran on her coat of gray.

"Call her." It was a voice behind him, and he spun around.

"Lyca?"

"Yes."

"What did you say?"

"I said call her. Call her by name."

"I don't know her name."

Lyca bent forward and made a gentle sound. "That is her name," she said.

Jason was not sure. Lyca was a strange girl, and the sound she had made was not like any name he'd ever heard.

"You call her," he said.

"No," Lyca said. "It is you she follows. Only you can bring her back." She moved away into the darkness.

Jason turned and looked down at the cat. He had no choice. He leaned forward and put his mouth close to her ear.

"Come on, baby," he whispered. "Come on," and made the gentle sound that Lyca had.

Nothing happened.

"Come on," Jason said, and again the gentle sound of the cat's name. And again. And once again. The cat moved; so little that he wasn't sure she had, and Jason called her name again.

This time she lifted up her head and looked at him with great loving eyes of green. He sat back and laughed. The others woke and saw him sitting there and laughing and the great cat getting slowly to her feet.

Then it was light, and time to go.

Again they roped together and worked their way upstream, pulling themselves up the sides of boulders, and sliding down again, trying to keep from cutting their hands on the sharp edges of the stones, yet having to hold on to keep from falling. Only the swamp cat seemed to be without concern, but even she slipped once or twice and scratched and clawed to keep from falling in the river.

It took the morning to reach a final bend, and, when they came around it, they stopped dead. The river continued for another quarter-mile, then went straight up. Or down, for it fell from great height in an awesome waterfall.

"It must be five hundred feet high," Jason said.

But the cliff from which it fell was even higher. The river had worn a deep cut, but, on each side of it, the cliff rose yet another fifteen hundred feet.

"I think that must be the way up," Sax said, and pointed to what looked like nothing more than a thin line which climbed diagonally up the face of the sheer rock wall, It seemed to end in a small dot of black. "That must be the tunnel entrance."

"You'd have to be a fly to climb that thing," Culter said.

Jason felt his palms grow cold and sweaty.

"No," Sax said. "It's probably much wider than it looks from here. There's no way to know till you get there."

"Look beyond the waterfall," Flos said.

The river cut formed a great "v" down in the cliff, and it was wide enough to let them see half a mile or so beyond the falls.

"It's a giant bridge," Culter said.

"It's some kind of castle," Sax said.

"It spans the whole gorge up there," Jason said.

Lyca's yellow eyes seemed to glitter.

"It is Zara Keep," she said.

VI
THE KEEPER

It took another hour to get to the base of the cliff. The rocks were smaller, which made the climbing even trickier. The chance of twisting or even breaking an ankle was increased. The noise of the falls mixed with the running of the river, and they could not communicate except with hand signals.

But finally they stood in a protected place close to what Sax had said might be the ledge they would have to climb to get up to the tunnel. It was just far enough away from the waterfall so they could hear each other if they shouted.

"Well," Sax said, "who's first?"

"I have a suggestion," Culter said. "Before we go climbing any ledges to some tunnel, let's assume it will be dark in there, which means we ought to get something we could use for a torch. I, for one, don't really want to get up there and have to come back down just because we forgot to bring a light."

They spread out and searched for branches, and Flos found one which could be broken into the right lengths. Culter used his knife to fray the ends so they would burn. They put them in their knapsacks and were ready for the climb.

All except Jason, who had been fighting off his fear as long as possible. "I can't make it," he said. "I'm sorry, but I just can't make it. You'll have to go without me. I'll try to find some other way up there."

"From what the old man said," Culter said, "any other way would take too long."

"I'm sorry," Jason said, and turned to walk away.

"It's the height, right?" Sax said.

Jason stopped.

"Well, listen," Sax said, "there are things we could try. I've spent a lot of time around cliffs. Not quite like this one, but at least this one has a ledge we can walk up. I've run into guys who were afraid of heights before. I think we can get you up there."

Jason looked at him. "How?" he said.

"Blindfolded," Sax said.

"No way," Jason said. "If I go up there, I want to see where I'm stepping."

"Let me show you," Sax said, and took out a handkerchief. "Sorry, I can't vouch for cleanliness," he said, "but it's the best I've got." He tied it around Jason's head. "Now hold onto me," Sax said, and put Jason's hand on his right arm. "Now take one step forward."

Jason hesitated.

"Come on," Sax said. "It was flat before you put the blindfold on; what makes you think it's changed just because you can't see?"

Jason stepped tentatively ahead.

"OK," Sax said. "Now take another one."

Jason did.

"Now keep doing what I tell you," and Sax led him to the bottom of the ledge and got him started up. "Hold it," he said, when Jason was about ten feet above the ground. "Stand perfectly still. How do you feel?"

"OK," Jason said. "But I don't know where I am. Up on one of the big boulders I think."

"Take off the blindfold," Sax said.

Jason took it off, and grabbed for the cliff wall.

"You're all right," Sax said. "Work your way down."

Jason was obviously shaken, but, step by step, he came back down.

The group stood around without saying anything, letting Jason make the move.

It took a few minutes, then he shrugged and said, "OK.

I'll try it, but you've got to tell me every move to make. I couldn't see a damned thing with that blindfold on.''

"Like how high you were, or how far down the ground was," Sax said.

Jason tried to smile. It came out very small. "Yeah," he said. "Something like that."

They roped together, with Sax in the lead in case there was hard climbing up ahead. He was followed by Flos, then Jason, with Lyca right behind, and Culter last.

"You may not believe this," Jason said, "but I was once a high iron man."

"What's that?" Flos asked.

"A guy who puts the girders up on skyscrapers," Jason said.

"What happened?" Culter said.

"I fell, and woke up here," Jason said, and the others seemed to understand.

"OK," Sax said. "We might as well take off," and he turned and started up the ledge.

It was not too steep at first, and was three or four feet wide. Sax strode up as though it were a highway.

"Hey!" Flos yelled. "Slow down!"

Sax looked back and said he was sorry, and the group began the climb.

Except for occasional small rocks and stones and pebbles which were slippery, it was not bad. Jason held the rope in both his hands and put one foot before the other at a steady pace. He kept pictures of a walk along a stream or through a field in his mind, and, except for the fact that they were going up, he could almost convince himself that it was easy. But he could still feel the trickle of sweat running down his face and chest, and knew it wasn't from the heat. The air was cold. The sweat was too.

They paused for breath after four hundred feet or so, and they all leaned back against the cliff and looked out at the countryside. All except Jason, who stood like a blind man, staring straight ahead into the darkness of the blindfold.

They could see the gorge they'd followed and the flooded river as it spread across the land. The buildings of Zaratown were like some toy, and they tried to look beyond, each searching for the place where he had come from. Sax looking for the quarry, Flos the fields, and Culter for the cottage of Bladen. Only Lyca and Jason were not searching. Lyca knew her hill was hidden by the mountains, and Jason was just standing there waiting to go on.

The quarry was behind a hill, the field too far away, and the cottage concealed by the woods.

Maybe it's just as well, Culter thought, and said aloud, "Well, everybody ready?" And they climbed on.

The ledge grew narrow as they went, and they had to go more slowly, look for footholds carefully, and lean in toward the wall. None of them looked down. Lyca moved up close behind Jason, and told him where to step. He did exactly what she said, and kept up with the rest.

Then Sax stopped. The group gathered behind him, strung out along the face of the cliff.

"Something's happened to the ledge," he said, and the wind whipped his words back to them.

"Can we keep going?" Culter said.

"Yes," Sax said. "But it'll be like real rock climbing here. You're going to have to face the cliff, and use your hands and fingers. I can't see how long this part goes on because it turns a corner up ahead, but, if it doesn't get much worse, we'll make it."

"I'll slow you down," Jason said.

"Don't worry," Sax said. "Just follow our directions. Flos can help you place your hands. Lyca can tell you where to put your feet. Just do what they say, and use your sense of touch, and you'll be OK."

Jason didn't answer.

"I'll go on ahead and see if I can find a place to anchor us," Sax said, and started out. Flat against the wall, working his right foot forward until he found a solid place, then shifting his weight slowly, moving his hands, and doing it all over again, move by move, and soon he was around a corner and they couldn't see him, just the rope stretching out across the rock.

"Here I go," Flos said, and tried to do what Sax had done. After each shifting of her weight, she looked back and helped Jason place his hands.

Jason's mind was now focused on his fingers and his toes, and he let nothing else come in. He didn't feel the wind or the roughness of the cliff against his chest. No sounds registered except what Flos and Lyca told him. He was nowhere, in a black world where he clung with his nails and leather moccasins. There was no time. He could have gone on doing this forever. Just so he didn't think.

The corner was the hardest. Flos felt around and found it smooth. There was no handhold.

"Lower," Sax called. "There's a crack lower down."

Flos moved her hand, and found the crack, and she worked herself around, and one more step and she was on the ledge again.

"That whole section must have fallen off some time ago," Sax said.

"I hope there isn't any more like that," Flos said.

"So far as I can see from here," Sax said, "it's pretty good up to the tunnel. If that place up there is where the tunnel is."

Flos looked up and saw what might be an indentation in the cliff. It was impossible to tell if it was an entrance to anything at all.

They talked Jason around the corner, then Lyca and Culter last. All stood together, not more than fifty feet below their goal.

"We might make it after all," Culter said.

"Doesn't look too bad," Sax said, and everyone felt better.

"Where's the cat?" Jason said.

Dead silence.

They had forgotten her.

"She was behind me," Culter said. "She seemed to be all right."

"What about that last part?" Flos said.

"I honestly forgot to look," Culter said. "I'll go back and see."

"No," Sax said. "I'll do it."

"Who made you leader of this outfit?" Culter said, feeling anger growing. It had been stupid not to check the cat and figure some way she could be brought with them. Now this big joker was telling everybody what to do.

"I'm the rock climber," Sax said. "I didn't mean to take over," and they were surprised to see him blush. "I just figured it was something I could do, so I should do it."

Culter struggled with the thought, then said, "Oh, hell. You're right. I can run circles around you in any city in the world, but I don't know a damn thing about rocks and climbing."

"I'll be glad to let you run it after we get there," Sax said.

Culter laughed. "I pass," he said. "I'm a loner, not a leader."

"We all are," Flos said, "but we have to use what strengths we've got to have any chance of making this at all."

"I'll get the cat," and Sax worked his way past the group and to the corner where the ledge had fallen off. "Tie me off," he said, and they made sure their end of the rope was well secured.

Sax reached out, found his grip, placed his foot, and moved quickly off and around the corner and was gone.

"How's he going to carry that big cat?" Flos asked, and no one answered. They waited.

"I should have told her to go home," Jason said. "I never thought about climbing this cliff."

"No," Lyca said. "She wanted to be with you. She would not have gone."

Jason wanted to ask how Lyca knew so much about his cat, but it was hardly the time. He would ask her when they were alone together, but he waited silently with the rest.

They heard a noise—stones rattling down the cliffside. Then it was quiet, all except the wind.

Another sound, and a hand came around the corner, feeling its way for the handhold. It found it, and the fingers dug in deep. Then a leg and foot, and, when it was in place, there was a grunt, and the rest of Sax wrenched itself around the corner.

With the great cat hanging on his back.

"My God!" Culter said, but there was nothing they could do to help.

They watched as Sax shifted his weight, found the next handhold, placed his foot, shifted weight, found the final hold, and with a mighty heave, moved to the ledge where they were standing.

He turned his back to the rest of the group, and the cat released her grip and slipped down to the ledge.

Sax bent forward and braced his hands on his knees and gulped deeply for his breath.

The cat crept up to where Jason stood and put her muzzle on his hand. Jason was slightly startled, then scratched the great cat's head.

"Whew!" Sax said finally. "That thing is heavy!"

"Your fingers are bleeding," Flos said, and touched his hands.

"It's a whole other thing to try to climb with a hundred fifty pounds hanging on your back," Sax said. "It tends to throw your balance off."

"Just a little," Culter said, and Sax looked at him and smiled.

"The hardest part was convincing the animal to do it in the first place," Sax said. "She wanted to climb the whole damn cliff just to get to us, and she would have tried if I hadn't gone back. She wasn't too impressed by my offer to carry her. I guess she figured I might not be strong enough. Half-way along, I figured she was right, but we made it anyway." He stood straight and grinned. Both hands were bloody.

"You should bandage them," Flos said.

"When we get to the top," Sax said. "Let's go."

The angle was steep, but the ledge was wide enough for them to walk instead of climb, and they were within ten yards of the opening when the first rumble came. They stopped, and looked at each other. The second rumble.

"What is it?" Jason asked, and lifted his hands to take away the blindfold.

"No," Sax said. "Don't take it off. Not yet."

"What was that sound?" Jason said.

"I don't know," Sax said. "I can't see anything."

A third rumble, but this time there were small stones falling from the cliff above them.

"It sounds like some kind of earthquake," Flos said.

"Then let's get out of here," Sax said, and the group climbed as fast as it could toward the opening.

They reached it, and, so far as they could tell, it was what they were looking for. A cave-like opening which might well turn into a tunnel. They moved into the entrance to avoid the falling stones.

They could go no deeper. The opening only went in a few feet before it was choked with rocks and boulders.

"Fulmin was right," Flos said. "The tunnel's blocked."

Before anyone could respond, there was another rumble, but this one twice as loud. The ground shook, and rocks fell, and there was a grinding sound, and then a crash. The whole group pressed hard against the rocks blocking the entrance to the tunnel to get away from what was happening out on the surface of the cliff.

The sound of rocks falling in the distance, then quiet. Even the wind seemed to have been afraid.

They waited. There were no more rumbles.

Sax was the first one who stood, and he walked back to the edge of the opening and looked out and down.

"Well," he said, with a strange look on his face, "I guess we're here for good."

The others moved to the edge and looked down. There was no ledge. The way that they had come up the face of the cliff just wasn't there, as though some giant hand had passed down the rock and wiped away the ledge completely.

"What's happened?" Jason said, and they realized he was still blindfolded.

"Nothing," Sax said. "We'll have to keep on going, that's all."

"I don't understand," Jason said. "Can I take this damn thing off?" He plucked at the blindfold.

"Yes," Sax said. "You won't be climbing anymore."

Jason ripped the handkerchief off his eyes, blinked a few times, then smiled. "Wow!" he said. "That's enough of that. Now what's all this stuff about being here for good?"

"I don't think you want to look," Sax said, "but, if you did, you'd see that our good ledge has disappeared. It's gone. Destroyed."

"So how do we get down?" Jason said.

"Through there," and Sax nodded at the blockage of rocks and boulders.

Jason looked. "Wonderful!" he said. "We're ten thousand feet up in the air, standing on a place no more than ten feet square, with no way down and no way forward."

"Something like that," Culter said.

"I'm so glad I came," Jason said, then saw that they were really worried. "Are you sure there's no way through those rocks?"

"We haven't really looked," Sax said. "That's my specialty, I guess, if no one minds," and he looked at Culter.

"Listen," Culter said, "when it comes to running through alleys or throwing knives, I'm your man. If you want to wrestle with rocks and climb cliffs for fun, that's your business and welcome to it."

Sax went over to the rocks and looked at them. He tilted his head to get another angle. Then he put his hands on each of them and stepped back and stood in silent thought.

"OK," he said at last.

"OK what?" Culter said.

"We can get through," Sax said.

"How can you tell?" Flos said. "You can't see through them, can you?"

"No," Sax said. "But I can feel cold air coming through the cracks, and that means there's a cave in there, and not too many rocks are in this pile. If you know anything about big rocks, you can see that these are not well placed. If I get the right grip, I can . . . oh, hell. Let me show you." He stepped close to one of the biggest boulders. "Now, if I put my hand here," and he stuck his hand into a crack, "and my other hand here," and his other hand went in, "and I get the proper leverage," and he seemed to feel around and set himself, "and, if all you guys will stand over there," and he nodded to a spot away from where he worked, and they all crowded where he indicated, "I can find out if I'm right," and his shoulders knotted and his arms bulged out, and the veins in his forehead swelled, and with a mighty heave, Sax lifted the boulder and pushed it away.

He stood for a few seconds breathing hard. Then grinned. "If I could do all that, we could get to the cave." They could see a black hole where the rock had been. They laughed.

*   *   *

"Might as well see what we've got here," Jason said, and went over to the hole and peered inside.

"What do you see?" Flos asked.

"Dark," Jason said, and pulled back out and straightened up. "Raw, unadulterated dark."

"But there's air to breathe," Sax said.

"Yes," Jason said, "although it kind of stinks. As though something died in there some time ago."

"Let's light a torch and see what we can see," Sax said, and took his own out of his pack, got out his tinderbox, struck steel against flint, and made a spark. The frayed end of the torch caught fire, and Sax guarded the small flame until it grew; then he turned toward the hole. "Here goes nothing," he said, and stuck the torch into the opening.

It went out.

"The air coming out is like a wind," he said. "I don't think we can keep the torches lit."

"Maybe after we get inside," Flos said. "Maybe it's because the opening is small out here, and it blows like that from some kind of suction."

"If we're lucky," Sax said, and they all stood looking at the hole. It was no more than two feet in diameter, and going in would mean crawling over small stones and rocks into the darkness.

"I'll go first," Jason said, and, before anyone could say a thing, he was down on his hands and knees, starting into the hole.

A deep growl, and a streak of gray, and the cat was beside him, its great paw against his legs. Jason pulled back out.

"What's eating you?" he said.

The cat growled again, then squeezed in ahead of him into the hole.

"She's not about to let you go in there without her first," Flos said.

"I won't argue," Jason said, then turned and followed the cat in.

"Ouch! These damn stones are sharp!" His voice was hollow.

They waited.

"Who's next?" Flos said.

"Let's wait a little longer," Sax said. "If we go in there now, and he wants to retreat, we'll trap him. He won't want anyone behind him in the hole."

Five minutes, then Culter knelt beside the hole, stuck his head in, and yelled, "Hey! How's it going?"

"You don't have to shout. I'm right here," and Jason stuck his head out of the hole, then crawled out completely. He was filthy.

"How far'd you go?" Sax asked.

"Far enough," Jason said. "This passageway is small for maybe thirty feet, then it opens up. I couldn't see a damn thing in there, so I came back to get a torch."

"And some company," Culter said.

"Well," Jason said, and grinned, "now that you mention it . . ."

"Where's the cat?" Flos asked.

"She's waiting inside," Jason said. "I figured she'd make a good watchdog, so I left her there."

"Watch*cat*," Culter said.

"Watch*something*, anyway," Jason said, and turned around and went back in the hole.

"Who's next?" Flos said.

"I'll go," Lyca said, and dropped silently down on all fours and moved into the tunnel.

Culter was about to volunteer when he realized that he felt strange. His fists were clenched and he was tense. He stood back to think it out.

Flos went next, and that left only Sax and Culter.

"After you," Sax said, and made a gesture for Culter to precede him.

"After *you*," Culter said, realizing it was the hole which was bothering him. "If a big ox like you gets stuck in that hole, we'll need someone in back to push while the rest pull."

It was meant as a joke, but Sax was huge, and he hardly could get in the opening.

"Lucky I don't suffer from claustrophobia," he said back to Culter as his feet disappeared inside.

"Right," Culter called, then knew what was the matter. A clear image of being caught in the small alleyway flashed in his head. The sense of being trapped with no way out. The closed-in pressure.

But this place was not like that. This had an opening. Jason had come back and said it opened up into a larger area. If Culter could just make it those thirty feet, he'd be all right.

He knelt down, felt the hard rock beneath his knees, and put his head into the hole. It was dark, but he could hear the scrabbling of Sax ahead of him. He concentrated on the sound, and crawled inside. The walls were rough, and he tried not to touch them. He felt each hand ahead and tried to find a level place to put it, then brought his knee up behind and worked his way along. His hands were slippery from sweat, but he would make it. There was no panic.

Sax got stuck. He called for help. Culter's way out was blocked. He could crawl backwards. He would have to soon. He could not stay in that place. He could feel the fear.

"It's OK!" Sax shouted and Culter heard him moving on.

Culter was drenched with sweat. He took deep breaths. What a great group, he thought. Jason's scared of heights, I can't stand small places, and Flos is terrified of snakes. That makes three out of five who are half crazy.

He had never been afraid of closed-in places in the past. He had spent time crawling through the sewers in his neighborhood when he was just a kid, and, later, when he needed to, he had run into anything to save his neck.

He moved his hand forward, and started on.

Jason had worked on skyscrapers. There was no way that he could be afraid of heights, but he was, now. Culter understood. He had been trapped in a small place when he had been kicked almost to death. Jason had fallen just before he came here. Flos was bitten by a rattlesnake.

"Each one of us has something related to the way he . . . the way he was brought here. Some weakness."

He could hear the others talking up ahead. He crawled forward, reached a curve, then saw the light.

"We made it," he said, and came out into a space bigger than the tunnel. He could stand up, and he knew he was smiling.

"Welcome to my lair, said the spider to the fly," Jason said, and Culter looked around.

Jason had lighted a torch, and Culter could see the room was large. He could also see that it was draped with spider webs. Every inch seemed covered with the strands, as though they had come out into the center of all spiders' nests.

He glanced up. The ceiling crawled with great black spiders, and they were coming down.

"Let's go!" Culter yelled.

"We were waiting for you," Jason said, and turned and looked into the webs. "There must be some way out of here, or those things," and he waved his torch up toward the ceiling, "would have died long ago." His torch bent in a slight wind.

"Follow the air," Sax said.

Right into the webs. Jason held the torch out to see if they would burn. They didn't. He looked back quickly, but no one could offer any help, so he started through the webs.

"Hurry up," Culter said, looking at the ceiling.

The spiders were more than halfway down.

"Can't you talk to them, Flos? The way you did with the hornets back in the woods?"

"I tried," Flos said, "but they are not like the other insects I have known. These seem to be from someplace else. I can't speak their language."

Jason was pushing forward, with Lyca, Flos, and Sax right behind. Culter came last. Looking up, with his knife in his hand.

A spider dropped. Culter caught it on his blade, then scraped it off. Another fell.

"Hurry up!" he yelled. "I can't fight these things with only one knife."

The spiders were about the size of dinner plates, with hairy legs and waving jaws. There were more than Culter dared to count, and they were almost down.

The webs were sticky. They clung to hair and face and hands and resisted wiping off. Each member of the group was covered, and the feeling of being wound tight in some kind of shroud was strong.

Jason thrashed around with the torch, saw the way it bent, and went the other way.

A spider dropped on Flos's neck. Sax yanked it off and threw it on the ground. It was too big to step on.

Now more and more were falling, but the light seemed to blind them, and they could only follow the jerking of their webs to lead them to their prey.

"I think I see something," Jason shouted.

"It's about time," Culter yelled back, and grabbed a spider from Sax's arm. The feel of the thing made his flesh crawl—long hairs and whipping legs and the mouth reaching to get its fangs into anyone. He threw the spider down and crowded close to Sax.

"It's the way out!" Jason said.

Something hit Culter on the shoulder. He twisted his head but couldn't see it. "Sax! Help me get this thing!" and Sax turned and yanked the spider off of Culter. "Thanks," Culter said, then both of them were hit again and they were tearing spiders off themselves and each other.

"Let's move it!" Culter said. "We can't stand still," and they turned and made their way to where the others were.

Jason was right. There was an opening, and the five of them almost fell out into the tunnel on the other side.

"Whew!" Jason said, and tried to wipe some of the sticky web from his forehead and face.

"Maybe we'd better put some distance between ourselves and them," Culter said, and gestured back into the room of spiders.

"They don't seem to be following," Flos said. "It's almost as though it were some kind of nest."

"A kind I hope I never see again," Culter said, and scraped his hand against the smooth wall of the tunnel to get it clean. The web still stuck.

Then it hit him. "Hey!" he said. "This thing's no cave. This is man-made. Look at these walls, and the floor. They're smooth. They've been carved out of the rock."

And they had been. The tunnel was some ten feet wide and ten feet high, and extended into darkness.

"What about that room?" Sax said, and indicated the room with the spiders. "Why would a tunnel stop right there?"

"Maybe that was some kind of guardroom," Culter said. "If that opening we came through from the cliff was once a real way in here, they might have stationed guards there to keep people out. Now it's guarded by the spiders.''

"Well," Flos said, "there's only one way left to go, unless we go back there. We might as well try it.''

"Let's have more light," Culter said, and they took the time to light another torch. "Save the other three," he said, not lighting Flos's, Lyca's or Sax's. "We may need them when these two burn out.''

Jason was in front, with the cat and his torch, and Culter was in back with the second source of light.

"All set?" Jason said, and the cat growled.

"What's with her?" Sax said.

"Don't know," Jason said.

"Quiet!" Lyca said, and seemed to be listening.

The group stood silent.

"Something's coming," Lyca said, just as the cat growled again.

"Let's be ready for it when it gets here," Sax said, and the group spread out and faced the dark end of the tunnel.

The cat growled, and Jason reached down and held its muzzle.

They waited. Then saw something. Little lights in two rows, coming toward them. Culter counted six along each side. And a scraping sound.

"It is the mother," Lyca said, and her voice was shaking.

"The mother what?" Sax said.

"Spider, of course," Lyca said, and now the rest could see her, filling the tunnel from wall to wall, great hairy legs and hairy body moving right toward them. The lights that they had seen were reflections of their torches from her eyes. Two rows of eyes down either side, and each one looking at them.

"It's poisonous," Flos said. "It's some kind of *Latrodectus*.''

"What the hell is that?" Sax said.

"Black widow," Flos said.

They watched it come.

"How can we fight the thing?" Sax said. "Look at those fangs.''

"I have the knife," Culter said, and got it ready.

"Your sword might be even better," Jason said.

"Damn!" Culter said. "I forgot the thing. Bladen and the

old man said not to draw it till I needed it. I think this
situation qualifies," and he drew the sword.

They all looked at it, but none of them spoke.

There was no blade. The hilt was complete, but where the
long, sharp blade should have been there was only a stub
which held the hilt in the sheath.

Culter stared at the bladeless sword for a long moment.
There must be something wrong. Bladen would never play
such a terrible trick on him, especially telling him to use it
only when he really had to. That would mean danger, and to
send a man out into danger with a bladeless sword was
murder.

The old man had said the same thing in the clearing. Not to
draw the sword until he needed to.

He felt the bitter taste of anger in his throat. The sense of
having been betrayed, of thinking that he'd finally found a
family that loved him, and coming on the journey just for
them, because he couldn't face their being killed if the
Keepers won. Now he'd found just what he'd meant to them,
just how much they really cared.

Tears stung his eyes, but the anger grew and turned them
red. He turned to the spider almost on them. "Go to hell!"
he yelled and threw the handle of the sword.

Despite his rage and blindness, Culter's long training was
in his hand and arm, and the handle of the sword flew straight
toward the center of the spider's head.

But never got there. It stopped six inches short. The handle
held out in midair by some power none of them could see.

"We can't even touch it," Jason said, and held the cat
beside him.

The spider wasn't moving anymore. She was just standing
in the tunnel now, not coming forward. She was no more
than half a dozen feet away. Her two front feet curled back
towards her face, as though trying to get hold of the sword's
handle. There was liquid running down from where the sword
should have hit. It dripped black on the floor.

"Look at the handle," Jason said, and they could see it
vibrating, as though the blade were buried in something, and
the hilt was shaking from the blow.

The spider's legs began to give way, and the great hairy body started sinking to the floor.

"It's dying," Flos said.

They stood and watched until it was all over.

"What killed it?" Sax said.

No one could answer.

Culter stepped closer to the thing, and saw that, even with it dead, its protective magic was still working. The hilt of his sword was still six inches from its head.

He reached out, took hold of it and pulled. It didn't move. He pulled harder, then felt it slowly come, as though being pulled from something it was stuck in.

Something like the spider's head. Then the sword came free and there was the black liquid in a line a foot from where he held the handle. The liquid acting just like blood along a blade.

"It's invisible," Flos said.

Culter grinned, and held the sword up high, then brought it down and wiped it off against his trouser leg.

The blade was gone. He passed his hand through the place where it had been. Then laughed, and carefully put the hilt back in the sheath.

"Well," he said, turning to the group, "let's hit the road. Or tunnel, as the case may be," and he started along the wall past the great hairy legs.

He knew that Bladen hadn't let him down.

Culter led with his torch, and the others followed. Once past the body of the spider, the going wasn't bad. The tunnel maintained its width and height and went straight ahead. There were no more spiders' webs, nor any other trash for that matter. The tunnel was perfectly clean.

"I wonder who's got the janitor's concession here," Jason said, and the group laughed.

"Maybe we're so far underground that dirt and stuff can't get down here," Flos said.

"Maybe," Culter said, but wasn't sure.

They had gone what felt like half a mile when Culter stopped. "There's something up ahead along the wall," he said, and he tried to see exactly what it was.

"A door," Lyca said.

They moved closer. It was a door. Obviously solid, and very, very old. Great iron bands held it together, and the hinges were immense.

Sax stepped up and tried the handle. It didn't move. He pushed against the door itself. It didn't move.

"I could try to break it in," he said, but didn't sound too confident.

"What for?" Culter said. "So long as we have this main tunnel to follow, why waste time checking out this door?"

The rest agreed. From everything they could put together, the tunnel they were in was heading in the right direction. They continued on their way, passing other doors. Sax looked as though he'd like to try his strength, but they went on.

Then they found the first of the round holes. It was about eighteen inches in diameter and worn smooth around the edges. Culter held the torch down close, but couldn't see the bottom.

"Anybody got any bright ideas what this is?" Culter asked, but no one had.

The swamp cat moved close and sniffed the opening, and the hairs on her neck grew stiff, and her growl low.

"Maybe it's just as well we don't find out," Sax said, and the others tended to agree, although they didn't say so.

They found more holes like the first, in no apparent order, just every now and then, but each one was the same size, and each worn around the edges. The swamp cat growled at every one.

Ahead of them the tunnel ended in a blank wall. But when they got closer with the torchlight, they saw that there were openings on both sides of the dead end.

"It's a cross tunnel," Culter said. "We have a choice."

"Flip a coin," Sax said.

Jason seemed to be thinking. "Wait a second," he said. "These aren't the same."

"That's absolutely correct," Culter said. "One goes left and the other goes right. They couldn't be more different."

"No," Jason said. "That's not what I meant. What I meant was that the left one goes uphill, and the right one down."

He was right. The cross tunnel sloped down to the right.

"Which tells us what?" Culter said.

"I'm not sure," Jason said. "Let's look more closely," and he bent down to check the floor.

"Don't tell us there are more of those damned holes," Culter said.

"Something else," Jason said. "Look at this."

They gathered around his torch and looked down where he was pointing at a crack which ran along the center of the floor. But it was not a crack, it was a groove, as carefully made as the rest of the tunnel.

"Look down in it," Jason said.

They did.

"Looks like some kind of chain in there," Sax said.

"I don't understand it," Lyca said.

"I've seen something like that before," Flos said. "Let me think a second . . . San Francisco. That's where I saw it. In San Francisco. The cable cars."

"I think she's right," Culter said. "I never saw them, but this looks like some kind of machinery which could work like the cable cars."

"Then we can just stand here and wait for the next trolley," Sax said, and they all looked up at the giant standing there with a big grin.

"Leave the humor to professionals," Culter said, but then laughed.

Jason stayed down on the floor as though to learn something from the groove and chain.

"That would explain the slope of the tunnel," he said, "and the way this chain is worn on one side of the links more than the other, but it doesn't tell us what used it."

"Who cares?" Culter said. "We have to take it anyway, unless you want to go back to the spiders."

The thought brought shivers.

"Let's take the left tunnel," Jason said.

"The right one goes downhill," Culter said. "I vote for that."

"The Keep is up," Jason said. "If we go down, then we are going in the wrong direction."

It sounded logical.

"I told you guys that I was good back in the city, but I'm not much good out in the woods or inside mountains."

"We'll call on you when we get to Los Angeles," Jason said.

"Or Chicago," Lyca said.

"Or Boston," Sax added.

The mention of the cities of their home brought sudden silence, but they came out of it almost at once and gathered up their things.

"Does everyone agree that we go left and up?" Jason said. They all nodded. "Then let's go," Jason said, and started up the tunnel.

They were no more than a hundred yards along when he first heard it. The cat beside him had already stopped and was growling, and, just as he was about to tell her to shut up, the sound came down to him, almost as a vibration, too low to call a noise, but it became a noise and soon identifiable. Something was rolling down the tunnel toward them.

Jason turned and yelled for them to run, go back, get out of here, and there was a moment's confusion as they all tried to obey, and then they were all running hard and fast.

The noise was growing, getting closer, sounding now like wheels against the stone, like something very, very heavy coming down on metal wheels. They ran harder.

Jason was in back, and wasn't sure he'd make it. The cat bounded ahead, the thing behind him getting closer. He dropped his torch, and now could only see the bobbing one which Culter carried. It was some fifteen yards away, then suddenly went out.

Jason was running in the dark. The sound was now over him, right behind. He wouldn't make it.

Something yanked his arm, and he was flying through the air, and hit the floor and lay there, half unconscious. The noise was deafening, then past and fading. The very air was sucked right out behind it. Jason tried to sit up, and shook his head.

"Sorry about that," Sax said, standing over him, holding a torch. "I had to get you out of there."

Jason felt himself to see what he was missing, but, other

than bruises and his pride, he was all right. He slowly got to his feet.

"You didn't look as though you knew where to turn," Sax said. "I thought you were going to run right by."

"I would of, if you hadn't grabbed me," Jason said. "Thanks."

"No sweat," Sax said.

"You may not be sweating," Culter said, "but *something* stinks in here."

They didn't have to sniff to smell it. It was all around them.

"Garbage," Lyca said.

Sax went over to the cross tunnel where the wheeled vehicle had passed, and held his torch out. The walls of the tunnel were now lined with bits of trash and garbage.

Culter laughed. "We were almost run over by a *garbage truck*," he said. "I mean, of all the ways to go, that must be one of the worst."

"I think he's right," Flos said. "I think that's the Keep's way of emptying the garbage."

"Where does it go?" Culter said.

"The best I can figure," Sax said, "is that it goes down to that gorge we saw where the waterfall came from. There must be some kind of opening in the wall of the gorge, and this garbage is dumped out into the river."

"Then," said Jason, "if we follow the tunnel up to the left, we'll get to the Keep."

"Or get run over by another garbage wagon," Culter said. "There's no place to hide from those things."

"We don't know how far up it is until we find another tunnel or an exit," Flos said. "We were lucky this time that we were so close to this tunnel so we could get out of the way. The next time we might be caught in the middle."

"The problem is," Culter said, "that, if Sax is right and the other end is nothing but an opening over that gorge, then there's really no choice. We *have* to go left, and hope like hell we're in between the scheduled garbage runs."

A new noise. The sound of metal grating, rattling like chains.

"The chain!" Flos said, and went over to the cross tunnel and looked in carefully. "It's moving."

Sax had wandered a short way back the way they'd come, and now he trotted toward them. "Something else is moving too," he said, and pointed behind him.

They could see nothing, but then heard the sound of slithering.

"I think they're coming from those holes," Sax said.

"What are they?" Culter asked.

"I didn't wait to ask them," Sax said.

"It sounds as though a lot of them are coming this way," Lyca said.

"I think I know why," Flos said. "When we first got here, this whole place was spotless, then the garbage truck went past and now it stinks and there are all those bits and pieces of the trash around."

"You mean, whatever lives down in those holes is coming here to clean it up?" Culter said. "And possibly us in the process."

"Yes," Flos said. "I think that's it."

"If the size of those holes is any indication, I would have to agree," Sax said.

"Then that answers all our problems," Culter said. "We go left and run like hell."

"Maybe not," Jason said. "Listen."

The slithering was closer now down the old tunnel, but there was a new sound from the right; the sound of metal wheels again, but this time slower.

"I think it's coming back," Jason said.

"Right on time," said Culter.

"We hope," Jason said. "Maybe those things, whatever they are, wait until it's past, then they can eat whatever's left. If that's true, then we can hitch a ride and they won't touch us."

"I like your timing," Culter said. "Ten seconds one way or the other and we either have to run in front of the garbage truck, or we are eaten by the clean-up squad."

"Just keep your fingers crossed," Jason said. "Everybody get ready to jump."

"Jump where?"

"Into the garbage truck," Jason said.

"I can hardly wait," Culter said, but they stood as close as possible to the cross tunnel and listened to the sounds. Behind them was the slithering; coming from the right, the truck.

The swamp cat growled and raised her fur and was about to turn and fight, but Jason held her by the neck and calmed her.

"Come on, baby," Culter said, half under his breath. "If ever you had to be on time, it's now. Just keep on coming."

The noise of the garbage truck was loudest now. It was in front of them. It almost filled the tunnel by itself. There was hardly room between the roof and the top of the truck to squeeze inside.

"Grab on the back!" Jason yelled. "Watch the wheels!"

They grabbed and ran and jumped, and everyone was hanging on the back—except the cat, running behind them, but then she stopped as something long and thick and heavy held her right hind foot.

"It's got her!" Jason yelled, and was about to jump, when the cat whirled and swiped its terrible sharp claws. The long thing let go, and the cat bounded ahead.

"She'll be all right," Sax yelled. "But we can't stay here."

He was right. The handholds that they'd grabbed were slippery, and it was almost impossible to keep from falling off. The truck was moving much too fast for them to run behind it more than a few yards. If anyone fell off, he would be lost.

"Inside," Sax yelled over the noise of the metal wheels against the stone floor, and he reached up, found the top of the truck and pulled himself over. There was no more than six inches of clearance between his back and the ceiling, but he made it.

"Nobody else come in!" he yelled, and his voice was like an echo in the metal truck. "I've got an idea."

The rest hung on as best they could. Then Sax's head appeared above them over the back. He looked down and said, "Listen. You guys work your way over to the side." Jason followed his directions. "That's it. Now the rest of you." Everybody moved.

Sax's head disappeared; then they heard a grinding sound, and slowly the back of the truck tilted out. When it was open far enough, Sax yelled for them to come inside. They moved quickly, and he was about to let it fall back closed when Jason said, "Wait!" and called the cat. It sprinted to the back of the truck, leaped, caught hold, and clawed its way inside, just as Sax's strength gave out and the back slammed shut.

"Well," Culter said, looking around by the light of the torch he still held, "it's not the Queen Elizabeth Two, but it'll do."

"If you don't mind garbage," Flos said.

"When I think of that cleanup squad out there," Culter said, "I realize I could learn to *love* garbage."

The stink inside the truck was worse than outside, but they all were so filthy by now they almost didn't notice. They just sat down on the bottom of the truck and leaned back against the metal walls.

"Where do you suppose it's taking us?" Flos said.

"Where garbage comes from, silly," Culter said, and no one laughed.

It was good to rest, even against the slimy sides of the garbage truck. Culter held his torch between his legs, and that was the only light there was. The metal truck banged on and on, and the sound reverberated like a ceaseless drum. But no one paid attention; they just closed their eyes and ignored the noise.

Then the motion of the vehicle changed slightly. It seemed to turn, then kept turning. They had to change positions to keep from falling over on their sides.

"It's going up a spiral," Jason said.

"If it straightens out when it gets high enough," Sax said, "that should mean that it is going from the mountain to the Keep."

Which is what it did.

"I never thought we'd come in quite this way," Flos said. "But I guess no one will be expecting us."

"They won't be too happy when they see and smell us either," Culter said. "I never thought I'd want a bath so much."

The truck didn't slow. It just stopped, banging against the end of its long tunnel. The whole group landed in a pile at the front end, tangled tightly, and trying to get out as they slid on the slippery sides and fell back into each other.

The torch went out. "What happened?" someone said.

"We're there," Jason said, and swore at someone's elbow in his face.

"Where's there?" Flos asked, finally getting free enough to slide back down the floor of the truck and away from the others.

"We said it would be in the Keep," Sax said, and he, too, was free now, and everyone was straightened out.

"I know," Flos said, "but *where* in the Keep?"

"Wherever it is," Culter said, "it's damned dark."

They had been expecting to stop somewhere other than the tunnel, in some sub-kitchen, or any place with light, but it was full dark wherever they were now.

"Maybe we'd better get out," Lyca said.

"Let me check it out," Sax said, and they could hear him scramble up the side of the truck; then, "Damn!" and sliding down.

"What's up?" Culter said.

"The ceiling," Sax said. "I bumped my head. There isn't any space between the side of the truck and the ceiling here. We can't climb over to get out."

"Then we'll have to open the back again," Jason said.

"Yeah," Sax said. "Give me a second to get set for that." He moved to the back of the truck.

"I guess I'm ready," he said, then they heard him grunt and the sound of his shoes slipping on the bottom of the truck.

The others moved down to the back to be there when it opened.

But it didn't open.

"I can't move it," Sax said.

"You need some help?" Culter said. "Let me give you a hand."

"Thanks," Sax said. "But I don't think that's the problem. I think the damn thing's locked."

"Locked?" Flos said.

"Maybe some automatic mechanism," Sax said. "Something to keep the garbage from falling out. It must be triggered when the truck stops here."

The others tried to push the back open, but Sax was right. It wasn't stuck, it was firmly locked.

"Which leaves us in this box." Jason said. "We can't climb out, and we can't push the back open, so we might as well settle down and make ourselves at home."

"For how long?" Culter said, and began to feel the walls closing in on him.

"Until somebody needs to empty garbage," Flos said.

"Assuming this is the only garbage truck around, that shouldn't be too long," Sax said. "On the other hand, if they have a whole fleet of these things, we may be here a while."

Culter's palms were sweating. He sat down and closed his eyes and thought of open places. All he got were pictures of his city, with canyon walls and tight alleys, and rooms stuck in apartment houses. He tried to think of what it looked like from the highest building, but he'd never been up there and wasn't sure. Movies, he said to himself. Think of a movie, but it wasn't easy. The reality of where they were kept coming in.

"We could light a torch," Flos said.

"Let's save them," Jason answered. "We don't know what we'll run into up ahead, and we do know what's in here. Us."

They all sat down and leaned against the metal sides.

"Anybody hungry?" Sax said.

"Not with this smell," Flos said.

"We'd better save the food anyway," Lyca said. "We don't know when we'll find some more."

A terrible clang, a screech, sudden light, another clang, and something coming down. It was a giant pot of old cold soup that landed with a splash.

"Hey!" Sax yelled, and jumped to his feet. "What the hell do you think you're doing!"

The opening of light above them was being closed, but Sax's voice stopped it. It opened up again. There was a head up there, although it was almost impossible to look up into the light. The group sat blinking in the glare, and Sax was standing, shaking his great fist.

"Watch what you're doing, you jackass!" he shouted.

Voices shouting. More heads looking down. "Who are you?" yelled down at them.

"None of your damn business," Sax shouted up. He was trying to wipe the soup off his already filthy face.

"You're not supposed to play around with the equipment," the voice yelled. "Now get up here!"

"How?" Jason called, before Sax could swear again.

Their eyes adjusted to the light, and they could see a circular shaft above them.

"The way you got down in the first place," the voice said.

"We lost our rope," Jason said, and signaled the others to be quiet.

"Idiots!" and there was talking up above, some heads withdrawn, then back again, and a long rope came down. "Climb that!"

Sax grabbed the rope and pulled it tight. It held. "Who's first?" he said.

"I'll go," Jason said. "The only weapon I've got is this," and he held up his once-white right hand, "so they won't know I'm armed." He took the rope and tried to climb it, but his hands were slimy from the garbage, and he couldn't get a grip.

"Pull the rope up!" he shouted.

Someone above them did, and Jason was drawn up to the top. The others in the truck could not make out exactly what was being said, but Jason seemed to be talking fast. Then he swung himself out of sight, and the rope came down again.

"I'll go next," Culter said, and took the rope and was pulled up. Then Flos, then Lyca, but, when it came to Sax, it was a different matter.

"What's he tied the rope to?" one of the men up at the top asked Jason.

"Nothing," Jason said. "He's big, that's all."

It took five men, and even then they almost dropped Sax back into the truck. He caught the top edge of the opening and heaved himself up and over onto the floor.

They were obviously in some part of a kitchen; not the main room, but one with enough pots and pans and other things around to make it clear that food preparation was the point.

The opening was a double door built in the floor above the spot the garbage truck was in. There was a set of levers to one side which probably worked the mechanisms. There were also men. Culter estimated ten, but more were coming.

Sax got to his feet. The group moved close and stood together.

"How the hell did you jesters get down there?" one of the men asked. They were all dressed in dirty white uniforms, and all looked like cooks or helpers.

"It's a long story," Jason said. "We'll tell you some other time. Right now we've got to get back to our stations."

"You'd better wash some of that garbage off before you do," the man said.

"Right," Jason said. "We'll do that in our rooms."

A sound came from down inside the garbage truck. It was the swamp cat. The men in white looked down the hole at green eyes reflecting up. The cat growled.

"Get some of the guards," one man said. "We've got to kill that cat."

"No!" Jason said. "You don't have to kill her. She's tame. She's just a pet."

"Nobody ever had a swamp cat for a pet," one of the men said. "I saw one of those things once, when I was out in the swamp. They're the most deadly animal around here."

"But this one's tame," Jason said. "Let me show you."

"Not while I'm around," the man said, and pulled back from the opening.

"She won't hurt you," Jason said, and looked down in the hole. "Come!" he called.

The cat jumped, but was a foot short of the opening, and she fell back in the truck with a great noise. She tried again, and this time caught the edge of the hole, but couldn't quite pull herself up.

Sax moved quickly, grabbed it by the loose skin on the neck, and lifted. The cat stood on the kitchen floor, growling at the men in white.

"I told you they were mean," the man said who claimed

full knowledge of swamp cats. "Look at those teeth. That thing is dangerous. It should be killed."

But there was no one in the room who wanted to take on the cat, and she stood by Jason's side and lashed her tail.

"Let's get out of here," Flos whispered.

"There's a door over to our left," Culter said.

"We're going to our rooms now," Jason said, and the group moved slowly toward the door.

"Not so fast!" They turned and saw a massive, fat man standing there. Filling the whole doorway with his bulk, chins layered down his neck, and hands like sausages. His eyes didn't twinkle as so many fat men's do. The group stopped.

"Let's have your names," the fat man said, and somehow they knew he was boss of the whole kitchen. The others didn't say a word, and moved back from the group so the chief chef could deal with it in his own way.

Jason tried a bluff. "We haven't time for that," he said. "We're due at our stations now, and we have to wash ourselves before we get there," and he started toward the door, as though he'd push the man out of the way. The fat man didn't budge.

"What stations?" he said. "You don't look like any of the guards to me."

"One of them's a girl," said a voice from the cluster of white-coated cooks.

"We have no female guards," the fat man said. "Who *are* you?"

Jason looked at the others. They would have to fight. He wasn't sure what tactics they should use, and he'd have liked to have had time to pick the targets. "Get out of my way," he said, turning back to the fat man. "I don't want to have to hurt you."

The fat man looked amazed, then started laughing. Jason moved to him in three quick strides, lifted his white hand and grasped the fat man's wrist. Then he turned and bent, and the great body rolled across Jason's back and landed on the floor with a terrible soggy sound.

"Let's go," Jason yelled. "This is our chance," and he turned to the door.

Two spears aimed straight at him, with two guards behind

them. They moved into the room, and two more followed. Then more, until finally ten guards were lined up facing them, each with a spear.

"I think it's a little late," Culter said.

The blubber on the floor was moving now, rolling back and forth and making awful sounds. Everyone in the room was watching him. The fat man got his voice and screamed, demanding that someone help him to his feet.

Six of the cooks jumped forward, and, after difficulty finding handholds, they pulled him upright. The fat man's face was scarlet, and his chins bright red with rage. He pointed to the group.

"Kill them! Now! You hear me? Kill them now!"

The guards didn't move.

"I said, kill them!" and the fat man's face was even deeper red. "That is an order."

One of the guards lowered his spear, then spoke to the fat man.

"Hold your horses, Yashta. You may give the orders to your cooks, but not to us. We are guards, and we take orders from the Keeper."

The fat man's face was livid still, but he seemed to be trying to calm down. "Then let me have them," he said. "You can leave them here with me."

"And find pieces of them in the stew tonight?" the guard said, and laughed. "No, thanks, Yashta. No, we will take them to the Keeper now, and let him see them."

"I will give you the finest meal in your whole life if you will let me have this bunch for half an hour. Then you can do what you want with them after that."

"They would only be good for the garbage truck," the guard said.

"That would be perfect," the fat man said. "From garbage truck to garbage in only half an hour."

"They must go with us now," the guard said. "We've talked long enough." The spears were brought in closer to the group. "Move!" the guard said.

There was no point in fighting. The spears were too long and too sharp to deal with in that number. And if, somehow, they overcame the guards, the cooks were there, and some of them had knives. It would be hopeless.

"Lead on," Culter said.

Jason followed, and the cat walked beside him.

"Watch out for that cat!" one of the cooks yelled.

"The Keeper will be pleased with that," the head guard said. "It will be the first swamp cat ever brought in alive. I may even get promoted for this one. Now move! Through that door."

The group went through the door into the kitchen, through the kitchen to another one, through that to a hall, through the hall to stairs, and up, and through more halls, and up again, and through another hall, until "Halt!"

The head guard opened the massive door enough to slip inside. He was back in a few minutes.

"Go!" he said, and two guards flung the door wide open.

The group stepped forward, into a room so large they couldn't see its end. It had a high ceiling, with great torches flickering along the walls, but the light could hardly make a dent on that colossal space. It showed that there were rows of benches, all empty now, and four chairs which looked like thrones, each facing in toward the middle, with a central throne high above the others, with a column rising right behind it to the ceiling.

But it was not the room, or the four thrones, or even the central one which they saw now. It was the man who sat on it and looked at them.

Then each was hit hard on the head from the guards behind. "Bow!" the head guard said, and they walked forward with their heads bent down.

They were stopped when they had reached the foot of the great throne, and tripped from behind, so that each of them fell forward on the floor.

"You will show proper respect for Zaragoza, Keeper of Zara Keep!"

VII
The Tower

"Pick them up, so I can see them." Hands grabbed their arms and they were yanked back to their feet to stand facing the great throne and the man seated on it.

He was small, with tiny eyes which glinted red. He had almost no nose, and his mouth was twisted and misshapen. He wore a pure black cloak, and his boots reflected torch light from the walls.

"So these are the ones who claim to be part of the guards, but hide in the garbage truck beneath the kitchen," he said, and his teeth were rotten black inside his mouth.

None of them knew what to say, so they stood there silent.

"Which one of you can speak?" Zaragoza said.

"This one, sire." The head guard pushed Jason forward with his spear.

"Then speak," Zaragoza said. "I'm waiting."

"I have nothing to say," Jason said.

"Nothing to say? Nothing to say? Don't stand there making jokes with me! You have much to say, and I shall hear it all. You shall start with what you're doing in the Keep."

"We got here by mistake," Jason said, trying to concoct a story as fast as he could.

"By mistake? How could that be? How long have you been here?"

"We just got here," Jason said. "Only since this morning."

"This morning," Zaragoza said. "You got here this morning! And you expect me to believe that lie? You expect me to believe that you have pierced the spell which keeps all strangers out, and you just wandered up into the Keep while you were on an outing in the woods? Is that what you want me to believe?''

Jason knew he had made a mistake. He had no idea how long the spell against strangers had been in effect. Could the group have been hiding in the Keep for all that time and just now surface? It was worth a try.

"We have been here a long time," he said.

"A long time," Zaragoza said. "Yes. I imagine you have. You thought you could fool me with some nonsense about coming here by accident this morning. Now you will admit that you were sent here by the Council a long time ago, and you have been inside the Keep and spying all this time. Am I not correct?''

Either a liar or a spy. The sentence for either was probably death. Jason had no more to say.

"I asked you a question!" Zaragoza said. "I asked if you were sent here by the Council to spy on us, and have been hiding here all that time.''

Jason could feel the tip of the spear pressing into the small of his back. He tried to think of a clever answer. He could think of none.

"I can see that this will take us quite a while," Zaragoza said. "That is all right with me. We have a little time, and it will prove amusing. I shall enjoy . . .''

A door slammed open, and there was the sound of running feet, then a body falling on the floor.

"What is this! Who dares to come into my presence in such a manner?''

"Sire. I beg your pardon," and the voice sounded out of breath. "It is the Keeper, Wolten, sire. I was told to come at once and tell you he is here.''

"Wolten is here," Zaragoza said. "Very well. I shall go and greet him.''

"Excuse me, sire," the guard said. "What shall I do with these?'' He kicked Sax in the ankle to indicate just whom he meant.

"Throw them in the dungeon," Zaragoza said. "I shall get

back to them some other time." He paused and seemed to think. "Yes. I shall use them later, as a form of entertainment for the others when they all are here. They will find the questioning most interesting, I am sure."

He turned and walked through a door behind his throne.

"Move!" the guard said. They felt the spears again and started walking.

Through the hall, out the door, down corridors and hallways, past rooms and endless rooms, and down twisting stairs. Then along a long, straight passageway which Sax figured must cross over to the mountain, just as the garbage trolley had.

The walls were rougher now, and the air was cool. It got warmer as they went down even more.

At the bottom of a final staircase, they faced an iron gate.

The head guard stepped forward, and pounded on it with his spear. "Where is that idiot!" he mumbled, and pounded again.

There was the sound of footsteps coming, slowly, with a shuffling gait. The gate was opened, and the group stepped back. The spears pressed them forward toward a giant. Not a big man, such as Sax, but a true giant, maybe fifteen feet in height, with heavy face and arms and legs, and it stood filling up the passageway.

"Who wants Gok!" The voice was terrifying.

"The Keeper wants these locked up in a cell," the head guard said, and the group was pushed forward again. "He will want them back in a few days, however, and in good shape, so you take care of them."

"Gok always take care prisoners." His vacuum-cleaner-sized mouth opened up, and a sound came out which almost deafened everyone. It was his laughter.

Again the spears urged, and the group was forced through the gate. None of the guards followed them. It was as though they did not dare. The giant stood looking down at them, and they could understand the guards' fear.

The giant frowned, pointed down the hallway, then slammed the gate behind them. The force of the slam was almost enough to knock them to the floor.

"Go!" the giant said.

They went. They walked quickly to keep ahead of him, but not so fast he would mistake it for escape.

"Stop!" They were by what appeared to be a cell. The door was open.

"In!" They went in, and the giant closed the door, more softly than the gate, or the sound would have broken all their eardrums.

They heard him leave, and heard him call down the hall that they were locked in tight. They could hear no answer. They looked around the cell, then at each other.

"Well," Culter said finally, "I guess we're just about the worst saviors a Council ever had. We get caught before we even get into the Keep. Dragged out of a garbage truck, and thrown right into jail. I suppose we get the firing squad tomorrow, and that should wrap it up."

His attempt at humor didn't help.

"I think we have to answer questions before they kill us," Jason said.

"I forgot," Culter said. "That ought to be a laugh."

But no one did.

They welcomed the dark of the cell, as though none of them could look the others in the eye. The sense of depression was profound. The jokes Culter made were much too close to what was real, and they felt deeply guilty. The swamp cat rubbed against Jason's leg, but got no petting. It growled softly.

"How come they left her here?" Culter said from across the cell. "And all our other stuff? I've even got my sword."

"They're either very stupid," Sax said, "or very strong. I'll give you one guess which."

"What chance do you think either the cat or your sword would have against that giant out there?" Jason said.

"It depends," Culter said. "Which may be our strongest point."

"I think I missed something," Flos said. "What's our strongest point?"

"Our weakness," Culter said. "I mean, our *apparent* weakness. So long as everybody thinks we're weak, we'll be allowed to keep our stuff, including my sword. They don't know about Flos's being able to do things with plants, and Jason's healing, or even Sax's strength.'' He purposely said nothing about Lyca.

"You forget my right hand," Jason said. "It may surprise you someday."

"It already surprised me," Sax said.

"Then we're still not helpless," Culter said. "Not the greatest fighting force ever assembled, but still not helpless."

"Unless you consider being locked in some dungeon with a giant as a jailer helpless," Sax said.

"Details," Culter said, "just details." But he leaned back against the wall and sat there, quiet.

"What *will* happen to us?" Flos asked out of the darkness.

No one wanted to answer that.

Finally Jason said, "I think they mean to torture us to find out what we're doing here and why. Zaragoza said something about being a form of entertainment when the others get here. I don't know who the others are, but I can imagine what the entertainment is."

"That guy who ran in said something about Wolten being here. Wolten's one of the Keepers, isn't he?"

"That's what the man said," Culter said. "He called him the Keeper, Wolten, when he came to say that he was here."

"But 'others' is plural," Flos said. "What others did he mean?"

"Maybe the other Keepers," Jason said.

"They are coming here, and we'll be tortured as some kind of floor show," Culter said.

"Something like that," Jason said.

"Swell," Culter said.

There was silence, but not for long. Sounds came from outside the door, then it flew open and the light streamed in. They sat there blinking.

The giant crouched outside, blocking the door. Apparently he couldn't get inside the cell itself. "Eat!" he said, and his voice echoed in the room. He pushed a plank of wood inside the cell. It held five dishes of some kind of food.

The food was followed by the sound of something dragged across the stones, then shoved into the cell. It was a great washtub of some kind, and steam rose from it.

"Bath!" the giant said, and then withdrew his hand and slammed the door.

It was pitch dark again.

"Shall we light a torch?" Sax said.

"Can you wait a few minutes?" Flos said.

"Sure," Sax said. "For what?"

"For me to take a bath," Flos said, and there was the sound of someone moving in the room.

"Well," Culter said, with laughter in his voice, "we might as well let *the* girl bathe. According to the cooks, there's only one."

"Which one of us did they mean?" Lyca said.

"We'll never know," Culter said.

There was a splash, then sounds of someone in the tub and making waves.

"I don't care if they thought I was a boy or girl or tulip," Flos said from in the tub. "I'm tired of the smell."

"What about our clothes?" Culter said. "They stink as much as we do."

"Throw them in," Flos said, "and I'll wash them too."

"When we've *all* finished," Culter said, and started taking off his clothes.

"Hurry up before the water gets too cold," Jason said.

"There's room in here for everybody," Flos said.

"Then heads up!" Culter said, and moved to the side of the tub, threw one leg up, lifted himself over, and slid down into the warm.

"Oh yeah!" he said, and ducked his head below the surface.

Something banged him on the back, and he came up spluttering.

"Sorry about that," and the voice was Lyca's.

Culter gulped. "That's OK," he said, and then the tub was shaken hard by Sax's coming in, then Jason. It was a hot tub in a dungeon cell in Zara Keep.

"I hope that cat stays where she is," Culter said. "I don't want her trying to scrub my back."

The splashing and the ducking and the laughing slowed, and each agreed that they could get no cleaner without soap.

"Then let's do the laundry," Flos said.

They all got out.

"Where are my things?" Sax said. "I can't see in here."

"Let's light a torch," Jason said.

"We're not dressed," Culter said.

"Jason's right," Flos said. "There's no way to do the clothes by feel."

Sounds of moving around, then Jason said, "If it's all right with everybody, I'll light the torch."

Each one said yes. A scrape from the tinderbox, a spark, a small flame, then the torch was lit. Everybody felt embarrassed, until Flos walked to the tub and threw her clothing in.

"Let's go," she said. "I'm hungry. Let's let these soak while we eat."

The others did the same, and soon were crowded around the plank with its five bowls.

"They seem to have forgotten forks and spoons," Culter said, and dipped his fingers in his bowl. He put some in his mouth. "And salt," he said, but was surprised the food was not too bad at all.

The others ate, standing around naked, dipping fingers in and licking gravy off them.

The food and bath cheered them up, and they all helped with the washing. They hung their clothes over anything that stuck out from the wall—old iron rings which probably had held chains to hold the prisoners, sharp rock protrusions.

"There isn't any chance that any of these things trigger secret panels, is there?" Culter said, smiling, but hoping he was right.

"I've checked," Sax said. "These walls are solid."

"Just thought I'd ask," Culter said, but the question had brought back the sense of being in a dungeon.

The group used their packs to sit on and waited for their clothes to dry. The one torch burned and gave a flickering light.

The cell door banged, then opened, and the giant was outside. "Tub!" he said, and pointed one massive finger at the washtub. Then pointed to the plank. "Bowls!" he said.

They pushed the items closer to the door, and the giant dragged them out. Then his face appeared again and his finger pointed right at Sax.

"Come!" he said.

"How do we handle this?" Jason said.

No one answered. Culter put his hand on his sword's handle, but didn't draw the blade.

Sax stepped forward. "Don't do anything," he said. "This isn't the time to try a move. If I don't come back, there will still be four of you. Maybe you can do something later, but don't try anything while we're down here. It won't work." He moved to the door and stepped out in the hallway. The door slammed behind him. The torch sputtered in the wind and almost died, but caught again, and there was light to see each other, standing naked and looking at the door. They each felt the terrible sense of loss of Sax's going.

"He was right," Jason said finally. "There was no point in trying something then." He went to where his clothes were and put them on. The others did the same with theirs, and soon were dressed in soggy clothing.

"But what about now?" Culter said. "Isn't there something we can figure out to do? I mean, what if that big bastard comes and gets us, one by one? Do we just go with him and die?"

There was no answer. Anything that they could think of wouldn't work. There was no way to ambush the giant, for he never even came inside the cell. They could refuse to come out, but somehow they were sure he had a way to make them. Sax had said the walls were solid, but Flos went over them again in case she felt a spell. There was nothing.

"Try the door," Jason said.

"The door?" Flos said. "But what good would that do?"

"I have an idea," Jason said, but there wasn't time to put it into motion. There was a sound outside the cell, the door was opened, and Sax walked back inside. The door slammed shut. This time it put the torch out.

"What happened?" Flos said.

"Nothing," Sax said.

"I'll get this damn thing going again," Jason said.

"Let's wait," Sax said. "Let's get some sleep."

"Not till you tell us what that was about," Culter said.

"As I just said," Sax said, "nothing. It wasn't anything. The giant took me out and down the hall, where it was lighter; then he made me stand against the wall and he just looked at me.''

"Just looked at you," Culter said.

"Just looked at me. I don't have any clothes on, and felt like a fool, but nothing happened. He didn't do anything. He didn't say anything. Nothing.''

"Then what?''

"He brought me back here."

"And that's all?" Culter said.

"That's all," Sax said. "Now where are my clothes, and let's try to get some sleep. It's been a long day.''

They scrabbled around, working their packs into pillows, then the cell grew quiet as they settled down.

"Should we leave a guard?" Culter said.

"Against what?" Jason asked. "The giant?''

"Forget I asked," Culter said.

They began to fall asleep.

Something woke him, and Jason sat up slowly, his right hand moving out in front in the defense position.

"Shhh." Next to his ear.

It was Flos.

"I think I've found something," she whispered. "I didn't want to wake the others till I talked to you.''

"What did you find?''

"A weakness.''

"In what?''

"The door," Flos said. "I never got a chance to make sure, but it worried me, and I woke up a couple of minutes ago and checked. There's a weakness there.''

"How can you tell?" Jason said.

"I really don't know," Flos said, "but the door is made of wood, and somehow it tells me how it's put together. I can't explain it, even to myself.''

"This one is weak?" Jason said.

"Not really," Flos said, "but there is one spot where it is slightly rotted. I think that, if it's hit just right, it might break open.''

That woke Jason up as though cold water were thrown in his face.

"Show me," he said.

Flos took his hand and led him to the door in the dark. Then she brought it down and touched it to a place on the door's surface.

It felt just like the rest of the heavy door—firm and hard and totally invulnerable.

"You want me to hit this thing right here?" he said.

"If you're strong enough," Flos said. "That's where the weakness is."

"I can't feel any weakness," Jason said.

"You'll have to trust me," Flos said.

If she were wrong, Jason would smash his hand. To exert the force he would need to crack the door, he would have to concentrate his every power on the blow. If the door did not give, the bones in his hand and arm would.

"It'll make a lot of noise," he said.

"Can you do it?" Flos asked.

"I don't know," Jason said.

"We'd better get the others up anyway," Flos said. "If you can get us out of here, we'll have to run for it. We'd better all be ready." She coughed loudly.

"What makes you think that we're asleep?" Culter said from the darkness.

"With you two yelling at each other, nobody can sleep," Sax said.

"I'm ready," Lyca said, and the swamp cat growled.

"You want a light?" Sax asked.

"No," Jason said. "I can see this better in the dark." He began to concentrate, to gather all his energy in just one place, to see his hand as it broke through the door, to know just where to aim six inches on the other side, to feel the door split down the middle, to wipe out any doubts of his ability—and it took time.

The others waited quietly, their things packed and on their backs, their hands free, their legs ready to run.

Jason began to breathe more deeply. His right hand drew back very, very slowly. Then, lightning-like, it struck.

The door cracked down the center, groaned, creaked, moaned, then slowly fell into two parts out in the dungeon corridor.

"Let's go!" Jason yelled, and leaped through the opening, the swamp cat right behind him, the others coming through as fast as they could move.

"This way!" Jason said, and started running away from the gate where they had come in. He had no idea what he would find, but was almost certain that the giant would be by the gate. The other way was their only hope.

The footfalls of the running group sounded through the corridor, but there was nothing they could do to quiet them. Speed was what they needed now.

Cells lined the corridor, and darkness was increasing. The torches on the walls had not been lighted here. Jason could see nothing up ahead. The cat passed him, then seemed to slow.

"Move it!" he yelled behind her.

It was even darker now, and Jason knew they could not run much longer without light. He heard the cat's claws on the stone floor. They scratched as though she'd tried to stop and was still sliding. Jason tried to see in front of him. It was pure black. Then light, a flared light, and a torch was lit, and Jason stopped.

So did the others. The giant stood there holding up the light and smiling down at them, and they were helpless.

The great mouth opened, and the deafening laughter poured out around them. There was no point in running.

Culter drew his sword. The laughter increased as the giant saw there was no blade.

Culter stepped forward and raised his arm. The giant swallowed his laughter, held out his hand, and said, "Hold! Don't strike me with that bladeless sword."

But it was too late. Culter brought the handle sideways so the blade would slice across the giant's middle. It was the only blow that he could make. Nothing happened, except that Culter almost fell from the force of the stroke. He had missed.

"I said, hold," the giant said. "Do not waste your effort."

Culter regained his balance, took a deep breath, and lunged across the space between them. The point of the invisible blade was aimed directly at the giant's stomach.

His great hand came down and stopped Culter, but not before the handle almost touched him. Yet there was no sign the blade had penetrated.

Culter tried to step back. The giant held him.

"I have told you twice to hold," he said. "If you insist on trying to kill me with that sword handle, I shall be forced to take more drastic action." He lifted Culter in the air, turned, looked along the wall, found what he wanted, went to it, and hung Culter on a hook some five feet from the floor. Then the giant turned to the rest of the group.

"Does anyone else wish to try to kill me?" he said. "Possibly with a bow without an arrow. Or maybe a sling without a stone. Or a lance without a point."

No one moved, with the exception of Culter, who kicked with his legs to see if he could lift himself enough to unhook his jacket. It didn't work, and he hung there feeling like six kinds of fool, wondering what happened to his blade.

"That is good," the giant said. "Now we can talk. I am Gok," and paused, as though expecting them to say something.

Jason shrugged, and said, "I'm Jason."

The giant looked at the others. "And the rest?" he said.

There was something different about his voice from when he'd talked before. Flos looked carefully to make sure it was the same man.

"I'm Flos," she said, and the other two identified themselves.

"And the courageous young man with the bladeless sword, who attacks giants regardless?"

"None of your damn business," Culter mumbled.

"As you wish," the giant said. Then turned back to the others. "I see you have broken out of your cell. I was wondering if you could do that."

Jason couldn't understand why the jailer kept them there instead of locking them back up again. Was this giant another sadist who took pleasure in their troubles? Did he get bored down here, and look for games to play? Jason felt anger growing.

"We did it," he said. "Now what?"

The giant looked down at him and smiled. "I ask you one more question," he said. "Why are you here?"

"The Keeper tried that already," Jason said. "He promised to torture us to get the information. You wouldn't want to spoil it all for your friend, the boss, would you?"

The giant's features clouded with some kind of rage. Jason had no idea what he'd said, but stepped back in anticipation of a blow.

"He is no friend of mine," the giant said, and turned his head and spat upon the wall. "He is filth. He is evil," and he spat again.

The group stood in amazement at what the giant said. Nothing was making sense.

"I ask you why you are here because I have to know," the giant said. "I must know if the Council sent you. There is so little time."

Jason quickly sorted out the facts and knew it really didn't matter what they said. They were prisoners, and admitting that they had come from the Council would change nothing.

"Yes," he said. "We were sent by the Council."

"Shut up!" Sax said.

"It doesn't matter," Jason said.

"How do *you* know?" Sax said. "Let them find out the hard way."

For some reason, the giant laughed again, then sobered. "If you are from the Council, then you have come for the Crystal," he said.

"Don't answer that," Sax said.

"It was not a question," the giant said. "There would be only one purpose in sending anyone in here. It must be for the Crystal. You must have come from the Council, for no one except from another world could pass the magic spell which keeps out strangers. You have been brought from some other place and sent here by the Council for the Crystal. I am certain."

"What difference does it make to you?" Flos said. "How come you've changed so much? You sounded like some kind of moron when we first got here. Now you don't."

"I am not a dunce," the giant said, and laughed. "But sometimes it is good that others think I am. You ask what difference it makes for me to know about you. I shall tell you. If you succeed in this, then I am free."

They looked at him. Fifteen feet tall, ugly, bald, hands as big as basketballs, rough clothes and shoes, and standing in the corridor of the dungeon. But somehow not an enemy.

"Free from what?" Jason said.

"From here," the giant said. "I do not come from this land any more than you do. I was brought when the Masters first got here."

"The Masters!" Flos said. "You mean the same Masters who ruled here years and years ago? How could you be that old?"

"My race lives many, many centuries," the giant said. "I am still young, the way we measure time. I *was* brought here when the Masters came. I was very, very young then. I was to be some kind of playmate for their children."

"But they left a long time ago," Sax said.

"And left me here," the giant said. "They took nothing, including me and my family."

"Family!" Flos said. "Where is your family?"

"Split up within the other Keeps," the giant said. "My wife is in Sulg. My son is in Quum. My older daughter is in Wolt. My youngest is in Vect." There was a terrible deep sadness in his voice.

"Each is kept working for the Keeper of the Keep through threats on the lives of all the others. We each know that if any one of us tries to escape the others will be killed before we can get there to help them. I might be able to save one, or even two, but they would have time to kill the others. We can do nothing."

"They use you as jailers," Flos said.

"Yes," the giant said. "All but my youngest. She is too small for jailer. She serves as playmate for the children of Vecten, the Keeper."

"Each is a hostage for the others," Jason said.

"Yes," the giant said. "Exactly. But if they can be defeated in this conflict, then we will be free."

"And you can then return to your own land," Sax said.

"With luck," the giant said. "We possess no magic, but maybe we can find someone who does who can send us home."

Culter had calmed down to listen, but now spoke up. "If

you hate these Keepers so, how come you didn't do a thing to help us? Like escape, for instance.''

''A good question,'' the giant said. ''I had to know just who you were, and if you had any strength. If I had let you out, I would have found out nothing. I have been waiting here most of the night to see what you would do. You did it well, although you made a bit more noise than necessary.''

''We can argue about that later,'' Jason said. ''What happens now?''

''I tell you where the Crystal is,'' the giant said. ''You go get it.''

''That seems simple,'' Jason said.

''Hardly,'' the giant answered.

''Why don't *you* go get the Crystal?'' Flos asked.

''I am not allowed out of the dungeons,'' the giant said. ''If I were seen—and it is hard to imagine anyone not seeing me—if I were seen, I would be killed at once. Those are the orders.''

''We're not exactly welcome guests ourselves,'' Jason said. ''How do *we* get the Crystal?''

''You will use another route, for one thing,'' the giant said.

''How come you don't use *that* one yourself?'' Sax said suspiciously.

''You will understand that soon enough,'' the giant said. ''But we must waste no more time. The others are coming.''

''What others?'' Jason said.

''The other Keepers. They are all coming here.''

''We heard that Wolt was here already,'' Flos said.

''That is true. And Vect has arrived since you were brought down here. There are only Sulg and Quum left, and they are expected any time now.''

''What difference does it make if they are here or not?'' Flos said. ''I thought the problem was mainly Zaragoza.''

''It is,'' the giant said, ''but he needs their help. He cannot cast the spell he wants alone. He must have the other four, and they must work together. Each one must do his part, and then the aliens will come.''

''The warriors from another world?'' Flos said.

"Yes," the giant said. "The warriors. Once they are here, there is no hope for anyone. The Council cannot muster a defense strong enough to beat them. The people will be enslaved."

"You will never be allowed to see your family," Flos said.

The giant looked at her, then nodded.

"If we get the Crystal before they can cast the spell, then they can't bring the warriors here," Jason said.

"Yes," the giant said.

"Then let's move it," Jason said. "Which way to this different route?"

"Down," the giant said, and pointed at the floor.

"But the Keep is up," Sax said.

"Yes," the giant said. "First you must go down, to the heat pit."

"That sounds like something I could do without," Culter said. "And speaking of something I could do without, it's hanging on this wall! Get me down."

The giant seemed to have forgotten Culter, and quickly moved to lift him off the hook. "Tell me, young man," he said. "Why was it you thought you could harm me with that bladeless sword?"

"Because I killed a spider with it," Culter said, and realized how dumb that sounded. "It works sometimes," and he held the handle up and waved his hand across the place where the blade should be.

There was no blade. He shrugged, and put the handle back in the sheath.

"I do not understand," the giant said.

"That makes at least two of us," Culter said.

"You drew it when you didn't need to," Flos said.

"Huh?" Culter said.

"I said, you drew your sword when you didn't need to. There was no enemy to fight. Nothing was trying to kill you."

"What about *him*?" Culter said, then understood. "OK. He wasn't trying to kill me, but *I* didn't know that."

"Your sword did," Flos said.

"We've got to go," Jason said. "How do we get down to this heat pit?"

The giant told them how, the corridors to take, which stairs, and what they'd find there.

"I would come part of the way," he said, "but it is better if I stay here in case someone comes for you. So long as I am in the dungeon, the guards won't come inside to search."

"How many guards are there in the Keep?" Sax said.

"Not enough for a war," the giant said, "but too many to fight. About five hundred."

"In a place this size, they must be pretty scattered," Sax said.

"Yes. Most of them are assigned to stay close to the Keeper."

"That's *some* help," Sax said.

The giant looked at him and almost smiled. "You may make a good general someday," he said. "You ask many of the right questions."

"Where is the Crystal kept?" Jason said.

"At the top of the central tower," the giant said.

"If we get it, can we bring it back the same way we got in?"

"It would be better if you didn't," the giant said. "There is no way from here to the outside. It would be faster if you found some other exit."

"Then we may not see you again," Jason said.

"It is hard to know for sure what will happen," the giant said.

"In case we don't . . ." Jason stepped forward and held out his hand to shake.

The giant took it, very gently.

"I think you will need this many times before your task is over," he said, and held the pure white hand in the palm of his gigantic one. "But let us hope you will not need the other," and he nodded to the pure black hand of healing.

"How do you know about my hands?" Jason said.

"There are many where I come from with such hands," the giant said.

The thought was both amazing and exciting to Jason, but he would have to think about it later.

Each one came forward and shook hands, Sax last. The giant seemed to hold his longer. Sax looked up at him, then said, "How come you took me out of the cell, and not any of the others?"

The giant's eyes were soft, and he spoke in a low voice.

"You are much like my son," he said. "I simply wanted to look at you and think of him. He is bigger than you now, of course," and the others looked at Sax's six foot eight, two hundred eighty pounds, and almost laughed, "but you have much in common. Perhaps someday you'll meet him."

"I'd like to," Sax said.

The giant seemed to shake himself back to reality. "You must go now." He gave Jason his torch, and watched as they started down the corridor.

They reached a turning point, and looked back. The giant almost filled the hall, and was just a silhouette against the light behind him, but there was something gentle in that massive frame. They waved, and saw his hand come up and wave to them, then they turned and walked into the dark.

Down and around and around and down through the labyrinth of dungeons, obviously unused for years. They saw doors on both sides of the corridors, but they didn't even slow to look at them. They stopped once to get organized, however.

"He said something about a fan. How does it run?" Sax said.

"I don't know," Jason said.

"He said by the wind," Culter said.

"Down inside the mountain?"

"On *top* of the mountain, man," Culter said. "A windmill on top of the mountain driving a fan deep inside. OK?"

"You win."

"But why is it a problem?" Flos said.

"We'll see when we get there," Jason said, and they started off again.

It was warmer every level. They were all sweating now, and breathing with their mouths open.

"How much farther?" Flos asked.

"One more staircase, if I remember right," Jason said, and

they went down a twisting stair and stepped out into a room, or hardly a room. It was more of a cavern, a place too large to measure.

"Good heavens!" Flos said.

"Wrong direction," Culter said, and wiped his steaming face. "And a little warm for that."

"Where is that fan he talked about?" Sax said. "We could use a little air."

"I don't think it will help," Jason said.

"Well," Culter said, "we have to find it anyway. The giant said that was the only way to go."

They walked toward the center of the cave. A bright red glow came from somewhere in the floor. The heat was terrible, and getting worse.

"We'll die in here if we stay long," Flos said.

Nobody had the breath to answer. They reached the source of the glow, and couldn't stand it. A great crack ran the length of the floor, and from it came the light and heat which made this place. They could see no flames from where they were, but knew it must be hell-hot down in the crevice. There was no sign of any fan.

Jason motioned for them to move sideways along the crack to find some way to cross it. The giant had said on the other side, but there seemed no way to get there, and the heat would kill them if they stayed.

Then he saw it. What seemed to be a bridge of some sort arching up and over the great crack. The bottom of it glowed with the light of the flames below. It looked solid.

He pointed to the bridge, and they moved faster, but not fast enough. Something was there ahead of them. They stopped.

"What are they?" Jason said.

"Horrible!" Culter answered.

"Slugs," Flos said. "They are garden slugs."

"From whose garden!" Jason said. "The giant's?"

"I think he would have told us they were here if he had known," Flos said.

"That's not the point," Sax said. "How in hell do we get past them?"

"Well," Culter said, "we're certainly in hell, so you've

got the right location." He tried to laugh, but the heat took all his breath away. He coughed instead.

The things were by the bridge. They were hard to see, as all the light came from the crack behind them, but they seemed almost transparent as they slithered on the ground, leaving some kind of slimy trail behind them. Each one was at least eight feet long and six feet high.

"What do garden slugs eat?" Sax said.

"I don't know," Flos said. "These are big enough to eat most anything."

"Like five people," Jason said.

"And a cat," said Lyca.

The swamp cat was looking at the slugs, but didn't seem to know just what to do, as though she couldn't understand if they were good or bad, or how she should attack them if she had to.

"Well," Culter said, "I have only one suggestion," and he drew his sword. "I sure wish I knew when there was a blade on this thing," and he swung the handle in the air and ran across the floor toward the slugs.

The group followed, but Culter had a head start, and he reached them well before the others. He lifted the handle of the sword, stepped close to the nearest slug, and struck.

At first he thought he'd made another error, that there was no blade again. Then he realized that these things were made of some kind of soft and mushy stuff, and the blade was cutting deep into it.

The slug reared up and Culter was almost knocked backwards. He pulled the sword out, took better aim this time, and struck again, right down the center of the thing. It fell into a slimy heap and Culter looked around for others.

Jason ran up behind him. "Can you clear the bridge?" he said.

"I'll try," Culter said, and jumped toward the next great slug.

His sword was up, then down, and the thing pulled back. He saw the bridgehead, and worked his way toward it, hacking and slashing at whatever slithered in his path. The floor was running with the slime of dying slugs, and Culter almost slipped and fell. He was getting closer to the bridge, and closer to the edge of the crevice.

Only two left, and he lunged and skewered one, but the other didn't pull away. Instead, it moved toward him. He tried to withdraw the blade to defend against the second slug, but he couldn't pull out. The slug that it was stuck in twisted in its dying, and had caught the blade. Culter pulled again. He put his foot against the thing, but it sank in. The second one was almost on him.

A flash of flame beside him, and he saw Jason in the corner of his eye. He had shoved the torch in what must have been the great slug's face, for it pulled back as though mortally injured.

"That's it," Culter said. "We can use the bridge."

"There are others coming," Jason said, and now Culter could see movement behind the bodies he had killed. The sliding, slipping, and slithering of a thousand other slugs.

"Hurry!" he said. "Get across the bridge. I can hold them," and the group reached the bridge and started running across.

Culter worked his blade out from the dead slug, and moved backwards slowly. He felt the start of the arching bridge, and tried to figure what the best place for defense might be. If he stayed here the slugs could mass and possibly defeat him. He turned and ran up and over the bridge.

He took a position almost at the other end, where the bridge was narrowest, and where the slugs could not gang up. "Where's that fan supposed to be?" he called to the others.

"We're looking for it," Jason yelled.

The light was uneven in that place, and the heat waves tended to distort things, and they could hardly breathe at all, and now they had to search an endless cave for one lousy fan.

"There!" Jason yelled, and pointed.

It had not been hard to find—blades at least fifty feet across, and the whole thing mounted in the wall ahead of them, spinning slowly.

"We have to go through that!" Sax said.

"That's what the giant told us," Jason said.

"Then let's go," Sax said. The fan began to pick up

speed, and soon the blades were blurred, then invisible. "You say we have to go *through* that!"

"Yes," Jason said.

"How?" Flos asked.

"I don't know," Jason said.

"Hey, you guys, get a move on," Culter yelled. "Those damn things are coming," and the bridge was covered with the slimy slugs sliding toward him.

They approached the giant fan, but felt the suction pulling them into the blades. They stopped and looked at it.

"I guess it supplies the heat for the whole Keep," Jason said. "Gok said we were to go up through the heating ducts, but he didn't tell us how to stop the fan."

The blades slowed down again.

"I think Culter's right," Sax said. "I think it really does work from a windmill up on the mountain. That would explain why it goes fast, then slow. I guess it wouldn't even be working at all this time of year if it weren't for the rain making everything so cold."

"Not down here," Flos said. The sweat poured down her face. "We've got to do *some*thing."

They looked around for anything they might jam into the blades, but there was nothing, nothing but the yell from Culter as he lunged at the first slug.

"Anybody got any ideas?" Jason said.

"No," Flos said, and Lyca shook her head.

"Maybe," Sax said, and reached in his pocket. He pulled out a small stone.

"Somehow," Jason said, "I don't think that's quite big . . ."

"Shut up a second," Sax said, and held the stone tightly in his hand, with his eyes closed, trying to bring back the thoughts of Quadra—in the quarry, in the cottage, stomping to and from the village.

He could see her. First only a dim outline, then her whole body, finally her face, and she looked startled, as though someone had called her.

"I called you," Sax thought to the image. "I need your help."

"Where are you, boy?" Her voice was distant in his head.

"In Zara Keep," Sax said. "Down in the heat pit."

"I can hardly hear you," Quadra said.

"I need your strength," Sax said.

"It is yours," Quadra said. "I do not know how much will get through. I will do my best." Sax could see her close her eyes and fold her arms and stand perfectly still.

The strength came. Slowly, through his fingertips, then up his arms and into his body. It was like the night he'd met her, caught beneath the boulders. Maybe not so strong, but much greater than anything that Sax himself could generate. He let it flow, and his muscles grew harder and the tendons flexed.

"Hurry up!" Culter yelled from the foot of the bridge. "I'm not sure how long I can hold them!"

"We've got to do something now!" Jason said.

"I'm ready," Sax said, and started toward the fan.

The suction from the giant blades was terrible, but could not overcome him. He stopped only ten feet away. He waited.

The blades slowed as the windmill far above ran out of wind for just a moment. Sax watched carefully for any sign of speeding up, then, judging as accurately as he could, he leaped forward as the blades were at their slowest, grabbed one of them, and braced his feet.

He thought his arms would be torn from their sockets, but they held. He held the blade and strained against its pulling.

"NOW!" he yelled, "NOW!" and heard them coming.

Flos and Lyca, with Jason right behind.

"Through the blades into the duct," Sax yelled. "Hurry!"

Flos was through, then Lyca, then the swamp cat.

"Culter!" Jason yelled. "Come on!"

"I can't," Culter yelled back, and Sax felt the pressure building up as the wind freshened on the mountain top.

"Run!" Jason yelled.

"I'm stuck." Jason turned and looked back at Culter on the bridge.

He had moved back to the flat ground, but didn't seem to be able to walk. The slugs were coming off the arch and starting to surround him.

"I keep slipping!" Jason could now see some liquid all

around Culter's feet. As each slug died it melted into slime, which covered the stone floor.

Culter could still lift his feet, but the stuff was so slippery that he couldn't move. If he tried, he would fall, and to fall would mean the slugs would be on top of him.

"I . . . can't hold . . . this much longer," Sax said between tightened teeth.

"Hang on, for heaven's sake," Jason said, and grabbed the pack from Sax's back, ripped it open, found the coil of rope, and yanked it out. He whipped it above his head and yelled to Culter, "Grab it when it comes," and threw the coil, holding one end.

It missed.

Jason hauled it in and tried again. The weight of the slime which now stuck to it carried it even farther, and it fell by Culter's foot.

He reached down and grabbed it.

Jason didn't ask if he was ready, he just pulled as hard as he could. Culter was off balance, then down and sliding through the slime to the open floor. He let go of the rope, stood up, and ran through the stopped blades of the great fan, with Jason right behind him.

Sax knew that he was out of strength, but it didn't matter. They were all through. If he didn't make it, they could still get the Crystal from the Keep.

He felt something around his waist. It was Jason and the rope. He tied it tight, then jumped back into the duct. Sax felt the rope pull.

"Let go!" Jason yelled.

Sax had no choice. His muscles couldn't hold a second longer, and his fingers slid off the big blade and it began to turn. Jason and Culter pulled the rope and pulled Sax through the opening between the blades, just as the speed picked up and the edge of every blade became a whirling guillotine.

Sax lay on the floor and tried to get his breath. It was difficult, more so than simply being out of wind.

It *was* a wind. The fan was turning faster now, and the blast of air it generated tore his breath away. It threw the lighter of the group down on the floor and pushed them along. They tried to stop themselves but couldn't. The fan went faster. Even Sax's weight was not enough to hold him, and he started rolling over on the floor. Then over again, and he was rolling down the duct along with all the others.

Each one of them curled up as tightly as he could, but still they banged against the sides and scraped their flesh off. If they could avoid breaking their bones or something worse they would be out of this tornado soon.

It lessened, then almost stopped. Apparently, the fan had slowed again. Lyca was the first on her feet.

"Run," she said, "before it starts again," and she started running from the source of the wind.

"I can't see anything," Jason said, and the others there agreed.

"Light a torch," Sax said. They almost got it lit before the next blast came; it threw them off their feet and fifty yards along the duct before it slowed enough for them to stand.

"How wide is this thing?" Jason asked.

Sax reached to his left and touched a wall. His right arm wasn't long enough to touch the other. "More than six and a half feet," he said.

"Wait a second," Jason said, and felt along Sax's arm and took his hand. "You keep touching that wall, and I'll see if I can touch this one."

He could, and they estimated the duct was ten feet wide.

"Keep touching that wall, and I'll keep my hand on this, and we should be able to make fairly good time," Jason said, and began moving forward.

Culter did the same with Flos, and between them they could just touch the two walls, but it was enough. They followed Sax and Jason. They got far enough so that when the next strong wind blew they weren't blown over.

"But it sure is *hot*," Flos said, and her hands were slippery with sweat.

"Pretend it's just a sauna," Culter said.

"Somehow it doesn't work," Flos said. She squeezed his hand to tell him she was kidding.

Lyca was waiting up ahead with the swamp cat. "Which way?" she said.

"Let's try the light again," Sax said. This time they got it going.

There were five openings ahead of them. The main duct stopped here, and they would have to choose which route to take.

"Gok didn't mention this," Sax said.

"He probably didn't know about it," Jason said.

"Anybody got any ideas?" Culter said.

"Yes," Flos said. "I think I could use a hand. Jason's hand." She sat down suddenly.

They turned and looked at her, and saw her face was white and she was breathing deeply.

Jason moved to her and squatted down. "What's wrong?" he said.

"I think I sprained my ankle," Flos said.

Jason looked up at the others. "Let's take a little rest. I'll see what I can do for Flos, and the rest of you work out which way to go." He turned back to Flos and put his black left hand gently on her ankle.

"It was easy," Culter said.

"How come?" said Jason.

He had been able to heal Flos's ankle without too much trouble. It was not a true sprain, more of a twist, and he had taken the pain and swelling away in a few moments. Now it was time to decide the route.

"Each of these smaller ducts has a grate over it," Culter said. "Sax can only get one of them loose. Which means we take the farthest left." He waved his hand toward the duct he meant.

"I'm not sure I'm nuts about that way of choosing," Jason said.

"Tell us a better one," Culter said.

Jason couldn't think of any, so he shrugged, and said, "Let's go."

The opening on the far left was much smaller than the main one, no more than two feet wide and maybe five feet high.

"Here we go again," Culter mumbled, but concentrated on each step and didn't think about the size of where they were.

They went no more than twenty feet before Jason stopped. The rest bumped into each other.

"What's wrong?" Culter asked from the rear.

"It goes up here," Jason called back to him.

"Then go up," Culter said.

"Just making sure it's empty," Jason called, and Culter could hear some scrambling ahead.

"There's a ladder," Jason yelled, then each one moved forward a few feet and disappeared.

Culter reached the point where it went up, and looked up at Sax's feet above him. They almost blotted out the light from the torch Jason was carrying.

"If *I* were carrying the torch," Culter said, "everybody would climb a hell of a lot faster."

They went up, then stopped again.

"Hey!" Culter yelled when he hit Sax's foot with his head.

"Basement," Jason called down. "Old wine kegs, dust, and rats. Everybody out," and he moved on.

It was a basement room. Jason had climbed through the hot air vent and dropped down into it. The others followed. The place had obviously not been used in years.

Flos sneezed. "Dust," she explained.

"Let's figure things out for a minute," Jason said, "before we just keep climbing up shafts and running down ducts. Let's think of some sort of plan, or something."

"Where are we?" Culter asked.

"I'm glad you asked," Jason said. "I don't know. *But*— and I emphasize the 'but'—*but*, I have a vague idea. I think we're under one of the towers, and the odds are four to one it isn't the central one. Especially since everyone seems convinced the Crystal's in the central tower."

"Well," Sax said, "we can be pretty sure we're not under the east or south towers. I don't think we've come that far."

"The odds are getting better," Jason said. "I figure that we'll have to climb up high enough to get our bearings before we can know just where we are."

"Then how can we plan?" Flos said.

"Like this," and Jason knelt and started drawing in the dust with one white finger. "Here are the two mountains, on either side of the gorge, just as we saw them from down below, before we climbed that cliff. Before *you* climbed that cliff. I just went along for laughs.''

"OK," Sax said. "Those are the two mountains, with the river running in between."

Jason drew a square between the mountains.

"The Keep spans the river between the sides of the gorge, right?"

They all remembered seeing the Keep straddling the gorge, like some great bridge.

"According to the giant," Jason drew some smaller squares, "the Keep has five towers. One on each of the corners, and the central one where Zaragoza keeps the Crystal." He drew a square in the center of the larger square, then put the tip of his finger right in the middle of it. "There!" he said.

"You think we might be underneath one of those smaller towers," Flos said.

"Yes," Jason said. "Either the west or north, I don't know which," and he drew a "W" in one small square, and an "N" in another. "The trick is to get from whichever tower we are in into the central one without anybody seeing us."

"Then getting to the top of the central tower, finding the Crystal, getting down again, and finding some way out," Culter said.

"That's about it," Jason said.

"If it's that simple," Culter said, "what do we need a plan for? Let's go." He pretended to start back up to the vent.

"Wise guy," Jason said, and Culter turned around and grinned.

"Just thought I'd get things moving," he said, coming back and standing beside the others.

"Where was the heat pit on that map?" Flos said.

Jason drew an "X" in the middle of the western mountain. "In here. So was the dungeon and the garbage truck. Apparently they used the mountain for nasty stuff. There are passages from there into the Keep. We've been blown and walked and climbed through one to get here. That's the heating system. We went through the dungeon passage and the garbage one before. There may be others for all I know."

"That may be a way out," Sax said. "We'll have to check on that when the time comes."

"Is there anything to eat?" Flos said. Everybody looked at her. "Just asking," she said, and blushed.

"The answer's no," Jason said. "Sorry about that."

"Mind if I look around in here?" Flos said. No one did.

"So that's about it," Jason said. "I vote we just go up until we find some lookout point and find out where we are. I think it will be faster than wandering around looking for the central tower, and we sure as hell don't want to go out and ask someone."

They all agreed.

"Maybe these will help," Flos said, and held up two lanterns.

"Any oil in them?" Jason asked.

Flos sloshed them. "Some," she said.

"Then let's light them up." He took one and opened it and lighted it from the burning torch.

He turned to Lyca and said, "Here, hold this a second." Lyca pulled back from the lantern as though she were attacked.

"What's up?" Jason said. "I just want you to hold it for me for a second while I light the other one."

Lyca moved away, and stood alone in the dark shadows. Jason shrugged and handed the lantern to Culter, lighted the second one, and stood up.

"We all set now?" and he glanced at Lyca. She was looking at the floor as though ashamed. "Let's go," Jason said, and climbed back to the vent and out into the hot air duct.

The rest followed, with Culter and his lamp again in the rear.

Within seconds they were all sweating as they had been before. The duct was dusty and Flos sneezed again, but it was easier to climb carrying the lanterns rather than the torch.

"I wish they'd put some windows in these things," Culter said.

"Be quiet," Jason called. "There may be people on the other side of these walls."

"Then they're probably scared out of their wits," Culter said. "Hearing ghosts crawling around."

"Don't count on it," Jason said. "Especially as we go higher."

Culter shut up.

The climbing stopped, and they were crawling across a flat area.

"It's hotter here than it was before," Culter said to Sax's shoes ahead of him. He had found it helped his fear of being in small crowded spaces if he talked to someone. Even shoes.

It was hot, particularly the floor under their hands. Then the space opened up, and Culter could see the others gathering around a source of light. It was in the floor, and they were looking down. He reached the place, and looked in.

It was the smell that hit him first. Fresh bread!

"Wow!" he said, then covered his mouth with his hand, and whispered, "Sorry."

"It doesn't look as though anybody's there," Jason said.

"Their bread is," Culter said.

Flos just moaned.

"How come they have a vent up in the ceiling?" Culter said. "The hot air doesn't go down."

"I think they're using the heat from the ovens to add more heat to the whole system," Jason said.

"That makes sense," Culter said. "I think I'd like to meet those Masters sometime. Pretty smart clowns, if you ask me."

"Well," Jason said, "I guess we better go."

Culter looked at Flos and almost laughed.

Her face was nothing but sheer disappointment. So close to that fresh bread, and yet so far away.

"Let me try something," Culter said. "Give me your rope, somebody."

Sax reached back and gave him his.

Culter took out his knife, tied the rope to it, lay flat on his stomach, and started lowering the knife down into the room below, down toward the pile of fresh baked bread.

"Yes," Flos whispered.

The knife was almost there. Culter stopped it, and stood up. He gave himself some slack in the rope, then dropped it suddenly. The knife fell straight down and pierced the topmost loaf.

"Ha!" Culter said, and pulled the rope up quickly, the loaf of bread dangling from the end.

"It's something like fishing," Culter said. "Only different." The bread came through the hole and Culter took it off the knife and handed it to Flos. "Just a snack, my dear," he said, and smiled.

Actually the loaf was huge, and must have weighed five pounds.

"Let's eat while we travel," Jason said.

"Wait a second," Culter said, "I forgot dessert," and he lowered his knife again down into the bakery.

"We don't have time for games," Jason said, but Culter lay flat on his stomach guiding the blade down.

This time he didn't let it drop straight. He started it swinging back and forth, then let it drop at the right time, and said, "Bull's-eye!" Very carefully, he began to pull it up again.

Sax leaned over and looked. Culter had speared a whole stack of doughnuts, and was bringing them up slowly.

Something banged, and Culter stopped. The sound of voices down below.

Two men in white came in and stood right under where the group was hiding in the duct. Right above their heads were hanging six doughnuts. If they looked up, the whole venture might be over.

Nobody breathed.

The two men were arguing, and much too interested in what they were saying to pay more than slight attention to where they were. They began to move, and went toward the door, then out, and the doughnuts started up again.

"Forget them!" Jason whispered.

"Nuts to you," Culter said. "I haven't brought them this far just to let them fall." Then the doughnuts were through the opening and tucked into a pack, and they were on their way.

They were climbing. Ever since leaving the ceiling of the bakery, it had been all uphill, ladder after ladder, proving Jason had been right. They were in one of the towers, but no one knew which.

Culter hoped like hell it was the central one, but the vents they passed were much too small to crawl through into a room with windows where they could look out and learn just where they were.

Culter didn't relish doing this trip twice, and apparently the others had been thinking the same thing, for, when they stopped for breath, Flos said she sure wouldn't like to live up here and have to climb this every time she forgot her handkerchief. She sneezed, as if to prove her point.

"If you think you have trouble, look at her," Sax said, and pointed above to where the swamp cat lay draped over a higher rung. The poor animal's tongue was out and it was breathing hard.

"I don't think it's built for climbing ladders," Lyca said, and rubbed the cat's big head. She just looked at Lyca and panted.

"I'm afraid we can't wait," Jason said. They climbed on until Jason held his hand down with the palm out for silence.

There was a faint sound above them: voices.

Jason moved up very slowly to find the vent from which the sound was coming. He eased himself into a position from which he could see in.

The room was big, and took up the whole tower with the exception of a bulge, which Jason assumed was for the stairs, and the duct in which he stood. The rest of the space was devoted to a bedroom of great size, with luxurious appointments in it.

Two men straightening things up—patting the bed, fixing the logs in the fireplace—were talking to each other about when someone was expected.

"He should be here before we're through," one of the men said.

"You ever seen him?"

"Hell, they all looks alike to me," the first one said.

The other laughed.

"One Keeper's like the next one, hey?" he said, and kicked the big log into place.

"They'd each one take the whip to you as soon as look at you," the first one said. "It don't make much difference what they looks like."

"Well, I'd just as soon not be here when they come, so

let's get a move on,'' the second one said, and headed toward the door.

"Right you are," the first one said. He took a final look around, shrugged, spat into the fireplace, grinned, and went out the door. The other followed, closing it behind him.

Jason beckoned to Flos behind him, and whispered, "Let's go up a little more. We should be near the top, and we ought to be able to see from there." He turned and started climbing once again.

He only got a few feet further. The ladder stopped; or, rather, the hole stopped. The ladder seemed to continue.

"What's wrong?" Flos said.

"Trapdoor, I think," Jason said. He set himself and pushed up with his shoulder.

The ceiling opened up, and Jason climbed through and was standing on the floor above. There was light, and each one scrambled up and blinked and smiled.

"That's about as much tower climbing as I want for one day," Culter said.

"How did you figure on getting down?" Sax asked.

"Flying," Culter said.

"Oh," Sax said. "I never thought of that."

"Well," Culter said, "there's one Wright brother in every crowd, and I guess I'm it."

"Are you serious?" Flos said.

"If I had some aluminum tubing, some nylon rope, some thin steel cables, and a whole lot of nylon parachute material," Culter said, "and if I knew what I was doing, I could make a hang glider. But I don't have any of those things right now."

"And," Jason said, and they turned and saw him looking out a thin window, "it wouldn't do you much good anyway. You'd just have to climb the next one," and he pointed out the slit.

To the central tower, about a hundred yards away.

"I was right," Sax said. "This is the north tower."

"And there's the one we want," Flos said.

"That's it," Jason said. They each took turns looking out across the void to where the central tower stood.

"So now we turn around, go all the way down again,

somehow find a way between these towers, then climb all the way up to the top,'' Culter said. ''That tower's even higher than this one. You'll probably want me to climb that pole up there on top, too.''

''Maybe there's a shorter way,'' Flos said from the window. ''Look down.'' She made room for them.

A hundred feet straight down was what looked like the ground, but wasn't.

''It's the roof of the main part of the Keep,'' Jason said, ''all overgrown with bushes and trees and stuff.''

''It means we don't have to go all the way down,'' Flos said. ''If we can find a way out on that roof, we can cross over to the central tower, which would save a lot of work.''

Jason studied the problem. ''I think you're right,'' he said, then saw something move below them. It looked like a dog, but he couldn't quite be sure. He saw two others. ''They seem to use the roof as a kennel.''

''We can still get across, can't we?'' Flos said.

''I think so,'' Jason said. He decided to postpone worrying about the dogs he'd seen. He left the window, and started for the ladder to begin the climb down.

''Wait!'' It was Lyca. Looking through the slit toward the central tower. ''It is Zaragoza.''

They all moved quickly to where she was standing, but, when she made room for them, none of them could make out much more than something very dark high up on the tower. It could be a shadow, or the figure of a man. It was too far away.

''Are you certain?'' Jason asked.

''Yes,'' Lyca said. ''But,'' and she leaned forward to get a better look, ''he is going inside now.''

A sudden flash of lightning made them jump, and the crash of thunder echoed in the tower room.

''Wonderful weather for this time of year,'' Culter said, knowing the sound had made him nervous. ''Let's get out of this crow's nest.''

They all agreed, and Jason started down through the trap-door, then stopped. ''How would one of you like to go first?'' he said, looking embarrassed. ''I guess it's one thing to climb *up*, but it's something else climbing *down*.''

"I'll take it," Sax said, and the two of them switched positions.

"How about the cat?" Flos said.

"She got up," Jason said.

"But she may not get down," Flos said.

Sax adjusted his pack.

"Let me have yours," he said to Jason. He put it next to his. "The cat can come down after me. If she loses her footing, she can use my shoulders and the packs." He started down the ladder, but got no farther than one floor, where he waved the others to be still.

Then they all could hear the sound of someone in the room where the two men had straightened up. Sax was closest to the vent. He looked into the room, and listened carefully to two men inside. But these were not the same ones as before. These were dressed in finery, with flowing robes, and polished boots, and jewels around their throats.

"He is using you, sire," one of the men said.

"I know that, fool," the other said. He strode to the bed and threw his gloves down on it. "But there is nothing I can do. I have no strength to fight him. I have only a few hundred men. And you, of course."

The other man bowed slightly.

"Even with your brains and cunning, there is no way for me to achieve power over Zaragoza now."

"Sire," the other man said, "if I may make a suggestion. I quite agree that now is not the time to strike, that you do not have the necessary forces to overcome Zaragoza at this moment. But, sire, I suggest that you will soon have access to all the warriors that you could need."

"What warriors? How?"

"The warriors that Zaragoza will bring from the other world," the man said, "at the meeting he holds this very hour."

"But Zaragoza will control those men. It is *he* who is bringing them, although he needs our help to do it. Still, he holds the Crystal, and it will be him whom they obey."

"When they first arrive, sire; but I am certain there will be ways alter that, to get them to follow you."

"How?"

"I do not know, sire. I have some ideas, but it is still too soon to know which ones will work. I shall report to you the instant I have chosen one."

"In the meantime, I have to pretend to be friends with this slimy worm of a Zaragoza. Even his name disgusts me."

"Lord Quummo," the other man said, "it will be for only a few hours more. Then I shall know which way to go."

"Then don't just stand there babbling," Quummo said. "You should be finding a way to get those warriors to follow me!"

"At once, sire." He bowed low. "Your servant, Kar, hears and obeys." He began backing from the room, still bowing.

Flos inhaled loudly, as though she were going to sneeze again. The others looked at her. They were no more than a few feet from the vent's opening, and any loud noise would be heard within the room. Flos stuck her finger underneath her nose, and pressed. The sneeze seemed to go away. She smiled.

"Be back within the hour," Quummo said. "I want an answer then, you hear?"

"Yes, sire," Kar said. He had almost reached the door.

Lightning flashed. Flos sneezed—just as the thunder struck.

The men inside the room heard only the loud crash, and then the rolling as the noise moved down the valley. The group was frozen where they stood along the ladder. Even the cat stayed where she was.

"I want control of the whole army by the end of this day," Quummo said. "Is that understood?"

"Yes, sire." Kar reached the door, opened it, and withdrew from the room.

Quummo swore, then started pacing back and forth between the bed and door.

Sax looked back up at the others, made a sign for extra quiet, and began descending. The big cat was above him, and Sax had to place each of her feet so that she wouldn't slip.

The others moved carefully, and each peeked in the vent to see the man inside, Quummo, Keeper of Quum Keep. A tall, thin man with a terrible scar across one cheek, and eyes deep beneath black brows, his mouth like a knife wound, and a blade-sharp beard. His robe was scarlet, and his boots were black.

Flos shivered when she saw him, but they kept going, passed the room, and then each floor of the north tower until they reached a place Sax had noticed on the way up, but had not had a chance to investigate. Now he studied the outside wall of the duct and ran his fingers up along the seam between the stones.

"This was repaired here at one time," he said.

"What difference does that make?" Jason said from above him.

"I figure we're about at the level of the roof," Sax said. "We've got to find some way to get out there. There's no door in this damn duct, but I think there may have been one, once. Maybe when they were building the tower itself." His fingers continued to explore. Then he smiled.

"Got it," he said. "This is the place where it's been mended. This is where it's weak."

"Maybe weak to you," Jason said, leaning down the ladder and trying to see past the cat to what Sax was feeling, "but it looks like solid wall to me."

"I think it'll give," Sax said, "but let's listen for a second and see if anyone's around. I may have to make some noise."

The group was silent, and there was no other sound except a dog barking in the distance; the cat growled low.

"Take it easy, baby," Jason said, and scratched her head.

"I'm going to try it," Sax said, and started tapping with his hand along the crack he'd found. "I wish I had a hammer," he muttered to himself. "But this will have to do." He pulled back his great fist and gave the wall one awful blow.

"Damn!" Sax said, and shook his hand hard in the air.

The wall had moved. It had been shoved back about six inches in a single rectangular piece.

"Want some help?" Jason said.

"No," Sax said. "I got it now." He set his other hand against the wall, braced himself, and pushed.

The whole section moved, then fell outward with a terrific crash. Dust flew and stones rattled, and the group hung on the ladder without breathing.

Nothing happened.

"I guess they're either further down or way up there," Sax said, nodding to where they had come from. He leaned out the hole to see exactly where they were.

He had been right. The hole opened onto the roof, and Sax stepped through. He was standing behind tall bushes, and couldn't see a thing. Neither could he *be* seen, and that might prove to be a blessing.

He helped the others through, one at a time, and soon they were all standing, trying to see where they had come out. Through the branches they could just see bits of the central tower.

"Let's go," Sax said.

"Wait," Jason said. "Don't forget the dogs."

There was no sign of any now.

"Just take it easy," Jason said. "Those things looked big from up above."

The bushes were thick, and there were brambles in between, and the going wasn't very fast. They all tried to be as quiet as they could, but twigs snapped and thorns cut, and they made noises every now and then in spite of trying not to.

They were able to get halfway across the roof under the cover of the bushes before they stopped.

"We're going to have to make a run for it," Sax said, standing on the edge of their cover. "I think we're in luck, though. That looks like a door in the wall. We won't have to make our own." He shook his right hand again.

They had about fifty yards to run, then the bushes grew again around the base of the tower, and they would be safe. Sax was right. There was a door. There was no way to tell if it would open, or where it led to, but it gave them a chance of getting in without too much trouble.

"Who's first?" Sax said.

"I'll go," Culter said, and started to the front of the group.

"Wait!" Lyca said in a low voice.

"What's up?" Culter said. "I don't see anything. . . ."

"Shut up," Lyca said, and cocked her head to one side as though listening. The others stood motionless.

"The dogs," Lyca said. "They're coming."

"Then we'd better hurry up," Culter said.

"No!" Lyca said. "There are too many of them. You must go back."

"What do you mean 'you'?" Culter said.

"We can't go back," Flos said. "We haven't time."

"Then hide," Lyca said.

Culter heard something. All the rest did, too. A deep barking, and the sound of running feet. Black mastiffs, almost the size of ponies, were coming across the open roof toward them.

"My god," Culter said. "There must be fifty of them."

"Run!" Sax said.

"No!" Flos said. "There isn't time. Stand still!" She closed her eyes and crossed her arms, and deep lines grew on her forehead.

"We can't stay here!" Jason said.

"Look!" Culter said, and pointed to the ground.

The brambles had turned into living, writhing whips of thorns, and were growing up around them.

The dogs were fifty feet away.

The brambles lashed and twisted and were six feet high.

The dogs still came—then stopped. There was no way for them to get through solid nets of brambles, even though they could see five people caught inside.

They went mad. Froth foamed from their great jaws, and they ran around the bramble cage and tried to bite it. The thorns tore at their mouths, and they barked and howled.

"We can't stay here," Jason shouted over the din. "We don't have time, and someone is sure to hear those dogs and come to see about it."

"You want to step out there and try to reason with them?" Culter said. "I'll even lend you my sword, and you can see what you can do."

They were safe, but they were caught in their own trap. The swamp cat bristled at the sight of all those dogs, but she would not last five seconds if they turned her loose, nor would the rest of them, for that matter.

"Who's got a bright idea this time?" Culter said. "I seem to have hit a fighter's block."

No one answered. They stood and looked out at the dogs. Lyca moved. "I will go," she said, "if Flos can open a small space for me to get through." She stepped close to the brambles.

"They'll tear you apart before you get ten feet," Sax said. "You're not going anyplace."

"Yes," Lyca said. "I am the only one who can." She reached up and withdrew something from around her neck.

"With what?" Sax said.

Lyca didn't answer. She just stood there, then slowly started unbuttoning her dress. It slipped to the ground, but she was not naked. She was covered with soft silver fur.

"My god!" Culter said.

Lyca slowly lowered herself to all fours, and they could see her hands and feet had turned to paws. Her face was long and silver-furred, and her yellow eyes were angry. She looked at Flos and nodded to the brambles.

As though in a dream of disbelief, Flos made a motion with her hands and the brambles right in front of Lyca parted. The dogs saw it and gathered in a pack and charged.

They never reached their prey. The great silver wolf flashed through the gap straight to the dogs, and it was over in not more than half a minute. Great fangs tore into mastiff flesh, and blood flowed everywhere. The dogs behind pushed forward, and the ones in front pushed back. Dogs bit dogs, and there was fighting all across the clearing.

Then came the wolf's call. Lips pulled back and sitting on her haunches, the silver wolf howled up into the storm. The dogs panicked, and those that could still run made for the far side of the roof.

The wolf howled again, and it was done.

Flos closed her eyes, and the brambles slowly pulled apart and shrank back into bushes. The group moved forward to where the silver wolf still sat. The swamp cat growled, but stayed with Jason.

"Let's go," Sax said, still looking at the wolf. "They may be back, or somebody may have heard the fight."

The wolf looked up at him, then stood and trotted to the door that he had seen, and stood there as though guarding it for them.

They ran across to it, and Sax tried the handle. To everyone's surprise it opened.

"Inside," Sax said, and they ran in. "And you," Sax said to the great wolf, and it slipped inside the door. Sax came in and closed it behind him. They were on the landing of a spiral staircase.

"Up," Sax said, and started up the stairs. He stopped and came back down. "There's someone coming," he said.

"Then we go down," Jason said.

"We go in here," Culter said.

They turned to him. He was standing right across from the door they had come in, and he was holding another door open. It was small and looked unused, but it would hide them, and they quickly went inside.

Culter closed the door. Sax made a sign with his finger on his lips for silence, and they stood absolutely still until the sound of men on the staircase had faded.

"Now what?" Sax said.

"Where are we?" Culter said.

"What about Lyca?" Flos said, and they looked at her, then at the wolf.

"Can she turn back?" Culter said.

No one had to answer, for Lyca was now standing on her hind legs, and the silver fur was fading into skin.

"I brought your dress," Flos said, and helped the changing girl get into it.

Lyca wouldn't look at anyone.

"That was some trick," Culter said. "What course did you take in high school to learn that?"

"Are you all right?" Sax said, and stood beside her.

Lyca nodded.

"Except for your leg," Jason said, and knelt down beside her left leg and touched it with his black hand. There was blood on the calf. Jason closed his eyes and the blood stopped flowing. "It should be all right," he said, and stood up.

"Thank you," Flos said. "I mean, for driving off the dogs."

"I couldn't think of any other way," Lyca said.

"What's wrong with that one?" Culter said. "If I could have turned into an elephant, you would have seen the damnedest fight you ever saw. As it was, you did pretty well."

Lyca smiled, and everyone felt better.

"If you don't mind my asking the same question over and over again," Jason said, "where are we?"

"In the central tower," Sax said. "That's the most important part."

"What's this room, and what are we doing standing here?" Jason said.

They quickly looked around the space in which they stood, and saw that it was circular. Sax looked up. "It's like some kind of silo."

"Except for the rope hanging down," Culter said.

"The floor's made of wood," Jason said.

"The rope's attached to it."

"None of which tells us a damn thing," Culter said.

"It's too high to climb the rope," Sax said.

"Then let's try the stairs," Flos said.

"I've got the door," Culter said. He went to it, but couldn't find it. He could see the outline of the top, but there was no handle. "Hey!" he said, then understood. "This thing is moving!"

Up. Very slowly at first, then somewhat faster. The floor creaked underneath them, and the rope which hung in the center was taut. The iron ring to which it was tied was straight up.

"Something's pulling the floor up by the rope," Sax said. It made no sense.

"How did they know that we were here?" Flos said.

The same thought had occurred to others.

"I don't think they do," Jason said. "I think we just happen to be here when this thing's moving."

"What's it for?" Flos asked.

"It's like some elevator," Culter said. "We wanted to go up, and up we're going."

"You may be right," Jason said.

"About going up?" Culter said. "Of course I am."

"No," Jason said. "I mean about the elevator. I think that's what it is."

"You're nuts," Culter said. "They don't have elevators here. You must think you're home, or someplace."

"Ever heard of hydraulic elevators?" Jason said. "They

had those before they had electric ones. With all the water power around here, I don't think they'd have any trouble building one. Those Masters seem to have been pretty smart."

They had risen half a hundred feet.

"What happens at the top?" Culter said. "When we hit."

"I don't think we will," Jason said. "There's probably a pulley up there, and there has to be clearance for that. We'll just have to keep our eyes open."

They all looked up. Their lanterns only lighted a few feet above them, and they stared up into dark.

"Why is this thing moving?" Flos said. "If it really is some kind of elevator, I assume the floor's its roof. We didn't hear anybody get in below us."

"Then it must be going up to get someone," Culter said.

"We should shut up," Sax said. "We're getting pretty close to the top."

They stood and waited. Sax suddenly pointed to a dark shape on the wall above them. As they passed it, they could see it was a door.

They looked up again and ducked. A giant beam ran across the whole width of the elevator shaft. A large pulley hung down from the center of it.

The floor stopped moving. There was the sound of something underneath their feet, as though the door they had seen in the wall had opened, then voices. Sax motioned to the others frantically, and pointed to the beam. The floor on which they stood had stopped about three feet under it. Sax climbed onto it and sat down. The swamp cat followed, then the others. The beam was about a foot wide and covered with dust, but they could sit in a line without much trouble.

Culter looked at Sax and made a sign of question with his eyebrows. Sax pointed down. As though he were the operator, the floor began to fall away below them.

They watched it go; then each one seemed to realize just where he was, and grabbed hold of the beam and hung on tightly. The floor was fifty feet down now, and lost in the dark.

"Whose bright idea was it to get up here?" Culter said. "No offense, Sax, old buddy, but what the hell do we do now?"

"There should be some way out at the end of the beam," Sax said.

"Who says?" Culter said.

"It makes sense," Sax said. "They have to check the pulley sometime, so there has to be some way to get here."

"How about riding up on the roof of the elevator, checking out the pulley, then riding down again," Culter said.

"No good," Sax said. "What if the rope had broken, so the elevator wouldn't work? No, there's another way, and it's probably right in front of you."

"Then hand me a light," Culter said, and Jason passed him his lantern.

Sax was right. There was a small door at the end of the beam. Culter moved very very carefully, and reached it. He pushed hard. It didn't open.

"Kick it," Sax said.

Culter kicked it. Nothing happened.

"Try it again," Sax said.

"Nuts to you," Culter said. "I almost broke my foot the first time."

"Did you try pulling it?" Flos asked in a small voice.

"You some kind of wise guy?" Culter asked. He hadn't. He reached out and found the handle, and pulled on the door. It swung easily.

"I don't want to hear one damn word," Culter said, and slid quickly through the opening onto a landing of the spiral staircase. The others followed, with Jason sweating through the dust.

"Which way?" Culter said.

"Up, I guess," Sax said, and Jason nodded in agreement.

"Down, I think," Lyca said.

"How come?" said Flos.

"I think that elevator was for Zaragoza," Lyca said. "Those two men who passed us when we first got in the elevator shaft would have taken the elevator if they could have. I think it's probably just for the big shots. This is the central tower, so the big shot here should be Zaragoza. He got on below where we are now."

"Which might be his apartment," Jason said, "and the Crystal would be there."

"Yes," Lyca said. 'That's what I think."

"It sounds good to me," Jason said.

They went down slowly, without noise. At the next landing was a heavy door. Lyca listened at it, then shook her head. She could hear nothing inside. Sax tried to turn the handle. It was locked.

"Let me look at it," Culter said. "These things are big, but they're not necessarily well made." He knelt and studied the big lock. "No problem," he said, and drew his knife, worked it around the keyhole, and swore once. Then they all heard a click, and Culter stood up. "After you," he said, and turned the handle and the door swung in.

Lyca had been absolutely right. They were certainly in some big shot's apartment, and, comparing it with the one Quummo had been given, this had to belong to Zaragoza himself.

Everything was black velvet with satin trim, and thick carpets on the floor. There was a massive black-covered bed, and black furniture. If there had not been windows, all light would have been absorbed and the room would have been as dark as any cave. The room was so imposing that none of them wanted to step inside.

The swamp cat was the first to move, and walked into the middle of the room. Jason followed.

"Should we leave a guard?" Culter asked.

"What for?" Sax said. "If they catch us here, we're finished anyhow. There's no place to run or hide." They all went in.

"That must be the elevator," Jason said, and pointed to where a cylindrical bulge stood out from one wall. A door was in the middle of it, and a lever stuck out beside it.

"Not quite a push-button," Culter said, "but apparently effective."

"Where do we look?" Flos said, bringing everyone back to reality. "The Crystal's only supposed to be about the size of an egg, and Zaragoza could have put an egg almost anyplace."

They looked around the black decorated room. There was no sign of where the Crystal was.

"I never thought about having to look for it," Flos said.

"For some reason I always figured when we got here, we'd just pick it up and run."

"Or, at least, it should be displayed in some special case or something," Culter said. There was nothing of that sort in sight.

"We've got to start looking," Jason said. "We haven't got much time. That guy, Kar, said the meeting was going to be in an hour."

"*With*in the hour," Sax said. "Whatever that means."

"It means we've got to tear this place apart and find that Crystal," Culter said. They began their looking.

"This stuff is a mess," Flos said after a minute. "Look at the material on those chairs."

On close inspection, it was obvious that the material was very old and uncared-for. Worn places and long rips were not mended.

"This was the way the Masters left it years ago," Jason said. "The Keepers don't take care of it at all."

"Which means they may not be so smart after all," Sax said, "I keep thinking they made everything we've seen, but that's not true. They're just living here. The Masters did the building."

"Let's find the Crystal," Culter said. They went back to work.

Jason opened the large desk, and started rooting through the junk he found there. He stopped with a long roll of papers in his hand. With any luck . . . and he unrolled them flat out on the desk and bent to study the top one.

"Bingo!" he said.

"You found the Crystal?" Sax said from across the room.

"Yes and no," Jason said. "I think I found where it is kept."

"Then let's get it," Culter said.

"It's not here," Jason said.

"Not here!" Flos said, and came to Jason. "You mean we've gone through all of this and the Crystal wasn't here all along?"

"No," Jason said. "Look." They all gathered around and looked at where he pointed.

"I think that's it," he said. A small circle on a larger one, inside a larger one, inside a larger one.

"What is it?" Flos asked.

"The top of this tower," Jason said, and he looked up at the ceiling. "If I'm right, it's right up there."

"We were just there," Culter said. "I didn't see the Crystal."

"Above that," Jason said. "This is the very top. It's not even *in* the tower. This is the roof."

"Those are walls around the edge," Sax said, pointing to the plans again.

"Yes," Jason said.

"What's that in the middle?" Sax said. "Those other circles?"

"That's been drawn in with a different ink," Jason said. "Look." They bent and looked more closely. "See? That's a blacker ink, as though it's fresher. I think that's supposed to represent some kind of container or something, with the Crystal inside."

"That's a little farfetched for me," Sax said. "I mean, I'll go up and look, but two circles on a plan don't mean the Crystal's there."

"Well," Jason said, "it's the highest part of the highest tower, right? Everybody says it's at the highest part."

"OK," Sax said, "but that's not enough."

"There's always this," Jason said, and pointed beside the drawing of the tower, to the small lettering, almost hidden in the lines.

"Crystal," Sax read aloud, and saw the thin line with the arrow aimed right at the center of the tower, right where Jason said it was.

Sax straightened up. "Remind me," he said, and took a deep breath, "to beat you silly when we get out of here." Then he grinned, and Jason laughed.

"There was that minor clue of the lettering and arrow," he said, "but I'm sure I would have figured it out by myself."

"While you clowns are playing games," Culter said, "the meeting will be called to order and we'll have to fight a whole army to get out of here." He moved toward the door.

"Let's grab that Crystal and run like hell." He went out the door.

The others followed, and went up the spiral stairs, past the landing where they had come out from the elevator shaft, and up around at least another twenty feet into a room which filled the tower and held no more stairs.

"This seems to be it," Culter said.

Jason nodded toward a small ladder on the wall. "*That* seems to be it," he said.

Culter went to the ladder, looked up, and saw a trapdoor in the roof. "Here goes something, I hope," he said, and climbed up.

There was a slide bolt on the trapdoor, which he slid back, then pushed the door up part way and looked out. He lowered the door softly, and climbed down again. His face was white.

"I think you're right," he said to Jason. "There's a kind of pedestal out there. It's about twenty-five feet high, and it has some kind of silver ball on top of it. It could be something to hold the Crystal."

"Then let's go get it," Sax said, and started for the ladder.

"No!" Culter said. "Wait a second. That's not all that's there," and his voice was shaking. "The pedestal's in the center of the roof, as I just said. The wall is all around the outside, but there's something in between."

"What?" Flos asked in a low voice.

"The dragon," Culter said.

VIII
THE CRYSTAL

"You're kidding!" Jason said, but knew Culter wasn't. The group stood silent.

"Was it moving around?" Sax said, more to break the quiet rather than because he cared.

"No," Culter said. "He wasn't moving at all."

"Maybe he's dead," Flos said.

"I don't think so," Culter said.

"How about asleep?" Jason said.

"Possibly," Culter said.

Jason then began to ask Culter about specifics of where and how the dragon stood or sat or lay.

"Go look for yourself," Culter said.

Jason did. He went softly up the ladder, then very, very carefully raised the trapdoor a few inches and peered out. He couldn't see a thing, and it took him half a minute to realize that something lay right in his line of sight. He lifted the door a little higher, and saw what it was.

The dragon's tail. Jason hadn't considered that it might be that close, and he almost dropped the door. But he didn't, and, by raising it a foot or so more, he could see over the tail.

The rooftop was about thirty feet in diameter, with a low wall with crenellations all around. In the center, a tall pedestal—a kind of column—twenty or twenty-five feet high. On its top lay the silver ball Culter had mentioned.

Jason looked for some way up to it, and saw the edge of a

ladder built into the pedestal. Wrapped around the whole thing was the dragon.

It was almost impossible to estimate his size, for he was folded upon himself, with his head tucked underneath one wing. Jason guessed that if the dragon stood up now, he would be twenty-five feet long or more, and maybe ten feet high. God knew what his wingspan was. He stood for a few moments looking at the massive body. A dark, putrid color, with scales and skin and hair. The tail's end was almost an arrow point, and the smell was foul.

Jason could see him breathe, the great body lifting in regular motion. He was asleep. Jason lowered the trapdoor slowly, making no noise at all, and went back down the ladder to the others.

"Asleep," he said.

"How deeply do dragons sleep?" Flos asked.

"Who's the dragon expert?" Culter said.

"This is nuts," Jason said. "There are no dragons, so how the hell can anybody know how deep they sleep!"

"If there aren't any dragons," Culter said, "then we don't have a problem. Jason can just run upstairs and grab the Crystal and we're off. Right, Jason?"

"I mean, in the *real* world there aren't any dragons," Jason said.

"What world are we in now?" Flos asked.

"I have no idea," Jason said, "but I sure wish it were some other one right now."

"You didn't have to come," Sax said. "We were all given the choice."

Again the image of Inochi and Shi, and the days and nights in the swamp learning what they knew. The swamp seemed soft and friendly compared with this. But Sax was right; it was for their sakes Jason had come, and it was not the time to quit now.

"I could try to sneak up there and get the Crystal," Culter said. "If that damned lizard up there doesn't wake up, we may be OK after all."

"And if he does wake up?" Sax said. "How long do you figure you'll last out there with that?"

"I try not to figure odds like that," Culter said. "It's bad for my morale."

There was too little time for them to stand there talking till they had a foolproof plan, so they agreed that Culter could try getting past the dragon to the pedestal.

"We'll go up there too, in case he's a light sleeper," Sax said.

"The fewer people around, the better chance I've got," Culter said. "You watch me from the trapdoor. If things don't work out, then you can use Plan B."

"What's Plan B?" Sax asked.

"Any damn thing you can think of to get me out of there," Culter said, and went to the ladder. He started to draw his sword, then realized he needed both hands for climbing if he reached the pedestal. He took out his knife, put it between his teeth, waved and winked at the others, then climbed up to the trapdoor overhead.

He opened it very slowly, looked out, lifted it higher, started up, stopped, moved up again, and his feet disappeared over the edge. The trapdoor lowered, then dropped into place with a small bump.

Sax ran to the ladder, climbed up, and lifted the door a few inches. He had the same problem with the dragon's tail that Jason had, and had to raise the door higher than he really wanted to.

He could now see Culter standing a few feet away, watching the dragon carefully. There was no sign of movement, other than its breathing, and Culter seemed satisfied that it was still asleep. He took a few steps around the edge of the low stone wall, looking for a way to get to the pedestal without touching the dragon.

There was an opening on the far side, but it was next to the dragon's head. Yet there seemed to be no alternative, so Culter moved until he stood by it.

The dragon lay asleep. Culter started in toward the base of the pedestal.

Sax saw the dragon's tail lift slightly, then fall back. He looked at Culter to see if he had seen it, but Culter was staring intently at the dragon's head.

He took another step, and now was only five or six feet from the pedestal.

The tail moved again, and this time didn't fall back down.

Culter took two more quick steps and was at the pedestal. He looked up, moved around the base until he was under the ladder, then reached up and caught a rung and started climbing.

He was only four rungs up when the dragon woke. A great wing unfolded and slapped against the pedestal, against Culter. Sax thought that he must have been smashed against the stone. He threw the trapdoor open, and jumped out onto the roof.

But the dragon's wing was not heavy, more like canvas than bone, and, although it knocked Culter against the ladder, it didn't hurt him seriously. He was more in danger of swallowing his knife than anything.

The other wing unfolded and the dragon's head came out. The size was shocking—six feet long, and heavy, with great jaws and teeth which stuck out like a group of random knives of blackened steel, eyes bulging red, and nostrils like deep holes to Hell.

The head lifted, then slowly swung back and forth, as though the beast were not quite wide awake. He started to get to his feet, and lifted both wings up like great arms stretching. He obviously hadn't seen either Sax or Culter. Yet.

Sax wished that he had stayed inside, but it was too late. He ducked low and stayed still, hoping that the dragon would not see him. If the thing would fly away and hunt his breakfast, there might be time for Culter to grab the Crystal and get down. The only problem then would be getting out.

The dragon scrabbled in the gravel of the rooftop, trying to get his heavy legs under him to stand. He seemed an awkward thing, not like the soaring nightmare he had seen before. The wings flapped again, and again they hit the pedestal and Culter.

This time he was ready, and he held himself tight against the stone. The wings were rough, and he could feel the skin on both his arms scraped off as they lashed across him.

"Go away," he muttered to himself. "Go find a shark to play with at the beach. Or maybe you could fly into a cyclone just for fun."

But the dragon wasn't ready to take off. His stubby legs were having trouble getting set. His tail thrashed back and forth to shake the kinks out. He lifted his head and breathed out fire.

Sax froze. The blast of flame which came from that black mouth went forty feet or more, and would have roasted anything it touched. The odor it left was terrible.

Now he was awake, and the head was turning slowly as though taking census of its world. Culter was right in the dragon's line of sight.

"HEY!" Sax yelled. "Hey, you big, stinking, stupid snake! Hey! Look at me!" He started jumping up and down.

The dragon whipped his head around to see what made the noise, and Sax jumped for the open trapdoor. He grabbed the edge and flipped over and down inside.

"Culter's in trouble," he shouted at the others. "We've got to help." He looked around for something to fight with.

Jason didn't have to look. He ran to the ladder, climbed it fast, and pulled himself out on the roof. He found himself looking right into the dragon's face.

He hadn't used his fire on Sax, possibly because he was still sleepy, but he was waking up fast, and knew there were enemies about. Jason was one of them.

He drew back his head and opened his mouth. Culter jumped down onto the back of the dragon's neck, startling the beast. He turned to see what had hit him, but couldn't quite see Culter hanging on behind his head. He also couldn't see Culter take the knife from his mouth, lift it high, and stab it down into the dragon's neck.

The knife went in to the handle, and Culter twisted it to get it out. The dragon bent his head, then threw it back to rid itself of the thing on its neck. If Culter hadn't been holding to the handle of the knife, he would have been hurled off the tower rooftop to his death. He hung on, and tried to ride the storm.

Jason was moving now, looking for someplace where he could use his strength, some vital spot where a driving blow from his fingertips would paralyze the dragon's system. But how in hell did you pick a spot in a beast that never was?

What was vital and what wasn't? The scales and skin and hair all looked impenetrable.

The dragon whirled around, and Jason was almost hit by the great, heavy tail. The only chance he had of doing damage was up near the head. He ran around close to the wall to get to it.

The dragon was now standing up, his squat, heavy legs, with foot-long claws, digging into the rooftop to get firm holds. Culter clung to the neck, but knew he had to move or would soon be thrown off. He could not see Jason, and hoped something would happen to distract the beast.

The dragon lurched, as though struck by something underneath.

The swamp cat had followed Jason out, and saw an opening. She dashed in and ripped her claws into the dragon's belly, then leaped out from under, as the beast lifted his hind leg and clawed at where the cat had been.

Again the cat jumped in and ripped, and again the dragon clawed, but this time put his head down so he could see.

Culter jumped and caught the pedestal ladder, and hung on for life. Jason was on the other side of the rooftop, close to the dragon's head, but, with the attack from the swamp cat, the dragon might turn, and Jason would have missed his chance.

The swamp cat jumped out from underneath the dragon's belly, and the claws raked empty air. The head came up, fire shot out, and the dragon roared, exposing his throat for just a moment. Jason moved, and his white hand flashed out and buried itself deep in the dragon's windpipe.

The roar was broken to a gurgle, and the beast seemed to cough. His cough was terrible to hear and see, for flames came from his mouth and looked like burning blood. Then the head came down, and Jason just got out in time.

Culter started climbing as fast as he could. He was pretty sure the dragon could reach almost to the top of the pedestal, but he had to get the Crystal, and maybe the others could keep the thing from seeing him.

Anyway, it was safer climbing up than jumping down onto the beast.

He didn't make it. A final great cough from the dragon

whipped his wings into the air, and this time it was not the fabric of them which hit Culter, but the bony upper edge. It was hard and strong, and Culter felt himself let go and fall. He hit the roof beside the wall, and didn't move. He was unconscious.

The dragon now was using his tail to keep the swamp cat out from under. The cat ran back and forth trying to find an opening. The tail lashed with her, and it was a stalemate.

Jason could just see where Culter fell, but he was hidden behind the dragon's body. Jason waited for some sign of Culter getting up. There wasn't any.

A scream came from behind him, and he turned in time to see the swamp cat smashed against the wall by the tip of the dragon's tail. The cat picked herself up, but was limping now, and trying to retreat.

The dragon's head went back to throw its breath of fire. The cat made it to the trapdoor and inside, just as the flame streamed out and covered that side of the rooftop.

Sax almost caught both the cat's claws and the fire's roasting as he was climbing up the ladder from below. He ducked when the cat came down, and wasn't quite in the line of fire when the flames lighted up the opening above his head.

"I've got to get up there," he said.

"Wait a second," Lyca said, and knelt beside the wounded cat. It was as though they talked, then Lyca stood, and said, "Let me go first. I think I know how to fight it now." She took off her dress and was the silver wolf.

She was up the ladder in two bounds and out onto the roof. She saw only the dragon. Neither Culter nor Jason was in sight. The dragon's head was aimed toward the other side of the rooftop. He was lifting up in preparation for breathing fire.

The wolf sped to her right, then underneath the dragon, where she found the wounds the cat had made and tore her teeth into them. She was out again before the claws could rake.

The dragon's head was still raised when it felt the belly pain, and the flame of its breath flared into the air, not down on Culter's body where it would have gone.

Jason held on, then moved as quickly as he could. He was hanging by his fingers on the outside of the wall.

After the cat had ducked down through the trapdoor, the dragon had looked around and seen Culter. Jason had had to get to him before the dragon did, but the beast's body was between Jason and where Culter lay. Jason could have tried running over it, but that would have been suicide.

The only other way was by his hands around the wall. It would take time, but Jason hoped that someone else would come up from below and cause distraction. He looked over the wall beside him. The drop to the rooftop far below was two hundred feet at least. Jason felt sick, but there was nothing else to do. He climbed onto the wall, then started running along it as far as he could. The dragon would see him before he got to Culter.

The great head came around, and Jason dropped down on his hands and knees, then lowered his feet out over the edge. He had no time to think now, and he let himself down until he hung there by his fingers.

The dragon's head went over in the air above him, but the beast seemed too stupid to understand where Jason was. Jason moved sideways, hand by hand. The stones under his fingers were wet and slimy. The wind pulled at his body and his legs. He wouldn't make it. The dragon would find Culter, and all this would be in vain.

Flames shot into the air, and Jason could just see the dragon's head turning away from Culter's body. Jason knew that someone else had come to help.

He kept moving, and, when he thought he was where Culter lay, he pulled himself up. His right hand slipped and couldn't hold. His left hand could. He brought his right back up and heaved, and got up to the top, rolled over the wall, and fell down on the roof, right beside Culter.

Jason reached out with his left hand and touched Culter's head. Culter's eyes fluttered, then opened. Jason put his hand across Culter's mouth and signaled with his eyes to look up at the dragon's body next to them, with his head whipping around looking for what had been biting him.

Both of them moved slowly to their feet, but stayed crouched down as long as possible. Culter held the knife in his right hand. Jason held his right hand like a knife.

Jason noticed the handle of Culter's sword, still in the scabbard. He touched it, and Culter looked down, then at Jason, and tapped his forehead to say he was stupid. Jason nodded his agreement, and Culter drew his sword. It was still apparently bladeless, but neither of them doubted it would work.

The dragon was turning away from them to get a final blow at the silver wolf. Jason pointed up under its leg and looked at Culter. Culter saw what he meant, braced himself, then lunged. The sword sank in the soft place between leg and body. Culter pulled it out, and where the blade should have been was black and stinking blood.

Culter struck again. The dragon turned toward them, and Jason threw himself up at the neck. He got one arm around it and hung on. The other hand was poised. Again and again it struck until the dragon thrashed its head around, and Jason was thrown off.

He landed on Culter, and they both went down, though neither one was injured.

The wolf shot underneath and ripped the belly open. It was no longer a smooth surface with a few teethmarks, but a rotten mess of torn flesh hanging down, and the dragon's claws now raked his own belly.

The wolf was out and looking for her opening.

Culter was on his feet with the sword ready.

Jason waited for a clear shot at the throat.

None of them moved in time.

"HEY!" came a great bellow. "YOU STINKING WORM! LOOK AT ME!"

Sax stood on the low wall, waving both his arms up in the air and shouting. The dragon turned his head, drew back, and opened his mouth, and Sax bent down, lifted one of the stones that made the wall, and hurled it straight into the dragon's open mouth.

Flames and awful sounds came from the mouth now choking on the stone. The dragon thrashed. Culter and Jason leaped back and huddled near the wall. The wolf dashed to the trapdoor and down inside. Even Sax, seeing the results of what he'd done, jumped from the wall and ducked into the trapdoor opening.

The dragon couldn't get the great stone out. He lashed his head back and forth, and tried to scrape his neck along the wall, but the stone stayed in his throat.

He staggered, then started to fall, but pulled himself to stand once again. His black wings now spread and filled the sky, and he brought them down and made a wind which almost blew Culter and Jason off the roof.

The wings flapped again, and once again, and the beast began to rise. The wings were beating now, and the dragon flew up and higher in the air, and flames boiled from his mouth.

But the stone stayed in his throat. With one final thrust of his wings, he died. An awful scream, fire flowing from its open mouth, and the black form began to fall straight down toward the tower.

The black horror fell past Jason, and he watched it hit the roof below. The sound echoed through the Keep. Then all was still.

Jason had a strange sense that it was not the dragon's fault. It had been brought to this strange land, as he had, and was doing what was asked. Maybe, if he had been brought in by Fulmin, he would have been on their side, not against them.

Culter said, "He put up a good fight." Both of them knew that they shared the same feelings. "But," Culter said, "we've got to move it," and he went to the base of the pedestal and started climbing.

The others came out to the roof, and watched Culter reach the silver ball. He looked it over, found a catch, and opened it. He peered inside, then just stood, holding the ladder.

"Bring it down," Sax called up to him. "We've got to go." Culter closed the silver ball and climbed back down.

"You get it?" Sax said, going over to him.

"No," Culter said, and wiped blood and sweat from his forehead. "It isn't there."

The wind blew across the tower roof, but the group didn't notice. Rain fell, and they stood with it dripping down their faces. They were in shock.

"We're too late," Flos said finally. "Zaragoza must have the Crystal already. He is probably calling in the warriors from the other world right now."

"The meeting," Sax said.

"It must have been going on all the time you were fighting the dragon," Flos said.

Culter seemed to shake himself back to alertness. "How long does it take to do that kind of magic?" he asked. No one knew. "I can't believe it's something you can do in a few minutes," he went on. "Maybe there's still time to stop it."

"You want to find the meeting and walk right in and ask for the Crystal?" Jason said. "Gok said there were about five hundred guards in this place. That doesn't count whatever the other Keepers brought. We may have gotten lucky with the dragon, but there's no way we're going to beat five hundred guards."

Culter looked at him. "You want to quit?" he said.

"No," Jason said, "but I want some kind of plan that stands a chance of working."

"First, we have to find the meeting and see how far along it is," Flos said. "Then we can make our plans."

It was agreed. They all climbed down into the room below the rooftop, then down the winding stairs.

"Maybe we can get the elevator," Sax said, stopping by the small door leading out to the beam and pulley. "I could try to pull it up by hand."

"No way," Jason said. "I figure we may all die going up against those Keepers and their guards, but I'll be damned if I'm going to die from falling down some elevator shaft. No way. You guys stay here if you want to, but *I'm* going in style," and he passed them on the stairs and went down to Zaragoza's apartment one floor below.

They all caught up to him and found him standing by the elevator door, pulling on the lever.

A sound came from inside the shaft, then the door clicked.

"Going down," Jason said, and pulled the handle. The door opened, and the elevator was there. Jason stepped inside. "Anybody else?" The rest of them got in. "Now all I have to do," Jason said, "is figure out how to make the thing go down." He looked around.

"Try this," Culter said, and reached out and closed the door to the apartment, then shoved another lever inside the elevator. It started down. "Life is so simple when you know how it works," Culter said, and grinned.

"Lucky guess," Sax said.

"I thought so, myself," Culter said.

But the mood changed as the elevator descended. They had no idea where it would stop, or how they would find the meeting, or how far along the magic would have gotten.

Sounds of voices began coming up to them. They stood, quiet. The voices grew louder as the elevator kept descending. Culter drew his bladeless sword. Jason shifted back and forth, as though to get his balance. Flos played with a long strand of rope she held in her hand. Sax rubbed his palms against his sides to dry them. Lyca held the small wolf carving in both hands. The swamp cat paced.

The elevator stopped. They looked at each other. Then Jason stepped forward and pushed at the door.

It opened, and they were looking out into the throne room where they had first been taken to Zaragoza.

But this time they were right behind the throne, and the figure seated in front of them was Zaragoza himself.

On the podium in front of him was the Crystal. Zaragoza was reading aloud from a massive book on the podium. His voice reached through the hall, and they could see the faces of the guards. Apparently all five hundred of them had gathered for this great occasion. They sat on the benches looking up toward their leader.

On the four lesser thrones were seated four men who could only be the other Keepers. They could see the one in scarlet, and knew that it was Quummo.

Zaragoza stopped his reading, but didn't turn around. Quummo stood, then walked slowly to a lectern which was before his throne and held another book. He began to read aloud.

Apparently no one had heard them coming down, and no one had seen them, or they all were concentrating on the magic which would soon be done. The group stood in the elevator, not knowing what to do.

The reading continued. Quummo finished, turned, went back to his throne and sat down on it. Zaragoza started once again.

It was time to make their move. They couldn't stand all day inside the open elevator. Someone would see them, or, worse, the Keepers would finish what they'd come for, and the warriors would gather from another world.

Jason made a humming sound, and the group looked at him, then recognized the tune. Jason started singing in a loud voice, and marched out of the elevator right over to the throne. The others followed, singing "Yankee Doodle," as loudly as they could.

The music filled the hall, and every face looked up, and every face was stunned. The sudden interruption froze them right in their seats. The group reached Zaragoza, and Sax reached out and took him by the neck and lifted him straight up and held him dangling. No one dared to attack with their leader held captive.

Jason grabbed the Crystal from its resting place, and the whole group turned and marched back in the elevator.

"Wait!" Culter yelled, and he darted out and over to the book. His knife came out from underneath his shirt and he sliced out one of the giant pages, then crumpled it and stuck it in his pocket, ran back into the elevator, and closed the door behind him.

"Take her away," he said.

"Where?" Jason said.

"Well," Sax said, "we've been up already. Let's try down." He shook Zaragoza by the neck and said, "Is that right?"

Zaragoza didn't answer, because he didn't want to or because Sax held him by the throat. It didn't matter.

Jason shoved the lever down, and the elevator moved.

Now there was noise above them. The sound of shouts and orders being given and a pounding on the elevator door above their heads.

"Pay no attention," Culter said. "Some people just can't wait their turns without complaining."

The elevator didn't stop so long as Jason kept his hand down on the lever. "How far?" he said.

"All the way," Sax said. "We have to get down some-how, and this is easier than those damned ducts or the garbage truck."

But the elevator stopped of its own accord, and they first thought that the guards had reached the mechanism. Culter pushed the door they had reached, and it opened.

The Keep spanned the river between the two sides of the gorge, and they were on some kind of balcony which hung down underneath, two hundred feet above the swirling river. "Wrong floor," Jason said, and reached for the door to pull it shut. "Let's go back up a floor or two."

But it was too late. The elevator started jerking, as though someone were hauling on the rope.

"Get out!" Sax yelled, and dropped Zaragoza out onto the balcony. The rest jumped just as the elevator started up, being pulled by some force above.

The shaft was empty now, and they could hear the elevator bumping its way up.

"How about it, Mr. Zaragoza?" Sax said, and picked his prisoner up again and shook him. "How do we get out of here?"

Zaragoza started turning purple, and he pointed at Sax's fingers wrapped around his throat. Sax let up a little.

Zaragoza laughed. "There is no way, you fools. You have come to a dead end." That seemed to please him even more. His laughter got wilder. "A dead end," he repeated. "But I shall make certain it is not a fast one. It shall be slow and painful, and I shall watch every second of your dying."

Flos walked to the railing which ran along the edge of the balcony. She leaned over and looked down, then came back to the others. "It's too far to jump," she said. "We don't have the ropes anymore."

Zaragoza laughed again. "My men will be here any min-ute," he said. "They will come, but, if I am still alive, they will not kill you. I will save that until I have brought in the warriors."

There was really nothing they could do. They could fight against the first guards down, but they would not be able to hold out for long. Zaragoza would have the Crystal again, and he would bring the warriors, and the land would be his.

"Not quite that easy," Culter said.

"Why not?" Sax asked.

"Because I have one of the pages with the magic on it," Culter said, and pulled the crumpled parchment out. "If they don't have the spell, then they can't get the warriors. Right?"

Zaragoza wasn't laughing now. "Be careful with that," he said.

"Of course," Culter said, and waved the page around in the wind.

"No!" Zaragoza said. "Don't do that. It might blow away."

"Now you've got it," Culter said. "You're right on the ball."

"I don't know about any balls," Zaragoza said, "but don't lose that page."

"What's it worth to you?" Culter said.

"Anything," Zaragoza said, and grabbed for the page.

Culter yanked it out of reach, and Sax tightened his grip on the Keeper.

"Wait," Culter said. "Let him go. I want to hear his offer." Sax released him. "OK," Culter said. "What's the deal?"

"I will let you live," Zaragoza said, and started slowly toward the page in Culter's hand. "I will give you money and servants and a castle, if you will just give me that page."

"I like the sound of this," Culter said. "Keep talking."

"Don't listen to him," Flos said, stepping close to Culter. "He will use that page to bring the warriors. Then he will control the land and kill our friends."

"No," Zaragoza said. "That is not true. I simply need a few more men to keep order in my Keep. I would not hurt your friends."

He had almost reached Culter. The sound of men coming down the elevator shaft was clear.

"You're a liar," Culter said. "You would kill them and then kill us if I gave you this page. If we have to go, then this goes with us." He stepped to the edge of the balcony and held the page out over the abyss.

"NO!" Zaragoza screamed, and hurled himself toward the page. His knee hit the railing, and his momentum did the rest. With arms outstretched to grab the page of magic, Zaragoza went over the edge. His hand caught the page, and pulled it loose from Culter's grasp, and together Zaragoza and his magic fell.

The long, long scream was swallowed by the wind.

The elevator door sprang open, and guards rushed out. Behind them stood Quummo in his scarlet robe.

"Hold!" he shouted, and the guards stopped in their tracks. The group stood along the railing waiting.

"I want them alive," Quummo said. "They have a page of magic from the book. Take them, but alive."

The guards moved forward slowly.

"I guess this is it," Culter said.

"Unless, of course, we jump," Lyca said.

They looked at her.

"If we fight, we will all die here. If we let them take us, they will kill us when they find we haven't got the page. One of us might just survive the fall if he hit the river right."

They looked over the edge. The mist of the river was too thick even to see the water. There was no chance at all.

"Then let's get it over with," Culter said, and climbed up on the railing.

"Wait," Flos said. She got up beside him and took his hand. "Let's jump together."

They all stood on the railing as the first guard was five feet away.

"Take it easy, baby," Jason said to the great swamp cat, who sat on the floor and watched him. Then she jumped up on the railing right beside him. He rubbed her head and smiled.

"On three," Sax said.

"One."

"Two."

"Three!"

They jumped.

EPILOGUE

Dying was soft, but she was still hungry. The smell of something cooking was too much. Flos sat up.

"It will be ready in a moment," Physis said.

"You . . ." Flos gasped, then jumped up and ran and threw her arms around her mentor. "I . . ." She was crying. "I didn't . . ." But there was nothing to say.

"Exactly," Physis said, and laughed gently.

Then Flos was laughing, and she looked around. The clearing was almost full, or so it seemed. Sax and Culter and Jason and Lyca and the swamp cat and Fulmin, the old man, and a tall, thin man with a silver beard, and a tiny couple with oriental eyes, and a weathered woman with a scowl, and the wolves. The wolves half in the trees, as though not sure they would be welcome close to humans.

Flos turned back to Physis. "How?" she said. "I mean, how did we get here?"

"Fulmin," Physis said. "He was watching, and as soon as you were free of the Keep's spell, he transported you."

"But we never left the Keep," Flos said.

"You jumped," Physis said. "The air underneath the Keep was not enchanted. Fulmin could reach you there."

Flos looked at the old man. "I'm glad he never blinked," she said.

"So are we," Physis said. "Now the food is ready."

The group was starved. They sat in a circle and didn't

speak at all except to ask for more. The mentors stood off to one side and chatted.

Even the most screaming bellies became full finally. When they all sat back, Fulmin stepped forward.

"Were you successful?" he said.

The group was startled.

"You mean you don't know?" Flos said. "You waited all this time while we stuffed ourselves before you asked about the Crystal and the warriors?"

Fulmin looked at her and smiled. "There are some things which take precedence over others," he said. "Making sure that you were safe and sound came first."

"And," Culter said, "if we got the Crystal, everything was all right, and if we didn't, it made no difference anyhow."

Fulmin turned to him. "That too," he said.

The group laughed.

"Well," and Jason stood and reached into his pocket, "we did get the Crystal," and he pulled it out and gave it to Fulmin.

"You have done well," the old man said, and his eyes looked close to tears. "You may have saved our land and people."

"Actually," Sax said, "Culter did something which may be even more important. He destroyed part of the spell which would have brought the warriors here."

Fulmin looked at Culter.

"Excellent!" he said. "I was certain I had chosen well."

"Quality's easy to spot on a dark night in an alley," Culter said, but felt good about what he had done.

"There is one other thing." It was Lyca speaking. The rest looked at her. "Gok."

"The giant!" Sax said.

"And his family," Flos added.

There was a crashing just outside the clearing, and two trees were bent apart.

"We are free." It was Gok, holding two oaks open for a woman twelve feet tall to pass, followed by three others who could only be their children.

"We were able to free them while all the Keepers were at the meeting," Fulmin said.

"How did Gok get out of the dungeon?" Sax said. "I thought he was trapped in there."

"We did not know of Gok and his family until you found him," Fulmin said. "When we learned of their plight, we were able to act. There is no spell on the mountain where the dungeons are. We could transport him."

"Because the spell did not affect the mountain, I could help you when you called," Quadra said.

"Thank you for that," Sax said.

"It was only because you were too lazy to do the work yourself," Quadra said.

"It's nice to be back where people care about you," Sax said.

Suddenly the clearing became silent.

"I guess that's the final question," Jason said.

"Where do we go from here?" Flos said.

"I wasn't nuts about that alley," Culter said, "but it looks as though there isn't any choice."

Lyca moved closer to the wolves, but said nothing.

They all looked at Fulmin. The old man gathered his robe around him, as though to keep out a chill, then cleared his throat, and spoke.

"It is my responsibility, as the one who brought you here, to return you to your homes. If I do not do that, my powers will be taken from me, and I will be of no more use to the Council. There is no other way."

Flos felt tears rising. Jason rubbed his face and coughed. Culter looked at Bladen.

Sax said, "What'd you say?"

"I said that it is my responsibility to return you to your homes," Fulmin said. "I am sorry, but that is the way it . . ."

"To our homes," Sax said. "Those were your words."

"That is correct," the old man said. "That is my responsibility."

"Then there is no problem," Sax said, and went quickly to Quadra's side. "If you can put up with me," he said, looking down at her, "I am ready to go home."

Quadra looked up at him and almost smiled. She sniffed, and slapped his rump.

"What would I do with a great oaf like you around the

place? Hardly worth his salt. Spends most of his time in foolish talking. Asking questions. Taking up my time." Now tears were running down her cheeks, and she didn't bother wiping them. "But, if you insist, I suppose I could make room."

Sax turned to Fulmin. "I am going home," he said. "I won't need your help."

Fulmin seemed to ponder this.

Culter looked at Bladen, and the thin man nodded.

"I won't need help either," Culter said. "I've got work to do."

Flos went to Physis, and they stood with arms around each other's waists.

"I have so much to learn," Flos said. "Now we'll have time."

Jason looked across at Shi and Inochi. He wasn't sure if he would be welcomed back. He thought of times when he could have been nicer, could have shown what he really felt for them. His hands had kept him from too much affection, and now he stood there waiting for some sign.

Inochi came with tiny steps, looked up at him and said, "You are the only son we ever had. Your room is ready in our home."

Jason bent and kissed her, and walked with her to where Shi stood smiling.

"And the cat?" he said.

"And the cat," Shi said, and the great swamp cat came to them and sat beside her master.

They looked at Lyca. Her platinum hair gleamed silver, and her eyes shone in the evening light. Around her sat the wolves, and she was leader.

"Well," Fulmin said, and cleared his throat again, "there seems to be nothing more to say." He smiled. "I have brought you home."

The leaves in the clearing whispered, and they all looked up at the great clouds of red and orange and of gold streaming in the sky.

The storm was over.

Read this stirring preview to a brilliant
new Arthurian saga

FIRELORD
by Parke Godwin

"With its superb prose and sweeping imagination,
FIRELORD brings to life a realer King Arthur than
we have ever seen before. Parke Godwin is a major
find; a convincing researcher and a master novelist."
—Algis Budrys, Chicago *Sun-Times*

Here is the story of King Arthur, not as he might have been, but as he was—a real man of bone and blood, fire and dreams. Mighty warrior, great hero, passionate lover. All the enchantment of legend and powerful sweep of history are present—the bloody battles, the savagery and treachery of a nation forged out of the crumbling ruins of an empire. And there is stirring romance in the stories of the two women who loved him and betrayed him: Guinevere the Queen, great love of his life who shared his triumphs and his tragedy. And Morgana, lusty, earthy ruler of the Prydn, the Faerie-folk, who taught him a simpler way of life close to the earth and the ancient gods, and gave him his war name, Belrix: FIRE-LORD.

Trystan was the flawed best of a sad lot, working well for weeks at a time, drilling his men with sword and the new lances, then one day he'd not come out of his tent; that day would stretch to a second and third. No one could talk to him then. Once, when the days became a week, I went privately to his tent to shake him out of it. Trystan hunched over a table, red-eyed and oblivious, glaring at me, through me, at a ship of the mind and an Irish girl he brought home for a king but loved for himself. I gave it to him without sweet.

"You're the emperor's centurion. Sober up and square off or you'll have no command left."

Like so many of my generation, he affected to despise Latin. "Centurion, no less. Aren't we the proper Roman. Have you forgot your own tongue?"

"Have it your way, then. I don't need to see into a sack to know it's bursting or into your heart to know it's full of pain."

"Ah, listen to the sage of Severn." Trystan glowered at me, sodden. "You're not the man to speak of pain, never lost anything. You're a list of rules, a machine. Trip its lever and it rides. Pull the string, it gives commands."

"Ambrose-rix placed a trust in you, God knows why. Every patrol you miss means one more for me."

"I'll ride when I see fit. Now, get out. Get out! Call your little dog Bedivere and—"

"If you were the half of him," I said, "you'd be twice what you are."

Trystan drained his cup and pushed it aside, heaving

up from the table. His smile was murderous. "Twice, is it? What a lovely day to kill you, Arthur."

He was too drunk to be dangerous. One shove and he went down heavily. Trystan sat up, befuddled, then clambered back on his stool with the clumsy deliberateness of a mountebank's bear. He shook the cloud from his head, peering at me as if I were a stranger just arrived on unknown business. Then the blank expression crumpled into agony and his head dropped onto his arms. I heard a muffled sob. We're a mad and mournful race. Our storms are dark and furious and quickly past.

"You're right," Trystan sobbed. "I'm a scant, weak man who can't get one small woman out of his soul."

"Not weak, Tryst. Just a mite single-minded."

"Well, now." He wiped his swollen face and looked reflectively at me. Incredibly, he seemed to have forgotten it all. "Will you have a drink, Arthur?"

I couldn't help laughing. "Haven't you had enough, you horrible man?"

Trystan poured a short drink, stoppered the flagon tight and shoved it aside. "Just one to bid it all good-bye. What is it now, four days, five?"

"Six."

"Only one, then. My health wouldn't bear the sudden leaving off." He raised the cup: "Lady, lady, what an angel you were. And what a bloody bitch." He tossed it down. "I'll ride tomorrow, Arthur."

When Ambrosius found no real cooperation in Cador's tribunes, he decided to appoint one from among us. More confusion: Gawain and Agrivaine left for Cador's court, each to argue for the office. Peredur placidly assumed it would go to him. Trystan was drunk again and couldn't care less. After considerable delay at Eburacum, Ambrosius' order arrived with frosty congratulations from Cador.

To the rank of tribune of *alae*, Centurion Artorius Pendragon.

Now all their weaknesses were mine to contend with. The Orkney brothers called it favoritism, subtly seconded by the gracious but distant Cador, who implied more than he said. I set about the business of building them into a cohort, overseeing their training and haphazard supply, fighting uphill against men who saw me as an inferior. No, Gawain, more important to have provender for the horses than a wagonload of wine. Agrivaine, where are the new cloaks your father promised? No, man, I never said King Lot was mean-spirited or even forgetful, but winter is coming. Prince Peredur, when you have quite heard mass and made confession, will you tell me why your men are so poorly fed with your own supply so close? (And tell me what you can find to confess and yourself not a drinker and nothing more female in your camp than a few goats.) Speak to your sister? Very well ... "Lady Guenevere, the third squadron needs fresh food. What they have on hand is spoiling. They can't do their job half-starved."

"But surely the men hunt," she wondered. "Surely they can always find fresh meat."

"If they weren't worn out from riding and if the Wall weren't hunted bare these three hundred years."

"You care about them." Guenevere touched my hand in compassion. "You care so much, and so do I. But the jewelry brought less than I hoped. My money is almost gone."

"My lords have always been unhappy under our tax system," Cador allowed regretfully. "It's hard to enforce payment."

I took advantage of my new rank to contradict him. "That's hard to understand, my lord, since the system has always allowed them to weasel out of paying in any one of half a dozen ways. And pass the burden on to the *civitates*. Why, your own Church has preached against this for eighty years!"

"Certain radical priests," Cador ceded smoothly.

"Radical and right, sir. We should un-protect those fat sons of—"

"Lord Arthur." Guenevere gently elided my profanity. "It would please me if you stayed to dine."

Please her? God, the sight of her was food enough, but I was needed back, though she gave me a smile worth a banquet.

"You're a stubborn man, Arthur Pendragon. Stubborn and loyal. Were a woman your own wife and fair as truth, I don't think she could keep you from duty."

Damn it, I blushed—and damn her, she enjoyed it.

"But come again, Lord Arthur."

Letters to Kay on leather and harness, reports to Ambrosius that would unavoidably be read at Eburacum before passing on: My lords Gawain and Agrivaine have improved their men at sword and lance, but their patrol methods are wasteful of men and time. Lord Trystan (my poor, demon-driven Tryst) is not yet properly committed to his office. Prince Peredur needs more assurance in decision. Prince this and Lord that, always holding my temper in check. If I lost that, I lost them and Ambrosius' purpose.

Where did I learn kingship? In the dust and ice and wind that blew across the Wall. In learning why the Saxon deserves his half of Britain. With all his royal blood, Cerdic would never have seen a crown if he couldn't first command a raiding keel. Since the Druids, we Britons have been too respectful of rank alone, too jealous of independence and meaningless distinction to work together. We are idealists wanting a god for a king, then fighting to be free of him. It will kill us in the end.

Then that wretched patrol when Bedivere twisted in the saddle, grazed by an arrow from a bow we never saw. He lay in fever for weeks, burning all day and sweating all night while he whimpered and raved and his body fought desperately against the poison. Back on patrol, letters, reports, bad food and too little of it, ignoring the insults behind my back.

"Here's a morsel straight from Cador. He says Pendragon got the command because his mother was Ambrosius' favorite niece. Not Uther's wife, his real mother. Her that was married to Gorlawse. A much-traveled woman, if you take my meaning, and mad as they come. Why else did Caius take the coronet and Arthur with no more lordship than the bare name of it?"

Nursing Bedivere through late winter into spring thaw when the sun peered timidly from lowering clouds or disappeared in sudden fog, and I could write Kay at last:

We're scarecrows in torn leather and tatty breeches, nothing like a uniform in the half thousand of us. Don't send the new ceremonials, I've no place to wear them. It's like plowing with bulls to get the work done, and I feel I was born in that miserable saddle, but we are a cohort.

Haven't we been here before? What place is this on the map?

The village was called Camlann. That hill is *Cnoch-nan-ain-neal.*

Music. The low, throaty sound of a flute curling in and out of my dreams.

I woke with my back cold against the damp ground, wrapped in a blanket of fog where there had been clear sky. Fool, dozing off like that with no more thought to danger than a recruit. Where was Bedivere? My horse was gone, too. I whistled his call, but got no answering whinny.

"Bedivere?"

I dared not call again. Whoever else might be close could hear just as well. Time to move. With drawn sword I made a guess at the patrol's direction. Mist could rise quickly on the moor, men and horses could blunder into bog, but this was the heaviest I'd ever seen, a blindness laid on the earth by a malicious god, thick as sheep's wool beyond ten feet.

The flute still drowsed in my ears, teasing and familiar, then thrilled in an odd little run. Who'd be tootling in this fog? A shepherd lulling his flock, keeping them near? This can't be the right direction. This way. No, this. No, you're going uphill, that not it. Bedivere, where are you?

"Back there, Arthur."

The voice was near and far at the same time. "Who's that? Who are you?"

Another run on the flute. "Forgetful man, didn't I say I'd meet you here?"

Frightened now, whirling about: "Damn you, where are you?"

"At the top of the hill, at the ring of stones. Come up, Arthur, to *Cnoch-nan-ain-neal*."

The music rose and fell in its quavering song, and far away, I heard a woman calling someone, keening with a sob in her voice as if she knew the loved would never come back.

The great stones stood like ghosts in the fog as I passed into their circle. The music was very near, but now I knew who played it.

"Merlin, where are you?"

"Here, Tribune."

The tall figure leaned against a strangely carved stone, wrapped in a travel-stained cloak, as dull and worn now as he had been incandescent long ago, but a man grown like myself. I felt no wonder or friendliness. A boy has time for miracles and magic, but a man has other things to do.

"You again, Merlin."

He breathed one half-sour note of finality through the flute and put it away. "Merlin will do for a name. I'm called that and other things, a part of things. That midge that deals with the mite of Arthur. Welcome to the hill of the fires."

I could use a fire; the fog was damp and chill. I shivered and felt empty. "Let me wake, Merlin. This is no time for games. I fell asleep bone weary. I could be taken."

Merlin pointed. "You have been taken."

To the right, the left, all around me among the upright stones squatted small figures, dim in the fog. I swung about, sword at guard.

"You devil, am I out of time?"

"For a time."

"Let me wake, really wake. Why do you mock me with riddles and magic?"

Merlin's lean, fatigue-lined features registered a kind of sadness. "There is no mockery."

"No? Don't I know I'm mad, seeing tomorrows for yesterdays, sleeping with a hundred ghosts at my ear? I saw Bedivere full grown before he was. I knew Ancellius."

"And he will betray you, Arthur—"

"Stop!"

"—as the Christ-man's Peter."

My fear poured out in anger. "You *boucca!* You air-thing, playing on my sickness like your flute. I could put this blade through the nothing of you—"

Quick as I was, Merlin parried my swing with a subtle twist of his body that hurled me forward off balance to sprawl against the stone. My muscles bunched to move —and froze, unable. I could only stare up at his narrow, watchful face. Behind him the circle of watchers waited. They were not all men. The small woman-figure rested her head against the shoulder of a huge dog, still as herself. They could all have been smaller stones in the fog.

Merlin smiled a little. "And still you don't know me. No wonder, there's little you have learned for sure. Why me, why this place, why the vision you call madness? Have I not shown you the king you will be?"

I shivered against the cold stone. "This is mad."

"If it is, so are you."

The whispering laughter of the watchers, like a rustle of leaves.

"You will be king, Arthur. There will be victories at first and a kind of defeat in the end, but that won't last. You'll be remembered. They'll sing your name through long, dark nights and darker centuries. They'll conjure with it, make you a legend and a god and sacrifice you as all god-kings are sacrificed. *Ave, Imperator*."

Merlin's eyes softened with some of the long-ago warmth. "You've learned to read men's failings, but not the heart that churns them out. A little imperfection, Tribune, a little human weakness. A love, a loss, and then how will the world look when this fog lifts?"

"What love? Guenevere?"

"In time," said Merlin. "When you've learned to love. She's only an ambition now, a reflection of you."

Merlin laid his fingertips on my damp forehead. "The carpenter had a bard's flair for poetry: 'Thou art Peter, a rock.' You are Druith, a fool, and upon this fool, I will carve something like . . . a heart."

He beckoned to the female figure in the fog. "Morgana."

The tiny woman glided closer to kneel beside me, skin the same coppery hue as Cador's prisoner, cheeks marked with the same ritual scars. Her sheepskin shawl covered only her shoulders, the short, fringed skirt very little at all. Her flat brown belly, veined with stretch marks, had borne child. She studied me with bold gray eyes, and I knew her from the last moments of dreams before waking, from the shadows beyond Cilurnum's watchfires, glimpsed as she slid around the corner of imagination, over the shoulders of other women whose faces were not half so well remembered even in my arms. A strong face that knew sorrow, joy and rage. But not beautiful.

"Very beautiful," Merlin answered the thought, "when you have eyes to see. And you, Morgana, what do you see?"

"One of the People," she said. "But it wears tallfolk clothes and smells of them."

"The fool needs you."

Morgana touched my cheek. "A's been too long from me. Only a child."

"Teach it, then."

She cupped my face in brown hands. "Many days did watch and want thee. Be thee so fair or far, do know our own. Hear of the Prydn, the First People. Your people. The beasts cut in these stones be elk and reindeer and others thee's never seen. When this land was half ice, the People were here; Earth's favored children who knew her secret names. Then tallfolk brought bronze to break our flint. Did learn the name of bronze and how to make it. Then more came, the red-hairs and yellow-hairs, with iron to break bronze."

Her voice compelled as the music of the flute. Most of her words I knew, a kind of British, but some were mere idea-sounds, as *flutter* describes the bird's beating wing.

"Iron took the land," said Morgana. "Iron hated our gods and called them devils, rubbed out our true name to steal our strength. Iron called us Faerie, made us part of the dark beyond their fires. When tallfolk are bigger, when they have iron-magic and all the good valley land, where can the People go but under the hill?"

Morgana raised her head to Merlin. "What does thee call it?"

"Druith," said Merlin softly. "A fool."

"And what must a see?"

"Too far and too much. A god-king who must burn for his people."

She flinched a little. "Cruel, even for tallfolk. Then know the way of things, Druith. All names go under the hill, stone before flint before bronze before iron, like waves on a shore."

Then Merlin asked, "What one thing can you teach it, one lesson to mark it a true man and your own forever?"

Her lips brushed across my cheek. "Poor Druith. New green leaf in a dry old world. Do know my own and what I'll teach thee."

She kissed my mouth, a long kiss that pressed the magic and the memory into me. The scent of her was sweet in my nostrils, and there were tears in her eyes and on my cheek were hers pressed against it so that I couldn't tell were they her tears or mine, so mixed with the joy and sorrow of her magic. I felt my chest go suddenly hollow with a vast, soft ache, an empty space that had to be filled with Morgana. Then I was—

Free!

Loosed, I

feel

myself

waking—

unfettered, returning to *true* self inside Artos-tallfolk. My Prydn soul throws off its bonds like a frayed rope and thrusts Artos into the prison where he's kept me so long. Free, stretching out my arms to my brothers, who come

out of the fog and lift me high on their shoulders like a
prize to take me home under the hill.

Read FIRELORD, on sale April 15, 1982
wherever Bantam paperbacks are sold.

FANTASY AND SCIENCE FICTION FAVORITES

Bantam brings you the recognized classics as well as the current favorites in fantasy and science fiction. Here you will find the beloved Conan books along with recent titles by the most respected authors in the genre.

☐	20281	WAR OF OMISSION Kevin O'Donnell	$2.50
☐	20488	THE HEROES OF ZARA	$2.50
		Guy Gregory	
☐	14428	LORD VALENTINE'S CASTLE	$2.95
		Robert Silverberg	
☐	01166	URSHURAK	$8.95
		Bros. Hildebrandt & Nichols	
☐	20156	BABEL-17 Samuel R. Delany	$2.50
☐	20063	GATES OF HEAVEN Paul Preuss	$2.25
☐	22562	NOVA Samuel R. Delany	$2.75
☐	20987	TRITON Samuel R. Delany	$2.95
☐	14861	DHALGREN Samuel R. Delany	$3.95
☐	20870	JEM Frederik Pohl	$2.95
☐	13837	CONAN & THE SPIDER GOD #5	$2.25
		de Camp & Pratt	
☐	13831	CONAN THE REBEL #6	$2.25
		Paul Anderson	
☐	14532	HIGH COUCH OF SILISTRA	$2.50
		Janet Morris	
☐	20722	DRAGONDRUMS Anne McCaffrey	$2.50
☐	22556	DRAGONSINGER Anne McCaffrey	$2.75
☐	22557	DRAGONSONG Anne McCaffrey	$2.75
☐	20914	MAN PLUS Frederik Pohl	$2.75
☐	14846	THE GOLDEN SWORD Janet Morris	$2.50
☐	20592	TIME STORM Gordon R. Dickson	$2.95